DARK VISIONS

A COLLECTION OF MODERN HORROR

VOLUME TWO

DARK VISIONS

A COLLECTION OF MODERN HORROR

VOLUME TWO

EDITED BY

ANTHONY RIVERA
SHARON LAWSON

GREY MATTER PRESS

DARK VISIONS
A COLLECTION OF MODERN HORROR - Volume Two
ISBN 978-1-940658-07-0

First Grey Matter Press Trade Paperback Edition - December 2013

Anthology Copyright © 2013 Grey Matter Press
Design Copyright © 2013 Grey Matter Press
All rights reserved

Grey Matter Press
greymatterpress.com

Grey Matter Press on Facebook
facebook.com/greymatterpress.com

Dark Visions Anthology
darkvisionsanthology.com

TO ALL OF YOU WHO EMBRACE
DARKNESS AND WHO HAVE
BELIEVED IN OUR VISION...

TABLE OF CONTENTS

JOHN C. FOSTER

The haunted birthplace of author John C. Foster is historic Sleepy Hollow, New York. As a result, he has been afraid of the dark for as long as he can remember.

An author of both taut thrillers and dark fiction, Foster spent many years of his life in the ersatz glow of Los Angeles, working in the entertainment and marketing industries before relocating to the relative sanity of New York City where he lives with his lady, Linda, and their cat, Lucy.

Foster's stories can be found in several anthologies, including *Under the Stairs* from Wicked East Press and *Big Book of New Short Horror* from Pill Hill Press, among others.

Foster recently completed his first novel, *Dead Men*, and is hard at work on his second, *The Isle*.

MISTER WHITE

BY JOHN C. FOSTER

"Who is Mister White?"

There was a pause and a crackle of static over the phone. Abel was about to speak again when the connection was severed.

"Um einen weiteren Anruf tätigen, legen Sie bitte—"

Abel hung up before the mechanical, feminine voice could finish telling him how to make another call. He turned back toward the crowd in the dimly lit bar, letting his gaze wander from face to face, his eyes stinging from the haze of smoke hovering beneath the low ceiling. He was grinning faintly and chuckling, as if he had just finished listening to a clever story.

He returned to his spot at the bar and ordered another beer. "Bitte," he said to the stocky bartender when a fresh pint glass was placed on the dark bar before him, adding another wet circle to the collection of moist rings that reminded him vaguely of the Olympic symbol.

Who is Mister White? Click.

He sipped, licking the foam off his upper lip and nodding

faintly at a man holding court with a stein in one hairy fist. He was at ease. A somewhat familiar face around this part of Schwedenplatz in the center of the city. It was warm inside and everyone was talking themselves into having at least one more drink before heading out into the snow.

Abel turned, leaning one elbow on the bar, another happy regular at Das Hupfen Schwein. He didn't look Austrian, but his wardrobe and hair looked as though it was possible that he came from Ireland or Scandinavia, and his flawless German refuted any possibility that he was American.

He forced himself to sip slowly, relaxing his shoulders, his apparent ease the result of long experience.

"Danke," he said to the barman's back, catching a glimpse of himself in the mirror behind the bar. Good. He looked anything but afraid.

* * *

The train clacked and rattled as it raced southbound along underground tracks toward the outskirts of Vienna. It was late, and only a few second-shift workers returning home shared the train with Abel. A big man reading the newspaper. A couple of city workers in stained coveralls hanging from the overhead rail. A woman in a domestic's uniform sat across from him.

Abel sank onto the bench, wrinkling his nose at a rank under-smell that infected the atmosphere on the car. He had already stepped off the train twice and boarded the next in line, keeping an eye out for familiar faces and postures. Indicators of interest.

There was nothing. Nothing at all out of place, but he still felt on edge. Maybe it was the smell.

"Who is Mister White?" He muttered in English, looking up to see the domestic eyeing him with a flat stare. He glanced over to see the two city workers giving him the once over as well. Or were they?

He forced himself to look away, studying the laces on his shoes and the slush puddle from the melting snow forming around them. He looked up and heard the city men in their coveralls talking to each other in guttural German. When he glanced across the aisle, the woman was still staring at him.

Abel closed his eyes, playing the language game to distract himself, listening to the two men. Austrians, by and large, had a liquid sound to their speech, and he placed the city men as immigrants from the eastern part of Germany.

He opened his eyes suddenly, and the woman was leaning her head back against the glass window, eyes closed. A slight string of drool adorned the corner of her mouth. He noticed that the floor beneath her feet was bone dry and wondered how long she had been riding the train.

Who is Mister White? Click.

Is it time to leave Vienna? He asked himself. *To shift the operation to another city?* He pictured Munich in the spring and chased that image with a memory of sipping brandy on the shore of Lake Geneva.

The car went black and Abel jerked in his seat, sweat beading on his forehead. The clacking roar overwhelmed his hearing, and he looked desperately to the left as something moved at the corner of his vision.

The lights came back on and Abel blinked, already aware that something was different. The big man with the paper, where was he? Abel heard the metallic clank of the door at the end of the car as it closed and could vaguely make out the big man walking away in the next car.

He sucked in a deep breath and let it out slowly, calming himself. He thought of the dinner he would have after the drop. A backstreet restaurant that kept its kitchen open late and served the most amazing platters of pork shoulder with roasted apples and spaetzle.

"Nachte station, Simmering," a voice barked from the speakers.

Abel rose and grabbed a hanging strap, fumbling the buttons on his long coat closed with the others.

The woman was watching him again. Dark skinned, hair escaping from the imprisoning bun on the back of her head. She hadn't bothered to wipe away the saliva from her mouth.

"Fuck you," Abel said with a congenial smile as he picked up his briefcase from the seat. "Have a fucking fuckity night."

The doors slid open and he stepped out onto the platform. A moment later the train hissed into motion and roared away. He caught a quick glimpse of the dark woman staring at him through the window, upraised middle finger pressed against the glass, then he was alone on the platform.

In the silence that followed, Abel knelt and placed his briefcase on the ground, pretending to tie his shoe while he carefully scanned his surroundings.

It was darker than the platforms near Vienna's nightspots. Dingier. Crumpled fast food wrappers and soft drink bottles were scattered about. Curling posters on the walls advertised performances that had gone dark a year ago, and he smelled the odor of finely aged urine.

The familiar disorder, at least by Austrian standards, reassured him. The stop at Simmering, the last stop on the line, did attract some visitors, but never eager ones.

Graveyards don't attract eager visitors.

* * *

Abel pulled his collar tight to keep the falling snow off of his neck and worked the lock pick with numb fingers. By the time he heard the click of the mechanism unlocking, he had aged several decades, his hair and beard coated with a dusting of white.

He slid through the maintenance gate and pulled it closed behind him.

The Zentralfriedhof was the largest graveyard in Vienna, home to the disintegrating remains of Beethoven and Brahms. Abel trudged in the opposite direction of those notables, ghosting between marble gravestones gone blue in the dark, the falling snow shrouding him, muffling his footsteps. As he descended deeper into the sea of the dead, the perimeter lights faded and the shadows seemed to boil and flow into dark lakes across his path.

It was said that there were more dead in Vienna than living, and Abel found it the perfect place to conduct business. He had worked with the Koecks before and knew that meeting in the cemetery gave the couple a not-so-subtle thrill.

The muffled crunch of his shoes through the snow had faded from his awareness when a sudden gust of wind blew a white curtain into his eyes. Wiping the wet coldness frantically away, Abel jerked back to see a tall figure staring down at him.

"Jesus," he said, the realization that he stood before a stone angel not coming swiftly enough to douse a surge of adrenaline.

He started forward impulsively, as if to curse at the angel, then stopped.

Crunch.

Was that a footstep? Abel turned slowly in place, rewinding the mental audio file and replaying it again. Was it his own footstep, the sound distorted by the increasingly heavy snowfall?

Unaware, he backed into the stone angel and looked straight up as his back met marble. It was a dark figure against the white, hook-nosed and deep-eyed. Judging.

Abel jerked away and his nose wrinkled as he scented the rank smell from the train again. A third-world odor of rotting flesh, blackened toes and gangrene.

"Ridiculous," he muttered. He was working himself up like a kid waiting for ghost stories around a campfire. Still, he thought he might take his coat to the dry cleaners tomorrow, because the scent did seem to be sticking with him.

"Abel? Sin sie das?" A woman's voice floated through the night. Abel grunted in disgust. *Amateurs.* Of course it was him, who else would be out here in this weather?

"Ja, ja," he said, breaking his own silence. Masha hadn't shouted yet, but she might if she was getting nervous, and the silly bitch had used his name.

He crunched his way toward the sound, thinking of the Go Bag back at his flat and the heavy automatic hidden inside among the cash and identification cards. Only amateurs carried weapons in his profession, or so he had been taught. But he kept one for a rainy day, or a snowy night.

"Abel? Sin sie das?"

Abel stopped, the hair on the back of his neck prickling. Something was wrong with the question.

He began to back away when he heard the rapid crunch of steps behind him and spun about, catching a quick glimpse of a white face that seemed to float in the darkness. Abel blinked snow from his eyes and looked again, but the row between the gravestones was empty.

"Abel? Sin sie das?" The voice came from somewhere beyond a vast, marble mausoleum. *Abel? Is that you?* Asked in exactly the same way, with exactly the same volume.

Break contact right now.

Abel darted into another row and began moving quickly away from the voice, not returning to his path of entry. He caught a slither of movement from the corner of his eye and heard a loud gasp followed by a splash. The gurgling sound was unmistakable.

Abel reversed directions, panic seeping in. He slipped and landed hard, the briefcase jarred from his grip.

Fuck it. He left it where it fell, scrambling on hands and knees.

"Abel? Sin sie das?"

"Shit," he said as he realized he had been herded right back to the meeting point. He clawed up to his feet, determined to sprint right through whatever was waiting for him. He ran, coat streaming, darting around the corner of the mausoleum.

"Oh hell," he said to Masha. His feet slid out from under him as he tried to stop and he fell again, the breath knocked from his lungs.

She had been crucified against the back of the mausoleum, railroad spikes driven through her outstretched wrists. Her chest was covered by a red bib flowing from the gaping tear in her throat, and a flashlight planted in the snow at her feet threw its light upward, transforming her horrified expression into a ghoulish mask of shadows and making the freezing blood on her blouse glisten like rubies.

"Abel? Sin—"

"No," he moaned over the recorded voice emanating from her coat pocket.

He turned away from her, crawling, the bonds holding back his panic shattering. He saw boots standing in his path and looked up to see the white face floating in the night.

"Don't," he shouted in the instant before the shadows swarmed at him and there was a bright flash of pain, then darkness.

* * *

A rattling rumble slowly became identifiable, and Abel felt a surge of nausea, his head throbbing. He felt like he was coming off of a three-day bender, but that didn't seem right.

He opened his eyes and just had time to see a young couple watching him when his stomach clenched and he doubled over, retching.

"Verdammt ekelhaft," the girl said, her face wrinkling in disgust.

"Lässt uns gehen," the boy said, grabbing her arm and pulling her towards the door to the next car.

He looked down at the string of vomit stretching from his mouth to the bench, his nose choked with a sweet, antiseptic smell.

I'm on a train, he thought, and then, *chloroform.*

Abel sat up blearily, clutching his aching head. His pants were wet with snowmelt and he shivered, struggling to clear the mental fog from his memory. He had the vague sense that it was very important he do so.

He wiped yellow bile from his mouth as the puddle of puke sent streamers down the bench towards his briefcase.

"Shit."

The door to the next car opened and a member of the Polizei stepped onto the car. He had the look of a man off duty, carrying his hat, tie undone.

"Bist du betrunken?" He snapped, eyes narrowing.

Abel shook his head, "Not drunk. Sick."

The cop gave him a doubtful look. "Sie, die sich sauber."

"I will, I'll use my coat." Abel realized he was speaking English and made a mental effort to switch languages.

He picked up his briefcase and something sloshed inside as he placed it on his lap. He had fumbled off his coat and was sopping up the vomit when he felt a warm wetness on his thigh. Red liquid was seeping from the briefcase.

Abel looked up instinctively at the Polizei officer, but the civil servant had turned away in disgust, and Abel quickly used his coat to smear away the blood.

As the train pulled into the lighted platform of the next station, the cop muttered a disgusted command over his shoulder. "Nach hause gehen und schlafen sie ab." *Go home and sleep it off.*

He stepped off the train and Abel tensed when another man started to step on, but the odor drove him back out in search of another car.

As the train resumed its clamorous transit, Abel looked down at his briefcase with dawning horror. *What the hell happened tonight?*

Trembling fingers worked the clasp open and he lifted the lid of the briefcase.

The severed human foot was resting in a sticky soup of blood. An amazing amount of blood. It dripped like red rain from the upper lid and Abel let out a high-pitched keening sound.

He remembered everything.

* * *

Abel's walk from the underground station to his flat was a paranoid dream set in motion. Every face turned to watch him, eyes shadowy pits like Masha's. White snow hats looked like skulls, and a man in a light-colored balaclava nearly gave him a heart attack when he stepped out of a doorway.

The befouled coat was in a public wastebasket somewhere behind him. He shivered as the snow coated his shoulders and cold reached through his sweater to drag icy claws across his ribs. He hung grimly onto his suitcase, unsure what forensic tell-tales he had left behind on it, hearing the foot thump and slosh as the case swung from his hand.

He wondered if the foot belonged to Masha or her husband, Ernst.

He had a brief thought to head straight out of the city, but with no money or identification, he wouldn't get far. And would likely freeze to death before long anyway. He had to risk returning to his flat, but when he came in sight of it, he couldn't force his feet to carry him across the street.

"Sie kann hier nicht schlafen," a voice barked at Abel from a window and he lurched hurriedly out of the doorway he had been huddling in, a frozen puppet with tangled strings. I can't sleep here? Why would he need to sleep when he was living a nightmare?

He stood in the street until headlights blazed through the increasing snowfall and a horn blared at him. Then he was stumbling across the road towards home.

* * *

"I'm surprised to see you alive," a gravelly voice said in the dark room.

Abel froze, staring at the single, red eye glaring at him. As his eyes adjusted he made out the hulking shape of the fat man.

"You hung up on me," Abel said, trying to sniff past the smell of the other's cigarette smoke to detect the odor of gangrene.

"You don't look well," the fat man said.

Abel turned on a reading light, but the fat man sitting at Abel's desk remained in shadows.

"Who is Mister White?" Abel asked, setting down the briefcase on one guest chair as he sat in the other. The fat man held out the pack of cigarettes, but Abel shook his head, afraid to show his shaking hands.

"Where did you hear that name?" The fat man asked.

"You know who he is then?"

"If you found his name, then it is already too late."

"Who is he?" Abel said, breathing deep. There was no rotting smell. He thought he might be safe for the moment.

"When you called, I thought it certain you would meet him tonight."

"Would I be alive if I had?"

The fat man's bald head shook slowly, connected to his massive shoulders by drooping jowls. "No." He exhaled a cloud of smoke. "But you do not look well."

Abel shrugged, imagining disgust. His face reflected it. "Amateurs," he said. "I'll have that cigarette now."

The fat man offered him the pack and rose as Abel slipped one free, his trembling almost unnoticeable.

"I will have a drink and you will as well," the fat man said, fetching a bottle of brandy and two glasses from a shelf. Abel lit and the fat man poured before moving ponderously to sit on the edge of the desk, which creaked noticeably. He wore a three-piece suit, very old world, the glittering length of a gold watch chain stretching across the immense expanse of his vest. Abel had heard that he suffered from gout and wondered if he carried a gun.

"I will speak and you will listen, and then we will plan. You have heard the name of Mister White and you are already on borrowed time."

"You said that already."

Abel dragged deep, the smoke mixing terribly with the taste in his mouth. He sipped and swirled the brandy, then sighed as warmth spread slowly down his throat and through his chest.

"Who watches the watchers?" The fat man mused, carefully tasting a sip of brandy. "A rhetorical question, but important in that it juxtaposes with my next question. When you were young, did you eat your peas and Brussels sprouts?"

Abel raised an eyebrow and finished his brandy. "Was that rhetorical too?"

"Did you clean your room? Did you mind your mother?"

"Do we have time for this?" Abel said, pouring another brandy for himself and wondering how many the big man had drunk already.

"What did your mother say when you did not mind her?"

Abel started to interrupt again, but the grim expression in the other man's eyes belied the levity of the questions.

The fat man harshly exhaled smoke and spoke through the cloud. "Never mind, I shall tell you what my mother said. She said that she would tell Mr. Haeckel and he would pay me a visit when I went to sleep."

The fat man rose and began pacing, his steps heavy. "He was an old man who lived several houses down the street, hideously maimed in an industrial accident and blind in one eye. Just an old man, yet my friends and I crafted terrible tales about him and ascribed powers to his ill-fitting glass eye in its bed of yellow pus. It got to the point where none of us would so much as walk past his house if we were alone."

The fat man paused to look out the window at the street below.

"I had forgotten Mr. Haeckel until just recently, convinced I had left him behind with distance and years. But I realized with your call tonight that he was not left behind at all."

The fat man turned around and his face had gone slack with horror, so dramatically that Abel thought he was having a stroke.

"Mister White is the Boogeyman," the fat man whispered. "Like Mr. Haeckel long ago, but all too real."

Abel stood and slammed his drink down on the desk, sloshing amber liquid onto the dark wood. "What the hell is this?"

"You and I have not eaten our Brussels sprouts. But worse for you, Abel, *you* have not cleaned your room or minded your mother, and I'm afraid she told Mister White."

"You're fucking insane," Abel said and rose, heading around the desk for the drawer hiding his Go Bag.

"Who watches the watchers?" The fat man said. "And who do they tell when an operative goes bad? Very, very bad?"

Abel rose with the leather satchel and saw the fat man pointing a small, black pistol at him, tiny in his giant fist.

"Put the bag down on the table and sit behind the desk," the fat man said. "When Mister White arrives, I will give you to him and tell him what you have done."

"You're dirty—" The pistol jerked sharply and Abel stopped speaking.

"Not like you, my boy, not like you, and I will be able to explain my own involvement away into nothing. Now sit."

Abel dropped the bag on the table and sat in the chair, still disturbingly warm from his unexpected guest.

The fat man moved around the desk and topped off Abel's drink. "Finish this, if you wish. Have more. I'm not sure it will help though, when Mister White comes for you."

He slid the drink to Abel, leaving a wet trail. "But it might."

Abel downed the drink in one, long swallow that set his

throat on fire and eyes watering. When he looked up, the fat man was staring down at the briefcase on the guest chair.

"Why is this dripping?" The fat man said.

Abel felt a fey wind blow through his mind, lifted by the brandy. His mouth twisted into a small, tight smile as the fat man bent to fumble open the catch with his free hand and lifted the lid. A coppery musk of blood filled the room as the fat man staggered back, eyes wide.

"Mister White is already here," Abel said.

"But—but—you're still alive."

Abel leaned back in the soft chair. "Maybe he wants *you*."

The fat man lifted the pistol and considered risking a shot, then turned and fled out the front door. Abel heard his thundering steps out in the hall and then on the stairs.

* * *

The clock struck midnight, and Abel stirred in the tiny cone of light from the reading lamp. The level in the bottle had descended considerably and he sat with an empty glass in one hand, a 9mm Spanish Llama pistol in the other.

Two hours had passed and he had not heard a sound save for the building creaking in the wind.

"Fuck you, Mister White."

He stood, having utterly failed to make sense of the evening. It felt as if he were trapped in one of the CIA's Cold War LSD experiments. The brandy didn't help, but he needed it to steady his nerves.

He carried the briefcase into the tiny bathroom and tossed the thing into the clawfoot tub, where he proceeded to douse it with rubbing alcohol, brandy and anything else that he thought might burn.

Smashing the smoke detector with the butt of the Llama, he lit a match and tossed it into the tub.

A cloud of yellow flame whooshed up and he staggered back in surprise. Oh, anyone looking in the tub would see the remains of the case, and forensics would be able to find blood traces, but any tells he had left on it would be gone. The apartment itself was under a false name and untraceable to him, no matter if he went to Geneva or Munich.

Once he was certain the fire was contained in the tub, he moved through the flat, grabbing essentials for his flight. The aroma of roasting pork wafted from the bathroom, and he briefly pictured Au Pied du Cochon—baked pig's foot—the chef's specialty at his backstreet haunt. His stomach rumbled and he briefly realized he had not eaten since lunch before remembering what was cooking in his tub.

Abel doubled over and threw up a hot stream of bile and brandy.

He had meant to stay and feed the small, charred bones of the foot into his toilet, but his stomach lurched at the thought, and he took a jacket and hat out of his closet instead.

"Good bye, Vienna," he said with a last look around the flat. Go Bag in hand and pistol in his jacket pocket, he stepped into the hall and pulled the door shut behind him.

"Es riecht lecker," an old woman's voice drifted down the hall. *It smells delicious.* Abel turned to see his neighbor peeking out of her door.

"I'll leave a plate outside your door when it's finished

cooking," Abel said over his shoulder before hurrying down two flights of stairs to the street door.

Munich or Geneva, hell, even Stockholm, whichever has the first flight out.

He stepped out into the cramped street and was immediately struck by a harsh, panting sound. He glanced into the alley adjacent to his building.

A grotesque Buddha sat cross-legged in the snow, his bald head glistening as the flakes melted on his scalp. He was globular, morbidly obese, his immense stomach plumped out to absurd proportions on his thighs, and his skin was so white it was nearly blue.

The illusion of his snow Buddha-hood would have been complete, if he had not been silently weeping.

Abel pulled the pistol from his pocket and held it low by his side, stopping a good ten feet from the naked, fat man.

"What the hell are you doing?" Abel said.

The fat man looked up and struggled to open his eyes against lashes that had frozen shut with tears.

"I—I—I," he stammered through chattering teeth.

Abel noticed a dark discoloration in the snow beneath the fat man as the Buddha lifted his huge belly with both hands, revealing the railroad spikes driven through both of his crossed ankles and into the ground.

"Puh…puh…please…" He whispered through his chattering, but Abel was already running away from him towards the main thoroughfare. His hat flew off his head and he didn't break stride, consumed with an overriding biological imperative to escape.

A taxi was idling at the curb as a couple disembarked. Abel nearly ran them down in his haste to catch it.

"Flughafen," Abel barked.

As the taxi pulled carefully away from the curb Abel was gripped with the conviction that Mister White was driving the car. That the head he could make out only in silhouette would turn around and he would see a pallid, murderous face staring back at him. He pressed the barrel of the Llama against the back of the driver's seat and asked, "Mister White?"

"Huh?" The driver said.

"You heard me, Mister White."

An oncoming car flashed headlights across the taxi's windshield, and Abel saw the man's dark skin and Rastafarian hair.

"Jesus," Abel said as he shuddered and sank back into the seat. The ride was slow and almost peaceful, the snow diffusing the city lights into a sea of glowing orbs. The car's heaters embraced him with their warmth, and he unbuttoned his coat with one hand, stuffing the pistol back in his pocket, soothed by the metronomic sweep of the windshield wipers.

The old-fashioned ringing startled him, and it took him several moments to realize it was a telephone sounding off right beside him.

Abel frantically patted the car seat looking for the source

The ringing stopped.

"Was ist das?" The driver asked over his shoulder.

"A cell phone," Abel said as his questing fingers picked up the rectangle of smooth plastic. "Excuse me," he said, switching to German. "Es ist ein handy."

It twisted in his hand and Abel almost dropped it. But it was just the vibration as it began ringing again.

The screen read CALLER UNKNOWN. Abel wanted to throw it out the window.

"Is it yours?" The driver said.

"Nein."

The driver held his hand back over the front seat and Abel handed it forward. The driver answered the phone, "Hallo?"

After a minute of conversation the driver hung up and pulled cautiously to the curb, sliding a little despite his care.

"What the hell are you doing?" Abel said.

The driver smiled and held up a hand in a *relax* gesture. "De last passengers, dey left it in de car."

His English was worse than his German.

Light filled the vehicle as another pulled up behind them. Abel twisted to see another taxi slide to a stop.

"Dey follow the GPS," the driver said, already getting out of the car. The door slammed shut, and Abel was frozen with indecision.

Steal the taxi? Wait for the driver? Get out and run? His thinking was muddied by terror and he wished he had not consumed so much brandy. *Get out and shoot them all?*

His breath fogged the rear window as he tried to watch his driver talking to the person who emerged from the other car. He wiped at it frantically, leaving smears, obscuring the figures.

Anything could be happening back there.

Normally he would immediately follow training and take the simplest route to break contact, but he was terrified into immobility. Utterly uncertain. It was as if he had been manipulated into a position where his years of experience were unavailable.

He reached for the door handle and pulled, but the door was locked. Holding onto the gun, he fumbled at the door until he found the button and heard it unlock. He reached for the handle just as the driver's door opened with a blast of cold air, the driver huddling inside quickly.

Abel pivoted in his seat and lifted his pistol. "Alright Mister—"

The Rastafarian cab driver turned, eyes white and huge as he saw the pistol.

"Drive," Abel said.

"What? You can have—"

"Drive or I'll blow your motherfucking head off!" Spit flew from Abel's mouth.

The driver turned and keyed the ignition, starter engine screaming as he turned it over too long in his panic.

"Drive!"

The driver stomped on the gas and the tires spun up a rooster tail of slush. Suddenly they caught and the car surged forward, fishtailing.

Right into the path of an oncoming lumber truck.

Abel screamed as he looked at the blinding headlights and the half-seen grill like a huge mouth full of metal teeth.

The sound of the head-on collision was like nothing he had ever heard, and he slammed into the back of the front seat, teeth clacking shut on his tongue, ribs cracking, vaguely aware of the taxi rocketing backward in an uncontrolled spin until it crashed into an immovable object and hurled out a deadly swath of hub caps, shards of metal and exploding tires.

Stunned, Abel was unable to give any meaning to the time it took to pull himself up from the back seat. He wiped at some sort of bony meal stuck in his hair. His mouth was filled with the taste of pennies, and a steady spatter of hot liquid hit the back of the front seat as he beheld the driver.

A two-by-four had crashed through the windshield like a spear, smashing directly into the driver's mouth and penetrating through the back of his skull, exploding like a brain, blood and bone grenade, until the wood lodged in the rear window. The Rastafarian man hung from the two-by-four by his enlarged mouth, eyes still wide and white.

Abel dragged himself across the seat to the door and used both trembling hands to open it. He sprawled forward onto the snowy road as if trying to do a push up, but his hands shot out to either side in the slippery wet and he landed, face first.

Time had no meaning as of yet, and it took years to pull himself completely from the wreckage until he flopped full-length in the road. In the next century he was able to lift his head by painful degrees, focusing his eyes with a herculean effort.

He saw a pair of black shoes surrounded by white, just inches from his nose.

He tried to say, "No."

* * *

Bare branches scratched at the windowpane as Connecticut hunched under its first major snowstorm of the season. Warm in his study, Moores sipped his tea and watched the video from the dead-drop website.

A naked man sat inside a mirrored cube maybe ten feet on a side. His face was black and blue, nose horribly swollen and crusted with blood. His pale ribs also showed contusions indicating the likelihood of broken bones. There was no escape for the prisoner from the sight of his own degradation.

Moores had seen such injuries before. Seen them in person in his younger days. But the years had made him squeamish and he shifted nervously in his seat.

According to the time code running at the bottom of the screen, it had been two days since the man had awakened to find a straight razor beside him and heard an emotionless command from what Moores took to calling "The Voice."

"Shave off every inch of hair from your body, Abel."

Moores started at the name and leaned close to the screen.

After hours of pleading and pounding on the walls, Abel complied, weeping and trembling. When he missed a spot, The Voice was there to remind him. As a result, the man was left with scratches over much of his body. His eyebrows were scabbed hyphens, and his groin looked like hamburger.

"Very good," The Voice said when the grooming was finished. "I would like you to think for a while on this question. How much of yourself will you give away to stay alive, and at what point does your life cease to matter?"

The camera had shifted angles constantly through the next two days, often shooting from underneath where the blood smears were turning brown and the increasingly indiscreet puddles of urine dried.

Moores played back the video frame by frame after the razor disappeared, but noticed a brief discrepancy in the time code and again did not see The Voice. He accidentally let his gaze wander over the picture of his family on his desk. He turned it face down.

When heavy wire cutters appeared on the reflective floor,

Moores played the video back again, but The Voice remained a ghost. Abel awoke and cried tearlessly, without sound. Moores suspected he was too dehydrated to produce either.

"Do you have an answer to my question?" The Voice asked.

"Please let me go. Can't you please let me go?" Abel said, turning around and around until he was weaving dizzily.

"Is the answer one finger from your left hand? If it is, I will give you water."

"No! Please!" Abel screamed hoarsely and struggled to his feet. "Let me go…"

"I can't, Abel. You will be an example for others."

According to the time code, Abel cut the pinky off his left hand four hours and thirteen minutes later.

"Jesus Christ," Moores muttered, his long finger trembling as he pressed the pause button. He jerked when the phone on his desk rang. The light indicated it was his house line, not the secure line. He ignored it.

Abel was watered and his wounds were bandaged. The time code showed a longer gap at that point, and Moores realized that The Voice was concealing his identity, disrupting the feed while he attended to his prisoner.

When Abel was asked to cut off a second finger, he held out for only an hour, rocking himself like someone in the throes of severe dementia.

"Now write, Abel. Confess."

Moores watched as the man on screen used the bloody stump of his second finger to scrawl a crude graffiti of woe on the walls. Abel wrote and wrote until he was on his knees. Line after line of confession deviating into large, looping whorls of blood and tiny, cryptic scratches on the glass. Moores felt his own pulse begin to race as he copied what Abel was writing to the best of his ability. Even under duress Abel was employing a code, and Moores was able to extract a chilling name from the bloody script.

There was more in the confession and it would take a specialist to get it all. But there would never be a specialist. Moores had already decided to burn his notes once he learned everything he could.

Finally, Abel collapsed into a fetal position mumbling repeatedly, "Killmekillmekillme."

"I can't kill you yet. Forensics would tell when you had died and we have more work to do before."

Moores began to lose his sense of time and suspected that he was somehow trapped inside the cell with Abel. He barely spoke to his wife and daughter. In fact, he barely left his study at all, afraid to look up at the walls to discover they had become mirrors. Long after they were asleep, he crept through the house, *through his own house*, and retrieved the small automatic pistol from the box in the bedroom closet while his wife slept not five feet away, unknowing. He took a quiet shower to wash away sweat that smelled old and fearful, the 7mm pistol safe inside a plastic baggy on the soap dish.

Moores was back in his study with the door closed before his family awoke the next morning.

Abel made it through the remaining fingers on his left hand over the next few days, bandages and water appearing when he was a good boy. The words on the walls had run and were now like ruins buried beneath dried brown streaks.

On the fifth day, according to the time code, Abel picked up one of the stiffening fingers from the floor and ate it.

"Dear God…" Moores said. He had taken to keeping the blinds down and checking the perimeter security system every half hour or so. He wished he had a dog. The pistol was in the pocket of a heavy sweater he had been wearing non-stop. It clanked once against the kitchen counter during a rare trip outside his study.

"What's that, Donald?" His wife asked.

"Just my pipe," Moores said, patting the pocket.

"Hon?" She said, waiting for him to turn. "Is everything alright?"

"Of course it is," Moores said, rearranging his narrow face into a smile. "Just work."

Back in his study, the video rolling. "Consider the question, Abel," The Voice said. "Is the answer, your left foot? Or a phone number?"

The footage jumped and Abel was screaming at a wall, as if The Voice had just been inside with him. He was emaciated and crook-backed, subhuman. He turned to the cell phone on the floor, but couldn't hold it with his mangled hand. Ultimately, he wedged it between his knees and dialed a number.

The footage blurred and the time code jumped. The image steadied on Abel shaking a small hatchet in his right fist.

Abel's first blow was clumsy, tearing a flap of skin off the corner of his forehead. He staggered and fell, but bounced up with manic energy. Abel's second blow, even one handed, drove the steel head of the hatchet into the thin bone at his right temple with surprising force and he collapsed in a heap, red ooze seeping from the wound.

The time code indicated eight minutes of twitching before Abel went completely still.

Moores hit pause and covered his eyes, trying to banish his fear and gather his thoughts. He rewound the footage until the image of Abel crouching over the cell phone appeared. Moores paused it, using agency software to isolate and zoom in on the phone's damnably small screen. Either the camera's resolution or the software was insufficient and the enlarged number remained an indistinct blur.

Moores returned to his place in the video, thankfully near the end. He hit play, unaware of the reluctant moan drifting from his own mouth.

Rigor mortis had begun to twist and stiffen Abel's corpse when Moores noticed the tell-tale blur of a break in the recording. Automatically he ran the footage back frame by frame.

Moores sat up straight in his chair, knocking over a glass of water.

The reflections made it nearly impossible to see, and the light in the mirrored room had been turned off, but Moores could swear he saw the blurry outline of a man with a too-white face that seemed to float disembodied, looking directly at the camera.

The video footage abruptly ended. Moores deleted the file without hesitation and crumpled his paper notes in the large, glass ashtray, lighting them with a wooden match. The ball of paper curled and twisted like a live thing as it burned, and the smoke made Moores nauseous.

He decided he would have Kathleen take their daughter to her mother's home in Boston. He would brook no argument. He had already deleted the video file, but he needed to dispose of the hard drive completely. Next he would visit the bank deposit box—

The phone rang, and a small sound escaped him.

The house line, not his secure line. *Thank God the agency doesn't know yet,* he thought. *I still have time.*

Mind churning with action items, Moores strode from his office towards the staircase. He would tell Kathleen—

"Dad. Daaad!"

Moores pivoted as his daughter's voice called out from the kitchen, his feet like blocks of wood, ice water trickling down his spine.

He stepped into the bright, white space and saw his daughter holding the house phone.

"Dad—"

"Hang that up right now," he ordered. "Do it."

His daughter pressed the disconnect button and put the phone down on the kitchen counter.

"What's wrong, Dad?"

"Who was it?"

"Dad, what's—"

Moores cut her off with a slashing motion of his hand. "Who was it?"

The ring of the phone was shrill and too loud in Moores' ears. His daughter glanced at it.

"Same number," she said quietly.

The phone rang a second time, rattling on the counter.

"Did the caller identify himself?" Moores asked, abruptly short of breath. His daughter took his arm, frightened.

"He did," she said.

The phone rang a third time and Donald Moores fought back a scream.

"Dad," his daughter said. "Who is Mister White?"

CAROL HOLLAND MARCH

A fiction writer from Albuquerque, New Mexico, Carol Holland March has published her speculative stories in *Mirror Dance*, *Aurora Wolf*, *Stupefying Stories* and *The Colored Lens*. An excerpt of her novel, *The Dreamwalkers of Larreta*, appeared in the December edition of *Bosque (The Magazine)*.

March's evocative work focuses on the intersection of dreams, reality and time. And she frequently sets her stories in places where the veil is most thin.

She lives with two demanding dogs who give her all her ideas in exchange for treats and bike rides.

DREAMING IN AND OUT

BY CAROL HOLLAND MARCH

The darkness whispers in my ear as I stumble through a labyrinth of tunnels, a stone maze with rough walls as sharp as glass, curving one way, then the other. Too dark even for shadows, but I stumble on, my right hand trailing the rough rock, my left extended straight ahead. I crash against something hard and fall to my knees. Pain slices through my right leg. I smell blood. I don't want to think about what might be crawling in the darkness. I get up and stagger forward.

Light appears. The wall of the tunnel curves to the left. I move faster, crawl under a rocky ledge and come to an arch that leads into an open area. Light shines from an opening above—too high to reach—but enough to see by. I stand waiting for my eyes to adjust. A circular room, shadowed edges. An open pit in the center, full of white ashes. Around it a low wall, no more than a foot high, a circle of stones surrounding the pit. This circle was constructed by human hands, so there must be a door. A way in. A way out.

From the far side of the room something moves. A flash of

white. Out of the shadows a woman steps forward, moves toward the circle. She wears a long, white dress—plain, cotton, pure. She has red hair like mine, but longer, and she is older, with haunted eyes. I want to speak, but my throat constricts. I flatten myself against the wall of the cave. A sharp rock tears the thin material of my shirt and punctures the skin behind my heart. She walks toward the wall of stone, steps over it and kneels in the ashes. She looks straight at me as she slowly lowers the straps of her white dress to reveal the red gash where her left breast had been.

* * *

He wakes me with rough fingers pinching my nipples so hard it hurts. His body is heavy against my back, hard and sweaty. I try to roll away from him, but there is no room left on the bed.

"Stop," I say.

His right arm is under my shoulders, and with that hand he pinches me harder. His left hand moves down between my legs. I am not ready, but he pushes into me anyway. To get away, I roll onto the floor, get up and look back at him. He grins. He thinks this is a game.

"I have to go to work," I say.

"C'mon," he says. "It won't take long."

I go into the bathroom to shower.

On the bus into town I remember the woman in white. A shiver moves up my spine and through the back of my head. My ears pulse. It is not the first time I have dreamed of her.

* * *

Again, the labyrinth. My forehead throbs in rhythm with my breath. Pitch dark all around. No way to go but forward and pray not to fall into a pit that will disintegrate my flesh. When I see the light in the distance, I want to turn and run, but the light wins. I will face the mutilated woman. Perhaps she will show me the way to the surface. I duck under the ledge. See the pit. The wall. She walks out of the shadows, slowly, as if walking onto a stage where she will deliver the speech of her life. She steps across the wall. Kneels in the pile of white ash. Looks straight at me. I cringe against the wall of lava rock.

She lowers her dress. Both breasts are gone. I stare at the red gashes on her chest, uneven blue lines where crude stitches held her together. She raises her arms above her head. Her colorless mouth forms into a sweet smile that makes me want to scream.

"I waited for the Lord of Time," she says, in a voice that sounds like an echo in a cathedral long deserted by the gods of man.

I wake sweating. His hand is cupped around my left breast, his whiskey breath against my hair. What does he dream about? I wonder, as I untangle myself and go to watch the sun rise over the mountains from the window in the kitchen.

* * *

In the park I sit on a bench to watch the other women with their children. A little girl runs after her yellow ball that has rolled close to my feet. I reach down and pick up the round, plastic thing. It feels light and hopeful. We look at each other. She holds out her small hands. I throw the ball to her. She catches it but does not turn away.

"Thank you," she says in a solemn voice, as if she has been taught to be polite to strangers. "Do you want to play?"

"I don't know how," I say. It is true. But I also see her mother approaching, concerned about the strange woman talking to her daughter.

"You throw it," the child says. She throws me the ball. I catch it and throw it back.

"Come along, Emily," says her mother. Something about me has warned her.

The child smiles and turns away. I look at her mother over Emily's head. I do not smile. She is right to be wary.

I sit on the bench long after Emily and her mother have gone. People come and go. They play with their dogs and their children. They seem happy. I wonder how far I could get on the two hundred and twenty-two dollars I have secreted in the back of the bedroom closet, in the false bottom of a box filled with mismatched buttons.

He brought me to this city a year ago, for a better job, he said, but I know it was to remove me from everything familiar. My sister is two thousand miles away. I have no friends. Only on the one day when he works and I don't can I come to the park and pretend I am not a prisoner.

"You're crazy," Susan said when I told her I was leaving with him. "He doesn't love you. It's something else."

Now that I know she was right, it's too late. I wonder if Emily's mother is loved. I wonder if I will survive long enough to tell Susan she was right and that I will never leave home again. I wonder who the Lord of Time could be.

* * *

Darkness again. I bang my shins against the lava rocks, but I must hurry through the labyrinth. A cobweb catches my face. I brush at it furiously and go on. It seems a longer journey this time, more turns, different directions. I fear being lost and stop to pant, to still my heart. I quiet myself. The darkness around me grays. I can almost see the way. I must find her. I go on and, after two more turns, find the lighted archway. She is there, in the center of the circle, kneeling, head bowed to the ashes. The white dress is red-stained.

She raises her head and looks at me with eyes so huge I see the horror reflected in them. I am frozen, but she struggles to her feet, using only her right hand to balance herself. Her left hand is hidden in the folds of her stained dress. Standing, she picks at her hair, as if to make herself presentable. She presses down on her skirt to smooth it.

What has happened? I ask, although my lips don't move.

Her eyes are too big for tears. Slowly—so slowly—she moves her left arm out of the folds of her skirt.

I feel a scream building in me even though I know that in this dream I cannot speak aloud. Her arm is still dripping from where her hand was ripped off at the wrist. She wipes the blood on her skirt and averts her eyes.

"I waited too long," she whispers, and the sound reverberates around the gray stone walls as if she had shouted them again and again.

What did you wait for?

Two tears roll down her white face. "Eternity," she says.

* * *

He comes home late and screams at me because the meatloaf is dry.

"I'm sorry," I say and hate myself for cringing. I smell beer on his breath and understand to lower my eyes when I answer.

"You're useless," he sneers. "You can't cook. All you're good for is fucking."

"Let me go," I whisper, suddenly brave. "You can find someone better."

He pushes me against the stove. My head hits the wall where the clock ticks off the hours.

"Don't even think about it," he whispers against my throat. "If you leave, I'll find you. I'll find you and slice you up like a cow. Do you hear me, Jen? *Jennifer*?" He mocks me with my own name.

I nod and try not to breathe.

He releases me. When I stand up, he pushes me toward the bedroom. I think about grabbing a knife from the drawer and gutting him before he can take another step. I think about his blood pooling on the dingy white tiles. About watching him die. How his face would contort in disbelief. How his eyes would dim. About telling the police who would invade the apartment with their uniforms and nightsticks, their red faces, and thick hands poised over their guns.

I let him push me onto the bed and press my face into a pillow so I will not cry out.

* * *

The cave is not so dark this time. Do I really remember seeing this outcropping of rock before? Have I learned the way? Or does my dream-self perceive momentum where there is only repetition? This time I do not fall, and when I come to the archway she is waiting, silent and still, in the shadows. She steps over the wall. Kneels in the ashes. The blood has stopped dripping.

Who is the Lord of Time? I ask her.

She smiles. Awkwardly, with one hand, she pushes herself up and stands erect.

I move toward her. I go as far as the wall and stop.

"He comes," she says.

I notice something moving in the shadows. She shrinks back in the opposite direction, steps over the wall and out of the circle of ashes. From the shadows a swirling figure glides. It comes closer. I step back. It enters the circle and dances, its legs moving so quickly I cannot see them clearly. Its arms — so many arms — in synchronized measured moves, fly up and down, swing sideways in a kinesis that is clearly language I cannot speak. His matted hair swings in rhythm with his sinuous body as he crouches and leaps and bends. Around the stone wall, a huge multi-colored snake winds itself.

I am mesmerized by the dancing, but I hear the woman in white, who is backed against the stone wall to my left.

"It is an image," she says. "Too old to be useful."

As she speaks, the dancer shimmers and fades. It recomposes itself into a comic book Devil with a long, thin tail and tiny, black horns. Perfect for Halloween.

She laughs. I join her, and the image devolves into smoke. Out of the smoke a huge, shining angel forms, pale and translucent, with wings that stretch as far as the cave walls and a face so bright I turn away.

This one stops my laughter, but the woman in white is not impressed.

"Eternity cannot be won," she says, and the angel evaporates into a pool of white dust that settles into the ashes.

What is your name? I think to her.

She faces me and raises the one hand she has left. "Mira," she says. It is like a prayer.

From the ashes in the circle, something new is rising. It starts as a dusty cloud in the corner of my vision. I look directly at it and see from the pale dust a child appear, a boy, perhaps five years old, wearing a three-piece, tan suit with a yellow handkerchief in the pocket. He is dark-haired with bright green eyes and he comes toward me out of the cloud. He offers me a bouquet of yellow roses. I kneel to accept them and look into his eyes.

"Eternity is what you do," he says.

I take the roses and breathe in their scent. In their midst is a plastic handle. I pull it out. It is a hairbrush.

"Open it," he says.

I pull out the stiletto dagger concealed within the handle.

I wake suddenly, heart pounding.

He is snoring beside me. I go into the bathroom and look in the mirror. I look the same. Haggard. Old beyond my years. On the sink is a different hairbrush than the one I use every morning. It fits my hand perfectly. I do not tremble. I take the hairbrush in my left hand and pull with my right. The knife slides out without a sound. I stand there and balance the stiletto in my palm. I grip it and practice slashing downward. Then I grip it another way and practice slashing forward, as if he were standing in front of me and I am aiming at his throat.

As I walk back into the bedroom, I am strangely calm. The knife in my hand is hypnotic. It is so early and he is still drunk, not likely to awaken. I stand over him. I think of Susan. I think of Mira. I think of the little boy in the tan suit.

* * *

I dress quickly, in jeans and shirt, sweater and jacket, as if I am going somewhere farther than the park. I put on boots even though it is warm enough for shoes. From the closet, I retrieve my box of buttons and stuff the bills I have saved into the back pocket of my jeans. I put the box back in exactly the same place. I shove my purse into the backpack I got for the camping trips we never took and lock the door behind me.

I sit on my favorite bench and watch the people come and go. At lunchtime the park is crowded with children and dogs. Later, Emily and her mother come. Emily carries her yellow ball. I watch while a little boy in a tan suit approaches her. They toss the ball back and forth, giggling endlessly. When the game is over, all three walk past me. The little boy comes to my side as if he knows me. Emily's mother thinks he is my child and smiles at me. I smile back.

He is close enough to touch. When he casts his green eyes up at me, my heart pounds.

"It's almost time," he says.

I feel as though I am melting into the wooden bench.

* * *

She appeared as the light was fading. I thought she was old, but as she came closer, I saw she was near my age, but ragged and tired. She pushed a shopping cart filled with her belongings along the winding cement path. She wore a white dress, yellow with age and stained down the front, under a short, blue jacket at least two sizes too large. When she came to my bench she stopped and raised her eyebrows as if she were asking a question I had promised long ago to answer.

I pulled out my purse and offered her a five-dollar bill. She looked at it for a long moment before she accepted it with a chapped, red hand.

"For passage," she said. "If you're ready."

I wasn't sure what I was ready for, but I picked up my backpack and followed her through the park and down the street that led to the river which ran through the city and, eventually, all the way to the sea. The river was lined with a grassy area and old trees and walking trails with benches so older people could rest in the shade with their dogs.

She led me to a small wooden dock where four rowboats were moored. They bobbed gently in the green water. The small building advertising "BOATS FOR RENT" was locked, the proprietor gone for the day.

We sat together on a bench at the water's edge and watched a mother duck lead six ducklings downstream. Their tiny, yellow feet paddled through the water just as they were born to do. I watched the setting sun turn the green water golden, a few purple irises blooming on the far shore. I thought about the garden behind Susan's house and wondered if the tulips had come up.

I looked at the woman. She nodded as if she knew what I wanted to ask her.

"Time can be bent," she said, still without turning toward me. "But you do need a boat."

I pulled the bills from my pocket and tried to give them to her, but she shook her head.

"You have farther to go," she said. "You might need them."

"Thank you," I said.

"You had better start."

I was dubious about rowing, but I dropped my pack into the bottom of the nearest boat. I stepped in and fitted the oars into the oarlocks. I looked back at the woman sitting on the bench.

"Who are you?" I asked her.

She smiled then and shrugged once, as a grandmother might. I untied the single rope. The boat floated away from the dock.

I started rowing. It wasn't as hard as I had imagined. The little boat went downstream at a surprising clip. I turned around and waved and she waved back. The current took my little boat and I knew it would not be a straight trip across the river. I also knew I would land at the place where I was intended to go. But even so, I looked back again and again, until my boat had rounded the first curve of land and I could no longer see her sitting there as I rowed away in the deepening dusk toward the opposite shore.

CHAD MCKEE

Speculative fiction author Chad McKee is a biologist who moonlights as a writer of both poetry and prose.

McKee's work features taut characters and intricately woven tales of life on the edge. His stories can be found in the volumes *Best of House of Horror*, *Blood Rites*, *Day Terrors* and *D.O.A.: Extreme Horror Collection*, among others.

McKee is an American Southerner who currently resides in Oxford, England.

MOONLIGHTING

BY CHAD McKEE

Anne Frank was wrong, at least by half.

I read *The Diary of Anne Frank* in junior high. My teacher, always eager to encapsulate reading assignments into neat, digestible, carry-home messages, stressed that the moral of the story—well, her *life*, I guess—was that you could always find positives in the worst situations if you believed everyone had a little good inside them.

What Anne failed to note is that there are two sides to Man, the old two-halves-make-a-whole idea, where one is good and the other is, by definition, evil. The truth, of which Anne certainly knew in her own heart, was that Man held equal measures of both. Maybe some incremental imbalance of the two halves determines whether you are feeding beans to poor Indio kids in Guatemala or molesting ten-year-olds; but I would argue that the scales are tipped more often by the standard Machiavellian forces: love, power, fame, money.

My question is: where do I fit in? I'm not weighing down the tithing plate at Sunday Mass, but I'm also not grabbing the lot and stuffing it into my pocket. I don't have a criminal record, look at kiddie porn or swear in the presence of old ladies. I live in a tasteful apartment off Thirty-Eighth Street, close enough to the Upper West Side to flirt with the bourgeoisie, but far enough away to pretend I possess the grit of the proletariat. I *had* that grit once, but five years of aspiring higher had scraped it to a nearly translucent veneer. I have an attractive girlfriend who just graduated from NYU and is socially conscious enough to donate her time to the soup kitchens on Forty-Second Street. I am the model for the middle class, responsible, well kept, docile and predictable.

I've never made an honest assessment of my faults, my weaknesses. Possibly because whatever the symptoms may be—that extra drink when you don't need it, or a stop by the "gentleman's" club when you know your girl is waiting at home—they boil down to one central problem: boredom.

I think my old man had it—he took off when I was twelve. I don't know where or why, nor does my mother, and if I were to ask Dad he could probably only shrug his shoulders as well. Chasing something he didn't have. A wife and a kid didn't meet his standard of life so he left them behind without a word. The man was nothing if not decisive.

Maybe in the end that's why I fell in with the Men With No Faces and their Architects. Their *Game*, if you could name it such, seemed much more innocuous when I began to play it.

You're twenty-eight and think you've experienced some things. Drugs, sex and money, enjoyed in their ordinary vehicles, become mundane in an unexpectedly quick fashion for a man like me. Perhaps I can't generate an ordinary amount of passion—it's always been a mechanical process, like deriving electricity from running water—I need an outside source to make an excess.

So I keep my ears open. Word of something interesting always filters down to those who listen. Maybe it's my job. Stockbrokers are notoriously control starved and satisfaction focused. It's an imbalance of serotonin or something.

Those promising words reached the halls and cubicles of Bordeley, Cooper and Kendrik, the brokerage firm I work for, as the summer session was closing out. The economy was in a mild recession, but I had managed several portfolios to a point modestly above an even break. Tech stocks had tanked and had tried to pull the mutual funds into the red when new lawsuits went against a particular drug maker whose product was linked to heart attacks. Like most arcane bits of information, I caught wind of The Game through a cable of hearsay, word of mouth.

I'm always a little surprised at how many rumors are seeded with truth and how subtle digging moves you closer to the source with every germane question asked. Taboo subjects are spoken about in whispers and delivered in fragments. However, finding the stream of information on these topics is like detecting gravity surrounding objects with small masses: you may have to take careful measurements to find anything, but it's still there all the same.

My initiation to The Game was at the hand of a fellow stockbroker, Mickey Templeton. Mickey was a junior broker, a bond handler, but talented enough and on the rise. He had overcome a slow drawl born of Hickville, North Carolina or somewhere, though you could hear it sometimes when he was excited. He also possessed *cum laude* credentials from Columbia which placed him squarely within the vanguard of BCK-caliber members.

The Club was not so elite to exclude Southern ex-patriots from the lower ranks, although the Inner Circle itself was founded on a bedrock of New England breeding. In fact, some Northeastern connection seemed to be prerequisite for a job offer. I've wondered more than once if my Massachusetts upbringing smoothed over my Georgetown education.

Like most brokers, Mickey had a fire burning inside him. He kept a carefully neutral expression in most cases, sometimes augmented by a mask of studied concentration. At a casual glance, he had an unassuming look to him anyway: average build and height, clean cut. He had neatly groomed blonde hair, combed to the left in a conservative side part, a faint under-aroma of aftershave, and favored ties that accented his clear blue irises. A closer look and you could see the light sheen of sweat over his upper lip and occasionally at the edges of his carefully trimmed sideburns, as if his internal combustion couldn't be completely held at bay by a mere layer of skin. Mickey was always on simmer, especially when things got tight. Such was the case with most of us. The reality was that most in the brokering business excelled under stress because stress squeezed an extra measure of adrenaline out of your sympathetic nervous system.

Still, it was often not enough. Mickey had been hinting around for weeks about something he was involved in but wouldn't spit it out until a slow Friday at the end of September.

"You still want to know about my Friday nights?" he asked in a voice thicker and slower than usual.

"I can't wait," I said, though I noticed the accent. The market had just closed—four-thirty—and I was idly wondering if I should ring Allison. Last night she had hinted around about catching a show. I put her off, claiming stomach distress. I hate Broadway.

"Meet me at Dunn's in two hours."

I shrugged. Allison wouldn't like a guy's night out but I still wasn't sure about *The Rainmaker* or *Phantom of the Opera,* so I begged off once more. Her voice chilled at this, and I could feel the weight of my wallet lighten. There is an inverse relationship between a woman's anger and your finances.

Dunn's proved to be a blow-by. As soon as I took a seat, Mickey was helping me back up.

"Not here."

I asked what was going on, but he said it could wait. We caught a different cab in what turned out to be an epic ride, eventually stopping at a seedy Irish pub to the south, in Brooklyn.

"What are we doing out here?" I complained. I noted the accent in my own voice—South Boston—amplified in that whine. My accent is always strongest when I object to something.

"You'll see," Mickey said, his face pinched like a weasel as he spied the doorway to the pub. He also peered into an alleyway that ran along the left side of the building, a long line of dumpsters obstructing easy passage.

Once we entered the bar, Mickey immediately went to the can while I ensconced myself into a corner booth, Guinness in hand. Briefly I studied the table top, which had to have had a thousand personal marks of graffiti engraved into the wood. I looked around; the pub probably dated back to the turn of the century, which was possibly the last time it was dusted. The mirror hanging beside the table was opaque with filth.

Mickey returned and he ordered drinks, followed by a few

minutes of small talk. At some point Mickey produced a scrap of paper from his pocket. "Look at this," he said, pushing a note across the table.

May 10—
Bridgeport St—10:30 PM—Lancaster alleyway

"An address. This address? So what?" I asked.

Mickey sipped a watered whiskey, his usual. "That's a message. Today is the first time in three weeks I've heard anything."

"And?" The note meant nothing to me—I waited, lighting a Camel. At least the bar had ashtrays. Smoking indoors was outlawed in Manhattan, and you got plenty of dirty looks if you lit up on the streets.

"It's a kind of game," Mickey said. "Each week, sometimes less often, I'm sent to a different location—a bar, club, gas station, whatever."

"Okay. You were sent here," I said and gave a sarcastic sweep of my hand. "Beautiful Bridgeport. So what do you do?"

"I've been given instructions."

"For what?" I asked. "The alleyway?"

"That's right. That's where it will happen."

"What will?"

Mickey spread his hands excitedly. "I don't know. That's the beauty of it."

"Mickey, what the hell are you talking about?"

"I really can't explain," he said. "You have to see tonight. It's only a couple of hours to wait."

I cringed a little bit at the prospect of spending more time here than it takes to have a drink and a cigarette. As for Mr.

Templeton's Friday night plans, I'm not impressed yet.

"I'm not following you. Why the suspense?"

"Just be patient. You need to watch me."

I put down my beer and gave Mickey a doubtful frown. I was looking for the root of this wild goose chase, perhaps expecting a punch line. But Mickey's eyes showed neither mirth nor malice. You can always tell a man is not bullshitting if he can return an unflinching stare. Mickey returned my gaze without a blink. Whatever was going on, Mickey was serious.

"It's like a club," he continued after several heartbeats. "Like BCK, right?" That was an inside joke for the brokers who worked there. "A very exclusive club, man. It's high intensity. I think you might be into it."

"This has nothing to do with me," I said, nodding to the note.

"No," Mickey says. "Not yet."

I didn't know how to respond to this comment, so I didn't say anything for a minute. I get a funny feeling. "I don't know what you're getting at, but I can't say I'll be into it," I said, half as a joke. "Maybe I should shove off. Allison, you know?"

But Mickey only laughed. The sweat was on his lip and he loosened the collar of his Versace jacket. "It's not anything like that. Let's get another drink. Be patient," he repeated.

I suddenly resign myself to it all. Couldn't be worse than *Cats* or *Annie*. The waitress returned with another Guinness and a whiskey watered *and* on the rocks for Mickey.

"You're going to have to drink ten of those to get drunk," I commented.

"I don't want to get drunk. I want to stay alert, and you should too."

I shrugged. His night.

Time moves quickly in New York. The crush of bodies, the bustle of the wait staff, the lights and noise—they compress time somehow, making the leap from one hour to the next shorter than in other places. More than once I have looked at my watch and discovered large chunks of the day have simply disappeared. I took a moment to consider Mickey. His lazy posture and steady gaze, usually into his glass, were a façade. I knew he was thinking ahead to this meeting, whatever it was, and that little mist of sweat was bubbling over his lip. *Burning inside*, I thought. I wondered how Mickey liked North Carolina, with the cows and orange blossoms. And the quiet. There, time must stretch the hours apart like chasms.

We left for the alley ten minutes before the hour.

The alley adjacent to the bar actually moved continuously through the back ends of several businesses, most apparently shut for the night. Butcher shops and shoe cobblers. Clothes boutiques and small markets. I imagined they had been closed for hours. The alley was nearly silent, the sounds of the city muffled behind the insulation of concrete structures. I followed Mickey closely, who seemed to know where he was going. My drinking was catching up with me.

We turned a corner and suddenly Mickey stopped. He gestured quickly—and, I thought, furtively—to one of the dumpsters that bookended the alleyway. I didn't ask why. Mickey's features were a tight mask of anxiety. I moved to the left trash bin, giving me a view directly to the front and partly around the next corner. I felt a bit ridiculous and annoyed while cautiously moving through the bags of trash. My Ferragamo loafers were in immediate danger of ruin as I stepped into soggy, rotten deli refuse. The scent of beer and piss lingered prominently along the dumpster wall as well; I wondered if a bum had staked this claim along with the alley cats. The double bourbon I had taken before leaving the bar sat uneasily in my gut, but I didn't complain. You had to be drunk to enjoy this sort of foolishness.

Mickey moved a small distance ahead, and I peered around my hiding place discretely. What the hell was I doing? I was tempted to call out to him and demand he set me straight on what was going on. Seconds later Mickey stopped and stood stiffly erect. Shadows obscured the alley beyond, but I thought I could hear, very faintly, movement.

Then a man—it seemed—separated himself from the darkness. The appearance was so seamless that the man *materialized*. He wore dark clothing over a sturdy, solid-looking body. A mask or stocking distorted the features of his face. I felt the rush of adrenaline as my body instantly registered the fight-or-flight instinct. *Mugger*, I thought.

Large, hooded men in dark alleyways were, for city people, the things of nightmares. I cursed inwardly for being led into this dim section of alley, which was nowhere close to a main street. Alleys in New York were often like cities themselves, just as the subway tunnels were riddled with subterranean colonies of bums. People vanished in back alleys. I stared at the man indecisively, although Mickey, only a few feet away, stood placidly, apparently unafraid.

A heartbeat later, Mickey and the other man were walking deeper into the shadows. *Shit.*

I moved from behind the bin and padded forward, trying to keep my feet light. The pair walked quickly, requiring me to semi-jog to keep them in sight. I followed through the umbrella of shadow the man had appeared from and tensed as a cold feeling passed over my body. The anticipated strike of a pipe or slash of a blade didn't arrive, and I found myself in a better lit stretch of alley. Though I was kicking boxes now and making my presence obvious, the pair never looked back. They stopped after some distance, perhaps a block's worth, and another corner, before the dead end came.

But not a lonely one.

Two men, identical in size to the Shadow Man, stood like sentries. Or sentinels. They also wore dark clothes and stockings were pulled over their faces. What the hell was this?

Yet, I merely gave them a glance.

Behind them was a woman, blonde and attractive, her long legs and full breasts displayed plainly. In fact, as I focused on her, she was totally nude, her skin glowing faintly under the light cast from a solitary light bulb. She was also tied, gagged and bound against a board bolted into the wall. The two Sentinels flanked her in the tight space, which could hold no more than the three of them simultaneously. The woman was not struggling but was not rigid—she arched slightly, toward Mickey, and twisted from side to side. The movement could have been a small sign of struggle or, perhaps, of suggestion.

As my mind wrestled with the scenario, I felt the bloom of heat in my groin. I felt a flush coming on—I was aroused. I pulled my eyes from the woman, flinching. My thoughts returned to that…gyration. Was it titillation or something else?

Mickey still hadn't wavered from his position but his face was composed. I knew he wasn't surprised. This was The Game, right? He had been having these encounters for months. I relaxed. This was an exposition. Something I "might be into."

Mickey thought I was a pervert, which brought back my earlier annoyance, but what was he doing? Again, only a second between thoughts brought a new action.

One of the men moved in front of the prostrate woman, made a rapid, smooth movement, and was abruptly inside her. She made a groan that could be easily heard, even through the gag. The cry became muted grunts as the man continued to thrust, repetitively, like a machine. Eventually the woman became silent, and the man finished, emitting a grunt of his own, a sound of animalistic satisfaction. I searched for the woman's eyes but the man's bulk and the quality of light and distance prevented me. Mickey simply stood, expressionless.

As soon as the first man finished the next began. I felt my stomach roll as the man drove home his lust, but not gently; punishingly, a brutal grinding. I turned away several times, choosing to study the effluents of the dumpster. My earlier arousal was long gone, and the flush of alcohol and adrenaline were washed away, leaving me drained. Yet, I didn't leave. When I watched, the choreography of this act struck me as repellent but fascinating. Mickey continued to watch intensely. I found his rigidness spooky, like he'd been cast in a glaze and couldn't move. I couldn't tell for certain, but the bound woman's body seemed limp. She simply took the force of the blows, the hard, uncomfortable looking board under her spine bowing under their weight.

Finally, as I suspected, it was Mickey's turn. He had forced a stocking over his head. I felt a hollowness in my groin and was sickened that there had been anything there before. Mickey's performance was just as violent, although in a flash of profile, I saw his face was in a grimace. Or perhaps this was my imagination. The stocking distorted his features, making his face appear only half-formed. The thrusts continued and eventually ended in fruition, at which point Mickey dismounted and stripped off his mask, revealing a blank look.

That look haunted me for some reason. Was it that I knew this man? My girlfriend shopped with his girlfriend. I knew her well—we had all had drinks just a week or so back, the four of us. Did she know what Mickey had been doing?

Now that the men were no longer obscuring her, I had a good look at the woman. She stared ahead with no emotion. Her only movement was the quick rising and falling of her chest with each breath.

I didn't wait for Mickey and certainly not for the Sentinels. He later caught up to me in the alley and we shared a glance but no words passed between us for a time. I felt conflicting emotions: shock, annoyance, curiosity, even a little excitement I think. Mostly I felt sick.

My stomach churned from the booze, but I couldn't keep my eyes off of Mickey. I thought of people living double lives and never expected Mickey to be one of them. I expected him to be like me. Now I wasn't so sure. I felt that I didn't want to talk to him again.

I welcomed normal sounds of cars and people as we approached the streets.

* * *

Later, I revised my judgments. Clear decisions are rarely made on the battlefield. As a lay in my bed, safely tucked into my apartment, the night's activities began to eat at me.

Eventually, I came to a shocking conclusion: I never averted my eyes from Mickey's part. Because, in the end, reality is always better than fiction.

* * *

I don't know much about psychology, but the act in the back of the alley stirred something inside me. Something seedy, masked by the Brooks Brothers suit and the Armani aftershave. I had always found sex to be crude and basic and stimulating. *Primordial*, I guess one would say. Freud said that everyone needed food, sleep and sex—the mind and body expects them, craves them. The question is what happens when these things don't hold their place in the hierarchy of necessities?

My answer: Moonlighting. That's what I call it.

This Game was a stimulus, like the caffeine in your espresso, or a hammer to the knee during a reflex check. The response is fast, effective and left no ambiguity. The reaction was going to occur.

I thought about Mickey's show. Upon completing his part, he had simply turned and walked back down the alley the way he had come. I had already made my way to the mouth of the alley. There was some indecision as to whether I should enter the bar for another whisky or to hail a cab and go to *another* bar for a whiskey. Either way, that was happening; alone or not was the question.

Mickey caught up with me. He didn't speak at first, which was fine by me. He looked calm, almost tranquil. He had tucked his shirt-tail neatly into his pants and smoothed his shirt out. He looked somehow fresher now than when we arrived three hours earlier. He kept silent for some time, sensing my confusion. For my part, I remained neutral, or tried. A stone silence was my best defense when I had to order my thoughts. And if I had to order my thoughts I was in a state of shock, or damn near.

"You saw it?" he asked finally. He leaned on the pub's brick facing.

"What the hell was that about?" I asked, with more of an edge than I wanted.

Mickey gauged what parts outrage, shock or excitement were in my voice. He was measuring me. I knew then he was going to ask me how I liked it, and if I was interested. Already I had two responses in my head. The high-minded defense was first, to be delivered with a dash of outrage. I could outline how I wasn't into this sort of sick amusement, which may or may not be legal. Of course I didn't know if it was either. The idea of role-playing returned to me. And the uneasy recollection of my erection as the act was being committed.

But my hesitation to simply say "no, leave me out of this" was enough affirmation, and we both knew it.

The strange thing about the incident, thinking about it later, was the long-term effect. At the time, I likened the incident to seeing someone shot or to watching a suicide. One day you see a person alive and perhaps you exchange a few words at the mailbox, then the next day that same person throws himself from the roof of your apartment building. It's a trauma. You look out the window and no longer see the azalea bush planted there, but instead a crushed body lying in a pool of blood. Therein lies the swing of the pendulum. Do you deny the memory or does it take on a life of its own as you constantly relive it?

I experienced my own epiphany here. I was shaken, yes. But did I enjoy it? If it were staged, perhaps, though Mickey would never give me a straight answer. That would ruin the whole thing, wouldn't it? I thought about the incident as I managed mutual funds. I thought about it over drinks with the other brokers at the usual Tenth Avenue bars. I thought about it most when I was in bed with my girlfriend. Instead of Allison, I found myself imagining the woman in the alley, tied, gagged, vulnerable.

I realized then that I was the sort of person who could put aside, for some stretch of time, all the little moral and ethical questions surrounding something and just *enjoy* it. Maybe that's the definition of evil. You know it's wrong and for a moment in time simply don't care. You try to wrestle with such a concept and struggle with the enormity of it.

Perhaps I'm a bad person or a weak person. I'm not proud of it. But in the end, I called up Mickey and let him know I wanted to see more.

* * *

My initiation as a player in this Game was no less harrowing.

The mechanism of communication between the "players" and the "managers" was designed to be mysterious. Once I made my interest known, I had only to wait. Apparently Mickey had given his contact my description. I could only speculate as to how this information was sufficient for membership.

"I don't meet someone?" I asked.

"Never," said Mickey. "You only talk to other people connected, like myself."

"Do I talk to you for meeting places?"

"No, you'll get a note or a phone call."

"Did you give out my personal details?" I asked. "Or are these guys Big Brother or something?"

"You just have to see," Mickey said with a gleam in his eyes. "To know too much kind of spoils it, right?"

So it did. *Real or role playing?*

"Somebody will contact you. Once a week. Sometimes less. You'll be told to go somewhere—alone—and wait for another contact. Sometimes they come, sometimes they don't. But when they *do...*"

"Are they always like last week?"

"No," Mickey said. "Always different. Although sometimes similar," he added.

The whole thing seemed a bit melodramatic to me at first. I still enjoyed the mystery of it. I imagined various scenarios, fantasized about different women in different ways, enjoyed the intrigue.

My first assignment was to be quite a different beast.

* * *

Like alleyways, there are an amazing number of empty lots in New York. If you took an aerial shot of the city, you would see a patchwork of buildings separated by spots of cleared land between interchanges, around rail yards and near the rivers. Especially the East River. Look hard enough and you'll even find that most of those empty spaces were free of people as well. At least above ground. Half of the tenements in Lower

Brooklyn were like giant tombstones, overlooking stitches of earth where bodies had accumulated for centuries.

And I could see the grave in the boy's eyes—he was seeing his own death. The two men surrounding him could have been the same ones from the other night with Mickey. Their features were distorted enough by stockings to be unrecognizable, from eye color to teeth size. They were disturbingly homogenous, these Sentinels, like people cloned from the same DNA.

I wiped sweat from my eyes; I was nervous myself and wiped more sweat from my hands onto my slacks. I already regretted wearing them; the field was filled with will-o'-wisps that coated the cotton with an obvious layer of white, fur-like buds. Then again, why the hell was I even in the field?

The boy—man?—was young, a hair past twenty if that. He was lean to the point of what my mother used to call "rail-thin," ribs jutting out of his body in regular half-moons. He was dark enough to be Latin, and though the light was poor, I noticed sunken pockmarks along his face. A large but faded scorpion was inked into his bare back, rippling as the young man struggled angrily. In the moonlight I saw his eyes dart back and forth, no doubt looking for ways of flight.

With an odd confidence I didn't think he would be going anywhere. I was in control, following the Sentinels as they led me to the prisoner, already tied to a post in the middle of a field of weeds. I kept my stone face, though I was reeling inside. There seemed to be no sense in this. I wondered, why is this ferret-like boy tied up for me? I thought back to only minutes before. I had nearly turned and bolted when I saw where the note had taken me, to a lonely and decrepit section of the city that even the derelicts had forsaken. My internal alarms were screaming as the cab dropped me off a block or so ahead of my destination. No one walked the streets in this neighborhood, where squared-off industrial warehouses faced each other in long lines of threatening anonymity.

The Sentinels had arrived in their stealthy manner. One moment the street was empty, in the next two large men were behind me. They motioned for me to cross the street, which led to the opposite bank of the East River harbor. Neither spoke, but the tension in their posture suggested I should oblige them. My legs responded automatically by moving in the direction they pointed, though my brain was screaming, telling me to run back to the cab as fast as I could.

Eventually, when we reached what seemed to be the center of the field, we stopped. Not far in front of me the boy was tied to a tall post, possibly iron. I realized it was a man, not a woman. Jesus, what is this? This was not what I wanted. What has Mickey gotten me into, that bastard? Adrenaline kicked in as I began to consider just how much I might risk by playing this Game. *Run.* I couldn't make myself do it. Despite the size of the two men, I knew they would catch me if I tried to flee. Fear fueled the certainty I felt about that; my legs were nearly jelly as it was.

When it became apparent that I wasn't going to run, the man closest to me handed over a heavy object. A piece of metal with four finger holes—brass knuckles. The man also cut one of the boy's ties, freeing one of his arms. Instantly he lashed out at me with a scrawny forearm. His aim was poor and I easily dodged the punch. Another potential blow was avoided as he struck at me. The lashing that held his other arm was short, but firmly held the boy at bay, much like a chain on a rabid dog. For a time I simply avoided his attacks and held the brass knuckles like a set of keys to an unknown lock.

I'm not a violent man. My aggression has always been directed towards my job, the stocks I traded, busting the market. I play racquetball and jog when I feel tense. A glass of Powers whiskey on the rocks was more soothing than the thought of punching a man—much less actually doing it.

As I ticked off these thoughts in uniform, logical fashion, I felt a sting behind my left ear. I had been hit with something. I looked around and the boy was already cocking his arm again, ready for another strike. He held a rock, with a good-sized chunk of something protruding from it. A piece of concrete maybe. It was at this moment that my mind came to grips with the circumstances; I was to beat this kid or he was to beat me. The Sentinels simply stood there, in silent observation.

"Bastard!" the boy cried out as he threw the cement chip.

I ducked the throw easily; the chip of concrete was heavier than he could accurately toss, and it landed with a thud onto the sandy lot. My temper flared at the audacity of this boy. I had done nothing to him. *Why was he attacking me?* I thought, with genuine outrage.

Then I did a surprising thing. I slipped on the brass knuckles, clenched my fist tightly and delivered a blow to the kid's mouth. I didn't use all of my force or attempt to square myself. I just swung, instinctively.

Perhaps most surprising was the grisly crunch of his teeth breaking. Blood shot out of his mouth in projectile streams, as though his jugular ran though his lips. In a moment of retrospect, I mentally noted the satisfying *solidness* of impact and how such little force had produced such terrific damage. My fist was bloody, but not cut; the brass knuckles had done most of the work for me.

My victim continued to spit out blood, and I could see his two front teeth hanging awkwardly, like shutters loose on bad hinges. But he recovered quickly, almost fast enough to shatter my own nose as I admired my handiwork. I moved aside at the last moment and his fist grazed my shoulder. He stumbled as he lunged towards me, and I took the opportunity to bash him in the back of the head with the knuckles again.

The kid made a groaning sound as he reached behind his head, protecting the back of his skull. I smashed him in the head anyway, thinking I might be able to knock the poor son of a bitch out.

Each blow reinforced a contradiction in me—I wanted to stop, but not until it was done. Not death, just unconsciousness. I don't know why I made this distinction, or how knocking the guy into a coma suddenly was a good idea. I just did it—pummel a guy smaller than me, bound to a post, in some abandoned lot in Brooklyn.

What drives people to hurt others? As I worked up a sweat beating this guy, I thought it must simply be opportunity. Otherwise, why was I doing it?

The silent Sentinels to both sides of me might be a factor. They probably figured this is what I signed on to do. At the same time, this was no stage act, this was real. So if I rejected the scenario maybe I would be strapped to this pole and a role reversal would take place. I suddenly thought that maybe this young guy was a player who had tried to escape and this was his punishment. Maybe there was someone watching *me.*

I stopped the beating, now coldly aware of the brutality I was inflicting on this person. No way could this be role playing. That would be too sick anyway. The Sentinels said nothing and, for now, didn't move. Neither did the boy on the ground, though he was breathing. The scorpion on his back was splattered with blood.

I dropped the brass knuckles and turned away. Without looking back, I began the walk through the will-o'-wisps, bracing for a tackle or another concrete chip against my skull. But nothing came—nothing from the boy of course. He was alive. That's why I left. Had I stayed, would he have lived?

This is not the sort of question one asks of himself. You don't want to know the answer.

* * *

Shocking scenes remain vivid in the mind for a time, then gradually subside. Of course, memories may dim but they never disappear completely—not something appalling like knocking teeth out of a man's head. Those who are disappointed with the fading of this memory may become restive. Perhaps if you did it often enough the act would eventually become commonplace, a routine. You are then a beast. Maybe even the Nazis underwent this change when they hunted and imprisoned Jews, before coldly executing them. But for a stockbroker it's traumatic, and hence, you return to the man who threw himself from the roof in front of your den window. Does the memory haunt you? Or do you simply accept it? Rationalization of the act makes it easier for you to see the azaleas rather than the broken body.

The man I saw was likely a criminal of some sort, possibly in a gang. The scorpion tattoo—that seemed to spark some memory in me in regards to inner-city gang fighting. The Sentinels might have paid this guy to take a beating. That didn't seem right, though. Better to mug some bastard than to take a beating yourself. No gang member was going to lose teeth, especially to a scared-looking, khaki-wearing, upper-Westside type. No way. This guy was somehow collared off the street and delivered to me for a beating. He knew it. He would have killed me—he had tried. The thought occurred to me that I could be engaging in vigilante justice. Even that didn't seem right. *Why me?* Why Mickey and I were doing two totally different things was another.

He repeated his previous explanation, which in later weeks would become rote. We were having a drink in Brooklyn after a half-day of trading—it was Veteran's Day.

"It's different every time," he said. Knowing this wasn't enough, he added. "Look, I've had to do some pretty weird things myself. I delivered a gun last night."

"A *gun*?" I couldn't believe what I was hearing. I looked around the bar to see if anyone was listening. The other patrons were talking in a low murmur, producing the characteristic rumbling you hear when many people are speaking at once.

"I didn't use it," he said quietly, sipping his watered whiskey. "I just picked it up and tucked it away in the place they told me."

"Are you crazy? That gun could have been used in a murder."

"I know," he said. His lip was sweating. The thought was clearly exciting to him. "I was careful, though. Nothing can be traced to me."

"Well, this is too fucking crazy. I don't want this type of shit. I might have beat that man to death. You're running guns. I'm not a thug. I don't want to go to jail."

"I don't either," he said.

"Then what the hell are we doing here?"

But I knew, and so did Mickey.

"How did you feel when you hit that kid?" he asked after a moment.

I considered my words while I lit a cigarette. Obviously, I struggled with what I had done—at times I wore guilt like a scarlet letter, or tried to convince myself of that. The truth was that paranoia was no substitute for contrition, and as the days passed my concern was based solely on the idea of getting caught.

Allison had hardly noticed. I did finally see a Broadway show, placating her and our relationship, but she was none the wiser in concern to my nocturnal activities.

I thought back on that night often, and as my life stayed on its tracks so did my desire to get another note. Just to see what they might have in their bag of tricks.

"It's a game," Mickey said. "But a serious one. I think some people do get hurt. But if you play right, you have nothing to worry about. They take care of everything."

I suspected that much, yet his answer was unsatisfying. What struck me was the coordination of it all. How did they engineer everything at the right time and place? For that matter, what kept the players from telling everyone what they did? Obviously the fear of criminal charges was great enough to prevent the average person from doing this. Besides, the players had no idea who their puppet masters were. Or how far their crimes might extend. No doubt certain people would crack eventually, or blow their assignment. A more disturbing thought was that, given the violent nature of my *assignment*, I knew there could be other ways to shut someone up.

"We're pieces in a machine," I said.

"No, we *are* the machine."

I shook my head, not knowing at the time what he meant. That would become clear soon enough.

Mickey studied the headlines scrolling across the television above the bar. His lip was shining, but his face was milky pale. He didn't look good. I glanced at what he watching—some human interest story on the homeless—so he must have been reading the scrolling blurbs at the bottom of picture. Brokers did it automatically, as the stock prices were listed on the bottom line. I caught the tail end of one story—a judge who had ended up dead in his house. Suicide or murder, no one knew which. The next headline concerned a woman who stabbed her husband.

"Mickey," I said. "Who...enlisted you?"

He waited a short time before his answer, perhaps to phrase it in just the right way, but he simply said: "An old friend."

"Somebody from the South."

"He was."

"How did he approach you?"

"How did I approach *you*? If you know someone who might be into something like this..."

"I think this role playing shit is out of control," I said. The drink went to my head as I leaned towards Mickey for emphasis. "It's not *me*, even if sometimes I go along with it."

Mickey smiled a little as he stirred the remnants of his whiskey. For the first time I felt like he was truly keeping something from me.

"You want me to tell you it's just for fun, something that means nothing. You won't turn away from it as long as you are unsure. I can guarantee you that. That's the excitement. You don't know, no one really knows. The hell of it is this: you don't care either. What is there to go back to? If you stop now, is Allison going to be enough? I think you know the answer to that. And work? No, God no. I mean, money doesn't do it for you. Sex doesn't do it for you. You don't have to worry about where you're going to sleep or when you're going to eat. When all is normal, everyday things are boring and mundane, and you want more. When you already have everything, you have to make something more for yourself."

Mickey doesn't talk much and delivers sermons even less. He knew his analysis had hit home, and I felt, even then, that we were still on the same train, that he was projecting his own thoughts. So I asked, "How do you get out?"

"I don't honestly know," he said, and there was weariness there. "Leave town?"

I grunted and leaned back into the booth's aged-leather back.

"I have to take a leak," Mickey announced. "Stay the course. You know the way."

I drained my Guinness and a red-headed waitress was over quickly. She had a pretty smile with a picket fence of white bicuspids. I had a brief fantasy of taking her in the bar, right on the faux-cherry wood tabletop.

"Another?" she asked.

I had to meet Allison in an hour so I shook my head. She left the bill and I fished out my wallet from the inside pocket of my jacket.

The bill was there, but so was another piece of paper. A note, typed.

Hudson River Park, Pier 40 — 10:30 tomorrow

I looked around for the waitress, but she was out of sight. When I went into the restroom, Mickey was not there. I didn't know if the note was mine or his. When I returned to the table he had thrown down a twenty and left. Fast exits were not like Mickey.

I asked another waitress where her red-headed partner ran off to. She looked puzzled at this.

"I don't think any red heads work here," she said.

She was right, too, because I never saw the girl again.

* * *

Hudson River Park ran from Fifty-Ninth to the southern tip of Manhattan, running along its western boundary like a lamprey. The southernmost point ended near my neck of the woods, in the financial sector. The park itself was rather open and I felt exposed. I stood in a small square with four benches arranged on opposite sides of a plain of short centipede grass, now stunted and flattened by the oncoming of the fall chill. It met the definition of a "day park" — no one reputable was here at night, no lunching office workers or tourists milling about the concourse, or even the occasional pan-handler that infiltrated this far into Wall Street.

After half an hour of wandering about the place looking for the Sentinels, I began to feel like a pervert on the prowl. Even worse, I felt exposed. I kept expecting a cop to put a flashlight beam into my eyes. *What are you doing here? Oh, just enjoying the concourse, Officer.*

I almost shouted when I noticed the Sentinels. Two of them, hulking and characteristically silent. Their black shirts and stockings made them unidentifiable and stealthy. I believed they could literally be anywhere at night, looking upon their chosen prey like wolves blending into the forest underbrush.

No greetings were exchanged. Instead, I fell into place behind them as we moved towards a cluster of boats at the wharf. Eventually we boarded a smallish craft with a sail, akin to a Mariner. The floorboards creaked under our combined weight and gave the boat a mild list to the starboard side. I could hear a gentle wake of splashing water. The salt was thick in the air, along with the heady smell of gasoline. I didn't see an outboard motor, but the smell was there anyway. I suspected the boat had recently been docked.

My nerves stretched just a bit further when I was led into the tiny bulkhead. We all ducked our heads while descending a short flight of stairs. The salt air smell immediately left and a surprising aroma of perfume and fresh laundry struck me. The cabin was dark, but I could just make out the figure lying on a small bed tucked under the hull.

I breathed in deeply to swallow my shock. She lay there, barely clothed—blond, petite, fragile. Like a doll. She was bound, but I must have been accustomed to this because I hardly registered this as unusual or unexpected. The shock was how young she looked.

I took a tentative step closer as the Sentinels offered their faceless gaze. My eyes had adapted somewhat to the dim light, provided only by a weak nightlight plugged into a wall adapter. She was awake, but made no move either towards or away from me. The lack of light made it impossible to tell if she watched me with fear. But when I touched her shoulder lightly she trembled. Her chest sparkled when she moved her head. I looked closer. A necklace. A *Friends Forever* necklace, or half of one. Only a girl would wear such a thing. My finger tips brushed along her skin, soft and warm and perfect.

The Sentinels stood perfectly still as I examined the charm. I wouldn't look back to see them, but I knew they were waiting. Blocking the doorway. I couldn't leave. Running was no option here. The cabin felt very small with the heat of four bodies. The girl's mouth was not taped, and she was as mute and still as my guardians. She was probably a college student. At least that old, no doubt of legal age. Perhaps she did this for money. How could I know?

In the end, I was as gentle as I could be. A perfect gentlemen, really.

* * *

Afterwards, I was no longer guided by the faceless men. The notes stopped being locations and turned into instructions. *Move this package to this street. Buy a ticket to the* La Traviata *opera and leave it in a PO box.* The first time, I was told to keep a manila envelope with something heavy inside. It turned out to be a key. I had no idea to what. It was a heavy skeleton key, like one a jailor might carry. My mind considered the possibilities and produced numerous others, many sordid. I fortified myself with Powers, fighting off my own paranoia.

Mickey might have noticed, but I saw him less and less. I asked him to come to my apartment, the first potential visit in weeks. But he didn't show. In fact, no one other than myself had been in my apartment in weeks. Allison was busy with her social work. I was busy with mine.

* * *

Winters in New York were wet and cold, sometimes enough to snow, but usually just enough to freeze the dirt on the streets into a filthy, grey slush. Inevitably, the muddy ice made its way onto the sidewalk, fighting for space with the pedestrians as if it belonged there. At night, when people were in their homes and when even the homeless had fled to their shelters, the dirt reigned the streets along with trash blowing in a frozen wind that ripped your body heat away in cruel blasts.

The City That Never Sleeps was in slumber on this block. It was too early for the street sweepers and too late to see many cabbies. I was alone as the long hand of my watch swung to 3:30 am.

There had been a time when I was out this late regularly, particularly in college. Then came a job, then Allison. Well, no longer—she was now a note in my personal history. She had sensibly left after I continued to withdraw from any normal relationship. Perhaps some part of my eroded conscience wanted to protect her from The Game.

The end has been abrupt, even when expected. Her things were simply gone one day when I returned from work— her clothes, the Highwater wall clock, even her goddamned blender. Gone, without a word. She had surgically removed herself like a perfectly benign cancer. I couldn't really blame her—our nights had dwindled to a paltry handful. You could only take so many nights out that began in a café, reached its pinnacle at the cinema, and died quietly in bed, usually with each facing the opposite direction.

The wind had died down, allowing me to faintly hear a strand of ghostly musical notes trickling down from the apartment above the canopy. I revised my assessment of the street. Nothing really sleeps here, not if you look hard enough. Shadows cast from streetlamps and car lights revealed the creatures of the night. I know—I'm now one of them. We move furtively on missions best kept secret from those asleep at this hour.

I clutched at the message in my left coat pocket. It was greasy and crumpled from my grip, but I liked to feel it anyway—like a talisman, this scrap of paper. I reflected on how much power this sliver of tree flesh held.

Some people frequent bars. Others whorehouses. Some of those places were one in the same. They should have their own stockholders, as the business never falters, and their doors never stopped swinging to and fro. A day's pay went a long way here. Used to, anyway. Inflation. The Fed kept cutting interest rates and the dollar kept wilting away. Some at the firm predicted it was the dying breaths of the old greenback, whose life seemed to be slowly sucked away year by year. I wasn't so pessimistic, but my clients were. They had no stomach for tough times. I found that I soon came to despise them. But back to whorehouses—they were not a bygone establishment, and the Big Apple had more than its fair share.

I watched a stranger leave from one.

I observed his clothes. They were well-cut but tattered, like the man inside them. His worn face held a pair of sunken eyes and a moustache almost disguised by the heavy growth on his jowls. He was unkempt and drunk, staggering into a row of stinking garbage cans that lined the street. He weaved back onto the sidewalk, taking some of the dirty slush with him.

I tracked him easily. I found myself wishing he was more aware, less of an easy target.

I wondered why this drunk was important. His suit and tie, once expensive, were now worn. Leather shoes, long since scuffed beyond polish. No wedding ring, but that meant little at a brothel. A man gone to seed.

Grimly, I gripped the paper in my right hand and the gun in my left.

I was surprised when, earlier, I felt the gun beneath the seat of my car, bundled with the note. I was given instructions, and this man was the object. The gun was small but heavy, solid. I didn't have much experience with firearms and wondered what caliber it was. Dad had a gun and his brother owned a rifle for deer hunting. I remembered being surprised by that, as I considered hunting something only done by rednecks. Which would probably make Uncle Phil a redneck. But with a gun in your own hand…things *felt* different than I would have thought. *I* felt different. No revulsion, no fear. For a time, after pulling it from underneath the seat, I handled it gently, delicately adjusting the moving parts—the clip, the safety, the cocking action of the hammer. After a few moments of becoming accustomed with the mechanism, I felt confident. Strong.

At some point, the man sensed he was being followed and turned. "Lost, son?"

I stared into the light misting rain, silently, stoically. Had I a stocking I could have been a Sentinel.

Recognition filled him. His eyes grew unclouded with the realization. "Oh," he said. "I knew this day would come."

I said nothing, stalling.

Sweat and rain was making my grip on the pistol slippery. I squeezed tighter.

"This could be you," he said, ominously. "This *will* be you. Our Keepers are fickle people."

My gut clenched at the way he spat out the words. He knew about me. Perhaps he knew about the girl on the ship. Or the kid with the scorpion tattoo in the abandoned lot.

Self-preservation has a way of turning you into stone. All I had to do was raise the pistol.

The street was empty except for the shadows cast by the street lamps and those that hid within them. They were probable much like myself. The Fifty-Percent Rule. The Even-Odd Rule.

Like I said, mere opportunity can make a man act cruelly. Given the chance, maybe I would be the man who tracks down children like Anne Frank and makes them disappear. Maybe if she met me she would know I was an evil man, but could still see into some corner of my soul that hadn't been tainted with darkness. Or, maybe, I was only being human, an evolved animal that has yet to shed its animal urges. In that case, perhaps no one can truly be evil. I still do not know for certain.

The shot was accurate. I couldn't tell if the bullet had lodged in the head or if it had exited, but blood pooled rapidly under his body.

I rifled through his pockets—keys, gum, lint, a tattered twenty. A wallet was in his coat. Through the rain I read his license. I confirmed a name and it tickled something in my memory. Had I heard of him? A lawyer? A judge?

Mentally, I found myself tracking his downfall. Why target him now? He was the walking dead. His wallet did produce a photo of a younger man, before he had started graying. He held himself stiffly, but with dignity. He was important, once. One could tell from the arrogant tilt of his head, the penetrating gaze into the distance beyond the camera. A worthy man.

I looked once more at the body on the ground and no longer saw the resemblance. For one brief instant, I saw myself in his shoes—destitute, a nobody, a memory already fading. My feeling of power drained. I shook off the thought, though, cursing the dead man under my breath. I had done him a favor.

My job here was done now. There was an assigned place to drop my gun. I knew it would be picked up by someone else in The Game. I smiled, as I still called it that. Only, now The Game was to not be caught, to see how far I could go. The man on the ground had lost his edge and eventually his life. But really, he had been dead for a long time.

I kept the photo, though. Everyone needs a reminder of their place. I do know which half of humanity I favor—the strongest. Thus, I can't really consider myself evil.

But perhaps you wouldn't want to see me in a dark alley, either.

J. Daniel Stone

Author J. Daniel Stone has been making some big publishing waves in recent years. His work can be found in *Abomination Magazine* and in anthologies from Blood Bound Books, Pink Narcissus Press, Prime Books, *Icarus: The Magazine of Gay Speculative Fiction* and more.

Stone's debut novel, *The Absence of Light*, was released in 2013 by Villipede Publications.

His work has been reviewed by horror websites that include *Horrornews.net*, who said his stories are "lush and ultra-violent, thus which successfully invokes the great horror literature of the 1990's," and *Hellnotes* deemed his work "Psychologically Insightful."

The 25-year-old Stone was born and raised in New York City, does not eat meat, believes in equal rights and absorbs as much art and science as he can.

WORMHOLE

BY J. DANIEL STONE

"The oldest and strongest emotion of mankind is fear,
and the oldest and strongest kind of fear is fear of the unknown."
—H.P. Lovecraft

"I want to know what becomes of us when we die," Jason said to me. "The beautiful unknown; the fragile darkness."

His hectic whispers ignite the flame in my head: ectoplasm, orbs, vortices and elementals. Together, Jason and I experienced lazy dreams, poetic nights and warehouse hunts in the refurbished ghettos of Brooklyn. Thrift shop rags painted on our bones. Geiger counters and cigarette smoke trailing ghostly in Bushwick. Digital cameras clutched like pistols in Williamsburg.

Jason rambling again about the best ways to die and the ephemeral existences we suffer here on earth. He couldn't help himself as the social scene he followed was that of the warehouse children who thrived in poverty, existentialism and gloom. Parties of shadow, candelabras in every window and incense burning to kill the smell of the rats; artsy-fartsy tongues—the sound of their snarky voices made me hate them. But Jason's young face made up for it; the tight lips and frizzy black hair that tumbled over his wild, grey eyes made him incessantly innocent.

We'd just finished touring an underground gallery, one that made its name for capturing life in its utterly final stage: death. Photos slung up like ghoulish garlands in a forever-Halloween world, black and whites pinned to the musty walls showcasing long hallways of dust and vapor distilled in time, an empty doorway leading the viewer into the burnt husk of an insane asylum. Glittering things swarmed like stars, things that were said to be orbs and vortices, or the oily eyes of former, pissed off patients.

"That's the place," silver fingernails in his mouth. "I know those eyes…the windows to a black soul."

Those photos lit a fire of jealousy in my gut: the strength and precision, the limitless angles. Photographers creating magic by the click of a button, and it was something I just couldn't do. I'd been shooting my own photos since the day I realized that photography was my only escape, the tissue protecting my bones and the air to my angry lungs.

Ghost hunting seemed as rational as any other form. What a thrill it is to prove the existence of things most people believe are locked inside books and movies. How sad it is to live in one reality when there is so much out there that has yet to be discovered. I had broadened my knowledge of ghosts, echoes and elementals, reading books like *Darklore* and *House on Haunted Hill*. I bought the best equipment: temperature readers, Geiger counters, infrared motion exchangers and full-spectrum camcorders.

It was my big *fuck you* to the people who said I should be a good girl and leave boyish enchantments like death, the macabre and heavy metal music behind me. Enchantments, not influences, because all girls are supposed to be princesses, aren't they? But I am one of choice. I wanted to seek things that made others uneasy, the weird silhouette known as a girl. So I matched my code of dress with that of my soul, the color of a raven's wing: skinny, long legs wrapped tight in fishnet; hair dyed every shade of a permanent gloom; my skin never in the sun long enough to get any Vitamin D, pale to the point of being unhealthy.

Jason loved the way I dressed, said I was his black Madonna. Our friends thought we were a freaky couple, the kind that fucked in the subways or necked in the middle of Central Park—Elvira and her ragged prince of darkness. Yeah, right. We had tried to be lovers, memorizing the sharp curves of one another's faces, the pale, jutting bones beneath our skin, the eloquent circuitry of veins in our throats and hands. But Jason's mouth left the taste of putrescence on my palate, and his skin was like touching a fish left in the freezer too long.

Jason was more like the brother I never wanted but always needed by my side. I adored his fascination for the adventure of death. Naturally it became his only hobby, obsessed and oppressed by the memory of the bad-people-dressed-in-white, who pumped his mother with a syringe full of liquid sleep and locked her wretched form in the loony bin. She'd rotted her mind with the bottle so much that eventually suicide became her only way out, being that they'd forgotten to take away her belt when they brought her in.

But it wasn't that Jason wanted to die. He simply longed to

discover death; his soul breaking free from the living chrysalis we call bone and flesh was the ultimate freedom. After all, his mother had done it, and his plan was to meet her halfway. Jason often filled my head with stories of her, his hate and regret, the anguish that a child feels over a mother who never wanted to be a mother. Though she was deemed insane by the state and had fucked up his life beyond measure, Jason's mother was the only person in the world he ever talked about.

She was his personal poltergeist.

Oh, how he would recall the memory of her, those piercing blue eyes as if the tips of needles, and the twisted, dark red curls atop her head. When you love someone enough to hate them, you find that you become their slave, and everything you say and do revolves around them; you aim to please the insatiable. It's a sick but true part of the human condition.

And then there was me, the weird best friend trying to understand how she fit into the fucked up portrait of Jason's jaded life, the paltry ghost hunter willing to sell her soul to capture the dead, in any form, on film. Whenever I talked about ghosts, elementals or orbs, Jason's soft side showed its face. His speculative curiosity and love of aberrance flowered into a deep understanding that there truly is life after death. We connected greatly on that level.

But I didn't yearn for the ending of life like he did; rather, I simply wanted to prove that it existed with the click of my camera, bringing to life the final moment when a person closes their eyes and accepts that there is no light at the end. That's the moment when there's only the one great expectation: the big, wet dirt nap.

Looking Jason in the eyes was like a puzzle. I wanted to know what was going on in his head. In the spiraled valleys of that special brain, perhaps there would be a symphony of death written by careful hands.

Many people assumed we were nuts or watched one too many scary movies. I feel terrible for them and their small minds, so complacent to live their lives judging others when there are so many realities to explore. But the truth is that they hate themselves for not being able to break free of their societal chains, and they throw that hate around like a vicious poison, trying to condemn others to their self-loathed doom.

"When I am here death is not," Jason would say. *"When death is here I am not.* I want to find the middle ground!"

That's only a taste of the poetry he wrote in scrappy note-books until that horrible, purple hour called sunrise. The promise of poetry is so much greater than that of ghosts. It will always be there if you want it to be; ghosts have a mind of their own. I learned this as no matter the equipment and no matter how many hunts we went on, I never came up with any hard evidence. It drove me to become sick of my art, sick of never being gifted with the promise of orbs or vapors, not even a faint sparkle of dust. And so it was then that Jason dropped the bomb on me. He wanted to visit the insane asylum where his mother took her last, agonizing breath, where she had convinced herself that suicide was the only way out of her own head.

That was to be my big payoff. But the place had burnt down, destroyed by a relentless fire. Fiberglass walls ignite easily and are very common in the oldest buildings in the city, allowing the spread of the kind of fire that kills everything around it, dumbfounding the FDNY with how powerful a flame can be against their pathetic water-weapons.

"Why seek something that we'll all encounter? I mean, we're all going to die." I said this to him nonchalantly, but curiously looking forward to his answer.

Jason pulled on his crazy hair and lit a clove cigarette. His face became elated, Cheshire grin, and his insouciant, grey eyes marked me as he clicked his nails against a bottle of beer.

"We're all born into a temporary world," he said. "After our body and mind die, our soul becomes the spirit and joins our ancestors in the permanent world. I'm not seeking this end of *process* we call death. I'm merely its biggest fan."

Ever feel like you're being watched? Ever feel that tickle at the back of your neck? Everyone has. In the ghost hunting world it's called a vortex and is defined as a tiny explosion of energy. We wanted to feel the ultimate vortex—Jason's mother. So we stretched our faith to the point of no return, living by the firm belief that life after death was a reality and that it could all be caught on film. And why shouldn't we? People aren't curious enough to ask why they feel like they're being watched, too afraid of what might answer them through the depthless dark. People just don't want to know that this reality we sit in, this reality we blow holes in and deplete like it's some renewable resource, isn't the *only* one. They don't want to interrupt their careful equation of perfect hair, perfect wife, perfect kids and perfect life. The Born Again Americans.

I decided I was finally going to be somebody.

But I knew deep down that this was something that could lead us to the bitter end of our friendship, to the *big come down*.

Having too much faith in something can hurt you, can mock all that you stood for in first place. In this sense, faith is very much like a wormhole. It transports your mind to another place so you can stare at yourself as if through a glass wall, trying to break out, remembering when you once had your sanity.

* * *

It was mid-October and the mist was still a swirling-gray phantom atop the Hudson. We watched the water scintillate against the moon while drinking whiskey from the bottle. Oh that amber burn in our throats and how it helped us sleep!

Halloween was in full spring. Gossamer webs spread across tenement doors, black and orange lights pricked twilight like children's daggers. That night Jason and I left a calamitous heavy metal show of rattling guitars and whorls of psychedelic lights crucified by salient vocals. Mosh pits of sweaty bodies in torn clothing, costume jewelry and faces scarred by crazed makeup ruled the night. It was our wasted scene.

Dusk washed over the towering buildings like a great spill of quill ink. Our tussled hair whipped the star-wind as we sped down Tenth Avenue on our Mongoose bikes, cursing the busy city streets. Sharp limbs swathed in black, Souls on the Road, like Kerouac wrote. We tipped a scraggy street musician, who was shattering notes with his violin as if the tearing of clothes, and halted to glimpse at what we thought was a specter in a lone alleyway, finding it was only thick grease vapors pouring out of a food truck.

Down a half mile, zipping under the brand new High Line Park, and we smelled spicy smoke and heard the paranormal echoes of scuttling, crazed forms running into the nearest bar they could find.

"These kids get annoying," I told Jason.

"They run from the night as we run into it."

Jason leaned over to kiss me but I backed way. His breath was rancid even with the lace of whiskey and cloves. I saw his bad teeth jut from that heinous smile, smelled the gingivitis cloud every time he spoke. But I pitied him because I knew that when you're poor you don't have time for the dentist; the will to care is a phantom memory.

All that shines turns to rust.

It was then that our eyes became tortured by the dilapidated sights of the industrial section. The air was weighted with coal ash, diesel fumes and charred timber, the clear smell of a recent fire. Hidden between buildings so scarred by flame they shouldn't have been standing upright, buildings so old the next wind would send them crumbling to the cobblestone street, our insidious destination had been met.

We parked our bikes illegally and took a moment to gaze at the asylum tipping forward like a sentinel rising from a gravelly grave and judging the city before it. Bashed windows and a hundred-thousand glass shards glimmered against the cobble; the moon lit its bare-bone insides and I thought that this was as close to a 9/11 ghost as I had ever come. Chain links crisscrossed the huge front door, but Jason picked the lock and we were soon ducking beneath a heavy, black nylon cover.

"Take a picture!" Jason said. "Mother may be right here in all this cold fluorescence."

Gods, he was really always talking about her!

Finger on the shutter button of my digital camera and I soaked the huge foyer with a bright ball of light. A sibilant group of rats scurried from the light; black dust became unsettled and peppered our clothes. Unhappy with the results, pixels showing no promise of orbs, vortices or ectoplasms, we continued our journey into the asylum.

I imagined full skeletons alive on their feet, bones not like you'd think, not birdcage torsos white as the moon, skeletal hands reaching out for a place in purgatory or skulls with permanent grins. No, I imagined the dirtiest, grittiest whole skeletons seared like skewered meat, tiny bones curled in fetal positions avoiding the fire; osseous matter splattered like bird shit after jumping off the roof. Jason lit a poorly rolled joint of salvia, throwing fruity smoke loops in the air. I took a hit and it made me feel quite fruity right away, imbuing in my brain, playing tricks on my eyes. The first sign of a good salvia high is hallucination.

"There are things in this world that can't be explained by the rational mind," Jason said. "They have the power to appear or disappear when they want."

"No matter what, it's time to prove these suckers wrong, the zealots and the atheists."

Eyes like chips of moon and him holding me close, he agreed.

I've always believed in the *We are One* idea. There's no real logic behind it. When we die, we go back to that one universal soul. Our bodies and brains are simply the vessels in which we travel. All life is energy, time and space, thus we are all one in this tired game of death. But this went against everything

I stood for as a ghost hunter. I had to believe that there was something to capture, something that would make me a hero in the art world.

Jason pressed forward, humming "10,000 Days" by Tool, a song written for mothers across the globe. *"Daylight dims leaving cold fluorescence, difficult to see you in this light."* An ode to heartache, remembering each time she picked up that poisonous bottle. I couldn't understand why he loved someone who treated him so terribly, concerned with her own issues, her own drink, not her family. That's the real unknown if you ask me.

"I feel like I've been here, as a little boy," wilting bones touching the ashy floor.

Our Docs skidded across the complaining floorboards as we entered a room so dark, so utterly vacuous of light that I needed to switch to my full-spectrum recorder. I took it out of my backpack—a craggy, bulging, oval thing decorated with XXX stickers—and turned it on to see the room under a different angle and different light. It was then that I smelled the rotgut stench of piss-warm beer, the sweet and sour aroma of white wine.

The room itself was destroyed. The bed was turned upside down; doll heads with burnt hair and gouged eyes piled in every corner. There were so many, and all were missing their eyes. I read once that insane patients play with dolls to recreate the life they think should be living. But you can't behead every doll you have and live in peace outside these crumbling walls; such is why they're locked up. And finally, when I looked into the small LED screen, I saw something I shouldn't have seen—a pair of blinking, blue eyes. They were hidden behind a jungle of curly hair, and when I moved my view away from the screen I only saw that complete blackness again.

"Mom?" Jason called as if he knew. "This was your room, wasn't it?"

The eyes rolled in their spectral sockets and took one long, wet blink before vanishing. A faint, pale vapor rose around us, thick as ectoplasm. I suddenly recalled the pictures with all the eyes from the gallery and wondered if they had been taken here. When I came back to my senses we were doused in silence, and oh, if I could describe it. Not devoid of sound but the absence of it, pure nothingness, the way you would say black is the inexistence of color. But I knew we weren't alone; I knew her eyes were carefully marking us.

"I have the chills," Jason said. "I think I need to sit down."

"No."

I didn't want to sit. I wanted to move on, to get into the heart of the building. I felt so close to that pivotal point where a person meets their harrowing goal, their life's tragic dream, that I couldn't stop myself. Davy Jones' locker full of the blackest treasures. I had to cajole Jason to move, planting my hand against that impossibly sharp shoulder, my nails digging into his scrubby shirt. He replied by just staring at the doll heads, moving two pale fingers in and out of the hollowed eyes.

"I remember how she looked at me, before she turned to the bottle. She had a way of making me do anything she wanted."

Then he stood and we jetted out of the bedroom, taking the longest walking tour of our lives. Each corridor after that was weighted with the sense of loneliness, loss, the hope for a friend or family member to come to the rescue. But no one had ever came. I could feel it. Everywhere I turned was only a pitchy silence, the sound of dripping water, of a million collected tears. Chinese water torture to my American ears. It was then Jason proclaimed that we had come to the asylum in vain, that we weren't destined to see anything.

"I've let you down. I'm sorry," he said.

"I already saw something. Big, blue eyes behind curly hair. I smelled alcohol—"

"Don't tease me!"

"I'm not!"

My voice took on an echo that seemed to never end, dying at the furthest end of the hallway and curving into another part of the building until it was above us, rushing out into the still-dark night. I thought about something that I'd read in a book about ghost hunting, that we are all born into a temporary world known as the *spirit incubator*. I recalled Jason's words. *After the body and mind dies, our soul becomes the spirit and joins our ancestors in the permanent world*, the world Jason wanted to get into, the world I wanted to record on film and show off in all the galleries across lower Manhattan.

It was that very notion that drove me to my very unforgivable act. I begged Jason to call her out, tease the spirit, take away the incubator before hatch time. It's well known that if you fuck with the dead, they will fuck with you right back. Jason was a good boy and did as he was told, with the help of a jet-flame lighter and a quick pull off the salvia joint. He began to spit and cry, his face a white sphere of light against the pitch black. It was the drug that led the true Jason out of the closet, a scared little pup that had no closure due to the untimely death of his mother.

"She was my everything," he said, snot like worms running down his face.

I wiped the slime away with my hand, sparkling slush

against my pale palm, and I kissed Jason on the mouth—first time in a long time—and his lips burned, much like his voice. He kissed me back; a big, sloppy kiss that tasted of tears and boogers, and that was fine by me. I realized that I truly loved him and didn't want him to hurt. But it was time to get the show on the road.

Fuck faith and how it tricks the mind into believing there's something greater in the world than us, some great cosmic force in the shape of a puppeteer god. Nothing is greater than the *big come down*. Nothing is greater than the end of days, the loss of friends. The afterlife is yet another construct of mankind's fear of the unknown. Death is merely the end of life, and is nothing to fear, like pages in a book with a beginning, middle and an end, so predictable.

Get it?

No.

Jason didn't understand this. He never feared death because he was so set on finding his mother. But mother never wanted him, so he was left an effigy to burn in his own fucked up agony of never feeling the proper love of a parent.

"Come out," I heard him say over and over. *"Difficult to see you in this light."*

But then…

A pale void, angel's brilliance. Deep glow of a space and time that smashed all the rules of physics to jagged pieces of universe. Eyes moved rapid as bad thought, ones that I could only see through the view of my full-spectrum recorder. When I looked without the camera I saw only the inky black of the asylum. But not Jason.

"I see her…"

He darted away and didn't stop even as I begged him to turn around, to come back with me, that we'd seen it all and we needed to go. I didn't want to be alone, not in here, and I didn't want to follow him to that bane light. I couldn't. Was I truly a believer?

"This little light of mine, a gift you passed unto me. I'm gonna let it shine..."

Down the narrow, black hallway, I saw her showing Jason the way to the noose in the shape of a halo. I saw Jason stand atop the stool, his hair falling over his face, bony hands itching with a relief that I could not rationalize. Freedom into the arms of his savior?

It was that moment Jason kicked over the stool and I saw his trembling feet in midair. When they stopped moving I saw that this was no noose, but a *belt*. He'd found the beautiful unknown as I was made into a true believer. I realized that death is a shortcut through space and time, ending at the blunt finality of nothing. It's a road I cannot bear to take just yet.

The last I saw of them was the clasping of wispy hands as they disappeared into the fiery wormhole, leaving me alone in that dusky asylum, to question my sanity forever, the proof in my hands, but the loss of my friend like dead weight in my heart.

Never took life, but surely saved one.
Hallelujah, it's time for you to bring me home.

DAVID BLIXT

Living in Chicago with his wife and two children, Blixt describes himself as "actor, author, father and husband. In reverse order." His work is consistently described as 'intricate,' 'taut,' and 'breathtaking.'

An author of historical fiction, Blixt's work spans the early Roman Empire through Renaissance Italy to the Elizabethan era and combines his love of theatre with a deep respect for the quirks of history.

His recent novels include *Fortune's Fool*, a part of his Star-Cross'd series, and *Colossus: The Four Emperors*, the second volume in his Colossus series.

Blixt likes to "find the gaps in well-worn tales and fill them." As the Historical Novel Society said, "Be prepared to burn the midnight oil. It's well worth it."

REMEMBER ME

BY DAVID BLIXT

I was walking alone. It was hilly and I was tired. I don't remember now where I was going, or where I was coming from. It's all too hazy. Nor do I exactly remember my name. I remember having one, and I liked it. I like it now more that I can't remember it. I liked having a name.

What I do remember are the hooves. Charming. Old-fashioned. Clip-clop. Not like a racing horse, but of a shod mule. And there were voices. A low, rumbly voice, and a high whine like a child's, conversing. I turned and looked. Sure enough, along behind me came a single mule pulling an ancient, wooden coach. But I only saw one figure on the coach's seat. Maybe the child was inside.

I remember stepping to the side of the road so it could pass me, and I remember smiling in the way that says I won't ask you for a ride, but it would be really nice if you offered one.

The coachman was a fellow with a wide head that looked squeezed, fluffy tufts of whitish-blonde hair sticking out from under his pork-pie hat, and he had a fat, red nose. He should have been funny-looking, but behind the smoke of his long-stemmed pipe his eyes were intense, smoldering, ablaze—words fail me. Those eyes I'll remember all my life. I may not remember much else now, but those eyes…

The coachman smiled at the sight of me and gave a slight heave on the reins to pull up. The mule said, "Owich," and the coachman flickered a frown at the mule, but then went back to smiling.

"Hello there."

"Good morning," I answered.

"It is, truly. A very good morning. A fine morning, brisk and promising." His voice was deep and had an accent. Not a fancy accent. But an accent that made him at least sound smarter than me. Foreigners always sound smarter than natives, as long as they know the words.

The coachman's eyes twinkled as he looked me over. "You're much too young to be on this road all alone."

I have always looked younger than I am. I remember, when I had my own face, that it annoyed me that I could never grow a decent beard. Baby-faced, they said. Sweet, they said. Boyishly handsome, they said. So I think I was ruder than I might have been when I answered him. "I'm nearly eighteen."

I remember that made him frown. "I take it back. You're much too old." He seemed about to continue on, but I must've held up a hand, for he caught sight of my arm and looked me over with more scrutiny. "You look strong. Are you strong?"

"Strong enough," I said.

"Don't be strong," said the donkey out of the side of his mouth. He had a high, piping voice and was missing part of one ear.

The coachman flicked the reins idly, and the donkey looked abashed. "Strong, eh? Are you a hard worker?"

"I can be. But if I liked hard work, I'd've stayed at home."

He seemed to enjoy that.

"Well, if you ride with me, you won't have to work, will you? Just ride along, enjoy this lovely morning. And there might be gold in it at the end."

"For him," said the donkey.

The coachman turned to address the donkey. "Alexander, you're on the road to a beating."

"Won't be the first," replied the donkey.

"It might be the last," answered the coachman with promising intention. The donkey bowed his head.

"That's a neat trick," I remember saying.

"It was a trick, but not neat," mumbled the donkey.

I think I asked something like, "How do you get him to talk?"

"It's getting him to stop talking that's the problem," said the coachman. "What do you say? Want a lift?"

I knew even then I should have said no. Knew it in my bones. And the donkey was swinging his head from side to side. But I remember being angry at the world, full of rebellion and piss and vinegar, as my uncles would say. So I didn't even answer, only climbed up onto the seat beside the coachman.

He was very neat, but beneath the smell of the tobacco, there was something pungent and earthy. Not the clean smell of dirt. Something deeper, volcanic. It mingled with the smoke of his pipe and created a smell I think I've known all my life, but one that towns and candles kept away.

"Welcome aboard," said the coachman. "Onward, Alexander."

"Tally-ho," said Alexander gloomily.

* * *

The coachman liked to sing, but I can only remember him singing one song that whole day. *"At night they sleep, and I never sleep…"* I can't remember the rest.

At some point on the trip I asked the coachman about his talking donkey, and he corrected me. "Jackass. Alexander's a jackass."

Alexander looked back over his shoulder. "And you're a son of a—"

The coachman's short whip snapped and Alexander yelped, then carried on, mumbling to himself.

The coachman smiled at me. "Sorry. But he's in disgrace. Until he stops talking, he doesn't get his nice, white shoes back."

"Don't want shoes," grumbled the jackass. "Want feet." He sniffled.

"I think your jackass is going to cry," I said.

The coachman shrugged. "Let him cry. He'll laugh when he has some hay."

"Don't want hay," muttered Alexander, sniffling again. "Want feet."

"Who taught him to speak?"

The coachman shrugged. "Not I!"

"My mother," said Alexander sulkily. "My mother taught me to speak." Suddenly he kicked up his feet, lashing out at the coach. "I want my mommy!"

I remember the sound of the coachman's whip cracking hard through the air, opening a long seam in the donkey's skin. At once Alexander was silent. His legs came down and he picked up his pace.

I think I said something like, "Poor little guy."

Glaring, the coachman relit his pipe. "Don't waste your time pitying a jackass when he cries. He earned his tears. Now, tell me more about yourself! The day is fresh and the road is long. We won't reach my home until nightfall."

That was the first time he mentioned his home. I can't think now why it upset me the way it did. I think I asked to get down, but he offered to let me hold Alexander's reins. I took them, thinking to be kind to the poor animal, and forgot all about getting off the coach. There was power in driving it, a thrill, and after a while I ordered Alexander to go faster. The coachman laughed.

He was always fussing with his pipe. I couldn't remember ever seeing one like it, white and long and carved. I must have asked him what it was made of because I remember his proud answer. "A bone from a monstrous whale."

We crested a hill just as the sun was setting, and there before us was a structure of stone and wood. It was a huge place, bigger than a palace, bigger than a castle. Yet at first it seemed deserted. I remember thinking that I could hear the wind whistling through it, as though it were abandoned.

Then all at once the huge front gate swung open and a man appeared. He was massive, dressed all in black, with a slouched hat over his eyes. I can't remember seeing his face.

Turning to look over his shoulder, the dark man called out, "L'Omino!" In answer there were shuffling steps, and suddenly torches came to life, flickering and dancing in the fierce breeze that funneled through the home. They cast strange shadows. I remember thinking that the huge man's shadow had more life in it than the dark man who cast it. The shadow writhed and whirled and strained to break free of its links to the feet of the figure who now took control of Alexander.

"Good evening, Carlo," said the coachman as he leapt down from his seat.

"L'Omino." The dark man bowed. He had trouble forming the word, like he had a speech impediment. And his voice was rasping, like he'd smoked too much. I was close enough now to see his face. But I couldn't. Or maybe I didn't want to. I don't remember if I tried.

I do remember asking as we passed through the huge gate, "Lomino? Is that your name?"

The coachman laughed heartily. "Of course not! Carlo is Italian. It's their pet name for me. *'The Little Man.'* I suffer it, because they amuse me."

I think I turned to say goodbye to Alexander because I remember his sad eyes following me as we walked through the doors.

* * *

We were relaxing in a very comfortable room with an unseasonable fire in the hearth and some steaming drink that was warm in my hand. I don't remember anyone bringing the drink in, just the coachman offering it, and me accepting. I hadn't drunk it yet. It smelled strong.

The coachman was packing his pipe again. "So, you're strong. But you don't like work."

"No," I said. "I don't."

"Good for you. It's important for a man to know what he likes and what he doesn't. Self-knowledge is the key. The ripe fruit of human experience." He lit his tobacco with the tongs from the fireplace. He paused as he did it, to frown at me. "Do you know, before they said 'I'm smoking tobacco,' they used to say *drink?* 'I drink tobacco.' There was no word for what I'm doing now. Smoking is such the obvious word, but they viewed it a liquid. Isn't that interesting? Not seeing a thing for what it is? Not finding the right word? That's not a problem I have. I see things for what they are. I know the importance of words."

I remember looking into my goblet and at the thick, violet swirls in the liquid. "What was in the coach?"

"Excuse me?"

"The coach. What was in the coach? I never asked."

"No. You never did." The coachman took a long pull on his pipe and blew nine rings of smoke, one into another. I remember it clearly. It was very impressive. "A little of this, a little of that. I trade from time to time. But really I just like to ride my coach and meet interesting people on the way. If my coach were empty, I'd ride it just the same. Fortunately for me," he puffed, "that's never been the case."

"So you trade goods? Is that how you made your fortune?"

The coachman patted his belly while he laughed. "Whoever said I have a fortune?"

I remember waving my free hand at all the furnishings. There were tapestries on the wall that were so rich I could have sworn the figures moved in the firelight. There were silver dishes laid out upon an ancient, carved table that had wine-colored stains and pockmarks in the wood from age and use. And in the corner there was a little wooden puppet, hanging by strings. A marionette. For some reason I continue to remember that word. It is the only hopeful word I still have.

The coachman made a modest face. "I'm just lucky. I belong to an exclusive club, you see."

"A club?"

"A band, a cohort, a consortium. We have lots of names. But our job is to remember."

"Remember what?" I asked.

He gazed at me, and his eyes seemed very far away. "Everything."

"I don't understand."

The coachman spoke with grave pride. "It is the fondest wish of every man to be remembered after his death. That's my work. Taking death and turning it into everlasting remembrance."

"There's good money in that?"

"More than you can imagine. Oh, we cater to certain tastes, certain prized goods, though we'll really sell any old thing along the way. That's the great thing about remembering. You hold on to everything."

"Like that puppet?" I asked, pointing.

He turned to gaze silently at the puppet for a very long time. "Yes. He's there to remind me to remember. Always, to remember. The one that got away."

"Excuse me, I don't understand."

The coachman returned to his pipe. "I don't imagine you would."

He seemed grumpier now, and I remember trying to compliment him, restore his spirits. "And so by trading and remembering you can afford a fine home like this?"

"This? This is just my home away from home. My true home is the road. I travel a great deal. But I have little cottages like this spread all over the map. Of course, most of them are full of toys. I do love children. So honest. You could rightly call me the King of Toy Land. Ha! I even have partial interest in an island! A kind of resort, where young people make asses of themselves. Very profitable, though, these days I let my junior partners run it. Honest fellows, if a bit foxy. But they keep the gold rolling in. Perhaps you'd like to see it sometime?"

I don't think I answered, because I was busy tasting the drink. It was strange, but I knew I'd tasted it before somewhere. At least, I remember the bitter, metallic taste on my tongue.

"Good?" asked the coachman.

I nodded, though I wasn't sure if I liked it. Now I know better.

"You don't remember drinking anything like it, do you? It is a prized beverage among my fellows. As I say, an exclusive club. Membership has its privileges."

I remember asking, "Like what?"

"Oh, wealth, freedom, travel. Nothing to tie us down. But most of all, we've found the secret to peace. To being whole. The most important thing in all the world is finding that inner peace. I love to help in that. It's not just my pleasure. It's my calling." He gazed at me intensely. "Don't you ever want to feel whole, like there's a gaping emptiness in the center of you longing to be filled?"

Though I was feeling sleepy, I remember nodding.

"Say it. You have to say it."

I didn't understand why, but he was my host. "I want to feel whole."

Leaning back and puffing his long pipe, the coachman smiled like a cat wishing well upon its master. "And so you shall. Of course, I can only help with the process. Like they say, to really change you have to want to change. And it is a change, make no mistake. Well, 'a change is as good as a rest,' the old woman says." He puffed again, then suddenly stood like a man making up his mind. "I like you, lad. So much that I'm willing to buck the rules. Rules are made to be broken, eh? Would you like to become a member? Just give me your hand, and I'll help you find that peace. Help you be whole. Guide you towards finding yourself."

I remember this moment very clearly. Standing up, I remember reaching out my hand, and his grip on it, hot and dry and firm. We shook. It hurt my hand a little. Then my hand stopped hurting because he brought a knife out of his pocket, and in one sharp, upward cut, he sliced right through my wrist.

I remember stepping back, not really understanding or believing what had happened. I wasn't sleepy anymore, but there was still a kind of haze on the room. He kept on shaking my severed hand with a friendly smile and those narrowed, burning eyes. Then he held my hand back out to me.

"I said I would help you to find yourself. This is a start. The first piece, if you will. Here." He tossed me my hand, and I tried to catch it, but lacking one of my hands, I dropped it. "Oh dear. But never you mind, my lad. I told you, the inner pieces are the most important. And I can help you be whole." I remember that he started walking forward, his small knife still dripping my blood. "Lads, hold him. Let's make him whole."

The room was suddenly filled with more men like Carlo, dark, hulking men with unhappy shadows. I have no idea how long they'd been there. Maybe they'd been standing and watching us this whole time. But they took hold of me and laid me out across the stained and pockmarked wooden table. I may have struggled, I don't remember. If I did, it didn't matter.

"Whole hole hole," said the dark men. "Peace piece pieces."

And the coachman was singing again. *A holy man, a holey man, a wholly holey holy man.* He came close with the knife, and with several expert cuts he lifted the heart right out of me. Looking down at my chest, he said, "There now. I've made you a hole. And I've got your inner peace right here. Want it back? Too late. It's mine."

"It's not fair," I said.

"What's not fair?" asked the coachman, interested.

"I don't deserve this."

"Oh? And who gets their desserts? I agree, it's much too bad. You just got carried off down the wrong path. It only takes a few steps, more's the pity. But you could have gotten off the path you were on at any time. In this case, the path to Dis."

"Dis?"

"Distrust. Disbelief. Dismemberment. You stayed on your path to the bitter end. Which, by the bye, is the name of this house. Bitter End. Or is it Bite and Rend? I'm never sure. Ah well." With a nod to Carlo, he returned to his seat as the dark men started again.

I…don't like to remember what happened next. There were knives, but also saws with looping teeth as long as a crocodile's, and I think there was an axe and shears and some kind of whippy little blade barely as long as my fingernail. And I was awake and alive through it all. Something in the drink, I think.

I lay there watching as pieces of myself were removed. And

the coachman watched too, puffing on his pipe, drinking his tobacco, my beating heart in his hand. I think I cursed at him, and he clucked his tongue sympathetically.

When it was over, I lay in parts all across the massive table. I know they were parts because the coachman crossed over and began to lift them, one by one. I remember that clearly. He weighed them, measured them carefully, like a wife at market day.

"Well now, that's a good day's work if I do say so. Eh, Carlo?"

Carlo said nothing. It seemed strange, but in that moment he reminded me of Alexander. He was just as sad.

It was that pitying sadness, I think, that made me struggle. I remember trying to move. All the parts of my body twitched. The coachman cried out, "Oh ho! A flicker of fire still in you. Well done. Then you want what I have to offer. You want what I do. You want to be remembered."

"Why aren't I dead?"

"Because we must remember the dead, and you are not remembered." He leaned forward to look into one of my eyes. "Say it. Say it now."

"Say what?" I don't know how I was able to talk, with my jaw sawed off. But I heard the words clear and clean in the ear of mine that he was holding.

"Ask me to remember you."

"Remember?"

"That's all any of us can hope for, after death, isn't it? To be remembered? I told you, man's greatest wish. Immortality, even. And you won't be remembered like this," he waved his hands at the broken parts. "You'll be whole again." I tried to shake my head, and he laughed. "Ah! He can be taught. Very good. But I do mean what I say. If you want to be remembered, it won't be like this. You'll get all your pieces back, to grant you that inner peace. Serenity, even. Won't that be nice?"

"Yes. Please, it hurts…"

"It hurts because no one has remembered you. You want to be remembered, don't you?"

I thought of my mother, my father and uncles, of the girls I had loved but never told, of the untold, faceless millions I would never meet, get to know, love, hate, be bored by. I realized that he was right. More than anything, I wanted to be remembered.

"Yes… Please…"

"You must say it, remember?"

"Remember me," I said.

The coachman smiled a ferocious smile. "As you wish."

Lifting my heart from where it lay, he took it to the hearth and held it over the fire. His hand did not burn, but the poor heart in it was scorched through, blackening and hardening before my eyes. Seared through. And I felt it. I felt it from across the room as my heart grew black and hot and small.

When it looked like a lump of coal in his palm, he turned back to the table. "You heard him, boys. Remember him."

It was pain a thousand times worse than dying, being remembered. They took each piece of me, inside and out, and burned it black. Then they took them and stuffed every bit, searing hot, back where it belonged, melting and scalding each part into place. My lungs were black, my liver, my intestines. They seared my flesh, and through it all my nose worked well enough to smell my own burning.

When it was over and I could move again, I stood up. I was strong, and bigger than I would have thought, with all those blackened bits. Looking down at my hands and arms, they were huge, misshapen and darker than dark, darker than the night inside your eyelids. I took a step and found I was light. I was fast. I was strong. And completely without memory. Except for the coachman.

"There," said the coachman with a satisfied puff on his pipe. "You've been remembered for all eternity."

Later, when I found out my blackened tongue could still form words, Alexander explained to me the coachman's love of wordplay, the nature of his magic. How he revels in recruitment, in giving it the personal touch. How he cannot touch those who don't ask to be touched. How he lets everyone choose their fate. And how he loves to point out that the Devil is in the details.

I know I should be angry. But I can't remember why…

DAVID SIDDALL

David Siddall, originally from Chester, now lives in Liverpool, England.

A Network Rail signalman for nearly thirty years, inspiration for his writing comes from the places he has lived and worked–most especially the dark, bleak locations. Whether moor, mountain or derelict dockland, it is the wasteland of the soul that flowers his prose.

Siddall's work has been published in *Supernatural Tales*, *The Realm Beyond*, *Our Haunted World: Ghost Stories From Around the World* anthology, *Out of the Gutter*, *Mysterical-E*, *eNoir* and *Fickle Muses*.

THE FIRST YEARS

BY DAVID SIDDALL

The first years are the worst years. This I know, and though the thought leaves its imprint in a mind corrupted by time, I still feel a smile twist my lips. For those are the very words Anton said at my initiation.

Those first years, as the people held dearest—mother, father, brother, sister—pass into the oblivion of death, and then almost from memory as well. I was lucky, careful perhaps, for I never married or had children. The very thought of watching as illness and age mock tender flesh and render sharp and inquisitive minds into an incontinent mess fills me with a dread I can hardly articulate.

There was a girl, but that was a long, long time ago. She was sweetness, she was light. I close my eyes as I try to recollect her face, but it is no use. She is gone like a blown flower and only a fractured memory of her faded bloom remains. Thank God I was spared that. Ah, God! Now there is a matter that deserves consideration. But before that, there are other things that demand my attention.

Rising from my chair, I go to the window and push a corner of the curtain aside. They're there, just as I knew they would be there. Cowled, like the black novices we once jostled in the courtyard of the Jagiellonian in Krakow, they stand outside my gate in their North Face jackets, eyeing the fastness of my fortress with feral eyes, daring one another to enter and *tweak* the monster's tail.

There are four; sometimes there are more, seldom less. I know these boys, their pasty, weasel faces familiar to my eyes: Shane McClusky, the Bentine brothers and Liam Fitzroy. Tomorrow I will smell them, trace their pheromones and spore left in the saliva specked floor, each strand as distinctive as a mountain road once traversed through the Alps.

I drop the curtain and return to my chair. Seconds later I hear the letterbox rattle, the sound of racing feet upon my path, and then the sordid, pungent aroma of dog excrement reaches me from its splatter point on the doormat. Their hyena laughter follows and I close my eyes, place hands over my ears and shut out their world.

I'm an easy mark and have been ever since they moved me onto the estate: a shabby cul-de-sac of good intentions turned sour, where dreams lie like the detritus of life that litter every back garden. Yes, an easy mark; a man with no family or friends, a man who keeps himself to himself, an outsider who does not conform to the bounds of the society I have been thrust upon.

How I long for my basement flat with its dark corners and shadows, its squalor. There I was left to my own devices. Nobody expected me to talk, to interact or get involved in the petty antics of my neighbours. I was a forgotten man, or so I thought. But to survive one must bend to the system. And once in the system, no one is truly forgotten.

But all would have been well, the vagaries of life could have been smoothed over and some level of harmony achieved, if only that boy hadn't gone missing. And that was almost a year ago.

The police called, as they did to every house on the estate, and if not for my frail and vacant mind, maybe would have looked closer. Suspicions and eccentricities enhanced in the telling and fingers pointed by back-street philosophers and pebble-dash heroes would have ensured that. But what could a diseased, old man have done with a boy quickly approaching maturity?

I made them tea, shuffled back and forth, clucked my tongue in sympathy when mention of what the poor boy's mother—there was never any mention of the father—was going through. Then I saw them to the door. What did they expect, what did they see? I have learnt through the years that people see only what they want to see. And they saw only an old, old man whose acquaintances number more amongst the dead than those of the living. I must have made some impression on the young WPC, for a few days later Social Services visited.

Afternoon callers are largely ignored, but this one was persistent enough to rouse me from my afternoon slumber. Shying away from the light that crept from the open door, I stared through the crack. A face, round and unremarkable, looked back.

Her name was Kathy.

Her eyes fluttered as she consulted the clipboard in her hand.

"Mr. Samuels?"

I nodded assent while her large, bovine eyes dripped a practised sympathy.

"I've been asked to call. Check on your circumstances." Her face scrunched. "Make sure you're alright." Her foot was already in the door before she asked, "May I come in?"

What could I do but open the door wider. A lesson learned: you should never, never invite them into your home. She pursued me into the lounge, perched herself on a hard-backed chair and casually ran a finger through the dust on the table. She fixed me with an imitation smile while her eyes darted here and there, surveying my house and then me. Within seconds of entering my home, Kathy had decided I was incapable of looking after either.

And so to the interrogation. She opened her mouth but stopped. The smile slipped and her head craned forward as she scrutinised my face. A frown appeared, causing a series of fine lines to fracture the skin on her forehead.

"Your face," she said and circled a finger around her cheek to indicate. "There are…marks."

Though I take every precaution, my infrequent trips outside result in exposing myself to the harsh rigors of the sun.

"The light," I said. "With age comes sensitivity." I shrugged as if it was of no matter and settled back in my armchair. My old blanket had fallen and I took a moment to retrieve it and toss it over my legs. She watched the performance, before her eyes strayed to the unlit fire. "The bills," I said, and gestured helplessly.

She smiled as if she knew the way things were, but can they ever understand? Gazing around the room and the remnants of my life, she looked over the bookcase and Welsh dresser, mentally noted their cobwebbed surfaces and ticked the boxes on her mental spreadsheet. Her nose twitched. I live amongst decay and ruin, and the smell of an old man and his memories can sometimes be a little...*ripe.* She made a wilful effort to appear unaffected.

Sitting still, I watched her grind her ample buttocks into the seat while consulting the papers in her file.

"You live here alone, Mr. Samuels?

I made a small motion with my hand. "As you see."

"And you have no family?"

"Just I."

"That must be hard," she said, and I watched her face follow the well-practiced route of compassionate understanding. "How d'you manage with the bills, shopping, that sort of thing?"

"I do all I have to."

She frowned. "What about food? Are you eating?"

"I don't need much." And I don't. Maybe only once a year do I eat really well.

She consults the file. "And you moved here...?"

"Two years ago. When they destroyed my flat."

"During the construction of the Dock development?"

"Yes."

She looked up from her papers and leaned forward so that I caught a hint of her smell. She had bathed that morning, soap with a lavender base, and her hair...jasmine I think, and something else. Breathing deep, our eyes lock. Ferrous, metallic, like old pennies caught on the tongue. She was menstruating. This woman before me was bleeding even as we spoke. The joke was too much. There was a time when I would not have been able to contain myself, a time when I would have taken her and be damned with the consequences. But those days are over. With age comes wisdom as well as frailty. But she saw my lips curl and recoiled as if a window had opened into my mind and she could see right through me. But that is impossible. It took just a moment for her to regain her composure. Self-consciously she adjusted her skirt and rolled her shoulders. I made her uncomfortable, that much was obvious. I savoured the moment.

She tried again. "D'you not find it difficult living alone?"

"Difficult?" I said and shrugged. "No. But I hardly have a choice." Before the words left my mouth I regretted saying them. It was the opening she was looking for.

"But there is, Mr. Samuels, there is a choice." She dug into her bag and with a practised flourish handed me a leaflet, a flyer with a large photograph of a red-bricked Edwardian edifice—gables, porches and large gardens. With difficulty I read the banner: "AUTUMN LODGE." She had to be kidding. I looked up at her then, looked to see if this were some kind of a jest. But no, she was serious. My brows came together, my mouth twitched into a dry sneer, but before I could speak she held up a hand, forcing me to hesitate.

"Before you say anything," she said, "think. You would have a room of your own, someone to cook and clean, and most of all people of your own sort to..."

"People of my own sort?"

"Yes. You know." She moved her head back and forth trying to find the right word.

I found it for her. "Old?"

She grinned, not at all embarrassed.

"And you do have two bedrooms, Mr. Samuels. One of which isn't used. A family could make much better use of it."

Enough. Rising from my chair, I took her arm and led her to the door. I think she found my grip surprisingly strong for she winced as I thrust her into the street. Rubbing her arm she turned and made a final riposte.

"We can make a compulsory order, Mr, Samuels. If you're not fit enough to live on your own…"

I slammed the door in her face.

That was almost a year ago and nothing ever came of it. The boy was never found either. Soon after, the police presence dwindled then disappeared altogether. Talk was of the boy running off to London or some other far-flung place. I took little notice. The lives of the lower creatures are of little concern to me. But there are those whose suspicions are never assuaged and regardless of my frailty their fingers continued to point at my door. Maybe it was my indifference, or maybe it was my refusal to contribute to the neighbourly fund given to the mother to ease her pain. Whatever, silence and vacant stares followed; soon after, eggs were thrown at my window. And so it continues to this very day.

There have been other times when suspicion and hate has aroused passions to such a degree that it has been prudent to seek pastures new. But I was younger then and had friends, friends who understood and shared the burden. But they are gone, all of them are gone.

I leave the mess by the door and wearily climb the stairs to my bedroom. The room is in darkness. It's a good house on the edge of the estate, and if I crane my head, I can just see the river. Fast and free flowing, the lights on the far shore reflect off the dark water like a Monet watercolour.

But I have other, more important considerations and shift my gaze. Beyond my garden lies a piece of waste land. A fire smoulders in its centre, its golden embers marking a boundary, a warning perhaps, that this is territory you enter at your own peril. I leave the window and sit on the bed. Breathing deep and slow, I reach down into myself, tapping into the reserves set aside for the purpose I have in mind.

And so it begins.

The blood flows quicker, the heart beats faster; wave upon wave of power floods through me like the tide into an empty harbour. There is a rush of sensations, my skin pulses while a host of stimuli pepper a body lain dormant for far too long. My nose twitches, my own body odour caught in the fetid folds of unwashed clothing compete with the mould and damp that inhabit my nest. Through the open window wood smoke, diesel and petrol fumes, and finally the great wash of humanity staining the world with their individual, sordid aromas. I love it all.

There is a fly in my room. I feel it, sense it; each beat of its tiny wings sends pulses through the air. The hairs on my arms react to its movement. It comes close and I snatch it. Carefully I open my hand. A bluebottle, and it is a fat beast. Plump, juicy, it sharpens my appetite. But there is little time for such nonsense. I feel invigorated. There is life in these old bones yet.

Clothing myself in black, I take from the wardrobe my coat with the deep hood I use for special occasions and push the window wide. It is held back by the catch, but I have experimented and know I can squeeze my liquid body through the opening. I do. I am dark as the night, and for a moment I perch on the sill like a great, black crow. I watch the road, the waste ground and the houses opposite. A twitch of curtain or a car rolling past and my plans would be negated. Nothing. I spread my arms, lean forward and drop.

The wind snatches my thin body and I drift to the waste ground beyond my little garden. Crouching down on my haunches, I wait and survey the scene. My senses are sharp, instincts good. But it's so long since I satisfied my desire that I want to rush forward and take the first opportunity that comes my way. Nevertheless, I am a survivor and recognise the threats to my existence.

Controlling my emotions, I sniff the air, and amidst the myriad of competing odours, catch their scent. This is good, but already I have an idea of where they will be. Beyond the warren of residential streets that dominate their lives is an area of new build. Built on renovated dockland, it's a gated community of modern apartments, ornamental lakes and internal security. Outside the perimeter is a copse of trees and in it these boys have a den. A haven where they can smoke their illegal substances, abuse their bodies with the market leader in narcotic availability, and look out on the apartments with envious eyes and dream of the day when they have climbed the ladder of criminality and can afford the same.

I care not. I do not care what they do to their derelict bodies. I only know how sweet, how tender, their flesh is. If they only knew how fragile, how tenuous life is, then perhaps…

No. Perhaps not.

I follow their scent through the streets. Passing the public house on the corner I pause and listen. Inside a man is singing.

Tremulous and off key, his voice rises above the chatter and leaches into the night. He doesn't care, he is lost in the momentum of his ambition and hears not the laughter, only the applause. It lifts him for another week of blighted existence.

I leave him his desires and concentrate on my own.

At the end of the street, steps are cut into the rock. It's a shortcut to the once bustling docks and path below. I'm hurrying now, anticipation eating my insides like coffin worms consume a corpse, and take them two at a time. On my right an iron-barred fence guards the apartments, but only secrecy secures the boys their den. And their secrets I have already broached. Even now I smell them. Their musky aroma has been indelibly etched into my olfactory sense from the moment I first identified them as prey. Leaving the path I head into the trees. Fronds of fern and bramble bar my way, but the track, worn into the bare earth by trainer-clad feet, is clear.

My approach is unobserved. I have had many years to perfect my technique and catch them, the Bentine brothers, unguarded. By the soft, yellow light filtering through the trees, I see that their lair is a clearing, a circle free of vegetation. It's unimaginative, dirty and sordid. Coke tins and crisp packets litter the floor, and the sickly aroma of their cannabis habit clings to every bush, tree and plant. Scent marked like wild animals, their spore surrounds me.

The first stares at me, trying to understand, trying to fathom the intrusion and whether the apparition before him is a shadow or the Devil? I waste no time. Before he has time to think, I withdraw the heavy kitchen knife concealed within my sleeve and with one swift, backhanded motion, draw it across his neck where the internal carotid artery joins the skull.

The blade is so sharp, the cut so fine, that for a moment I fear I have miscalculated and slashed only air. In times past, my heavy-handed action has resulted in almost severing head from body. It is a fine art, a calculus of pressure, speed and penetration. Anton taught me much.

But I am mistaken. My aim is sure, and a moment later the skin opens like a lipless mouth and a geyser of blood erupts from the wound and arcs across the space to where I am standing. For a moment I am back, back at my initiation, for the first time experiencing the flower of humanity in its finest form. A beautiful moment, poetic and fulfilling, as like a newborn babe when I took to the teat and knew what it was to feel truly alive. Ah, the revelry that followed as I was welcomed to the fold.

I snap out of my reverie. Nostalgia. It can quite ruin the moment.

The arc of blood quickly dwindles and as the boy's heart pumps its last, he falls. There is a gentle crump as his lifeless body settles on the floor. And now I gaze to the other. He is the younger of the two and, transfixed by events, he stares at his dead brother. He hasn't moved or cried out and remains frozen to the spot. I have come across the phenomena before. Events so shocking, so bizarre, it renders some into such obsequious compliance they may as well be sheep being lead to slaughter. His fear is palpable. Already he has soiled himself, the sharp tang of fresh urine mixes with blood and older scents of the wood. A tingling arousal pockmarks every inch of my skin. No slashing blade here, just a small incision below the ear and a soft caress as I place my hungry lips to the opening.

Ecstasy. I close my eyes and drink deeply, savouring the rich, thick fluid. So thick it almost coagulates in my throat. Iron rich, metallic, and other things as well: a hint of garlic, chilli—the boy has eaten a kebab—and some narcotic that makes my head spin. I lift the boy higher, tilt my head further back so as to allow a greater flow of nourishment. My vision blurs, shapes whirl around the clearing until I am unsure of what is real and what is not.

Perhaps it is that which lulls, lowers my defences and finely honed sense of survival. But somewhere along the path a twig breaks. The noise disturbs me. I pause in my feeding and listen. A footfall disturbs the equilibrium of the wood, and I remove my lips from the boy's neck and sniff the air. The others have come.

Sated, full, I have no desire for confrontation and drop the Bentine boy. He collapses in on himself like a deflated balloon, an empty husk sucked dry by my need. I have enough presence of mind to dart into the undergrowth, to lose myself amongst the birch and alder, skimming left and right until I hear a cry behind.

"Fuck!"

It ruptures the air in its fury. Then there is silence. The Bentine brothers are found. I grin inanely. I am mad, insane with the joy of existence, and fly through the undergrowth faster than I have in years. I am restored, the nourishment has renewed me and I break free of the trees and run along the road until headlights capture my dancing shadow. A car swerves, the driver's hand clamps down on the horn and I leap aside, laughing at the ordeal. I am a demon of the night revelling in the glory of death. But it isn't wise, it isn't good; reports will reveal, "A black-clad figure was seen fleeing the scene." But I have little to fear. I bear little resemblance to the old man who resides on the Watling estate and can barely move from lounge to kitchen without assistance. Nevertheless, I force myself to slow. I lurk in doorways and shelters, creep amongst hedge-rows and keep away from the drunks, prostitutes and lonely who inhabit the night with the ghosts of their presence.

And so, circumspect and wary, I make my way home.

The estate is quiet—the alarm not yet raised—and sleeps under a blanket of ignorance. Skirting the edge of the waste ground and the fire which has dimmed to a dull glow, I climb the wooden fence of my property then up to my window.

At last I rest. And I wait.

It is less than an hour when I hear the car. It turns past my house and a sweep of light flashes across the drapes of my lounge. The police have arrived. Prising the corner of the curtain away from the window, I stand and watch. There are two, one of them I recognise. It is the same WPC who came to my house. They confer, walk uncertainly to the Bentine house and knock. News is never good when it comes at two o'clock in the morning.

A minute passes before the door opens. A woman, pyjama-clad and indignant, stands with her arms folded in the opening. I cannot hear but she gestures madly, vents her anger in a ritualistic display of perceived victimisation because her boys, her sweet, innocent boys, would never, ever be involved in the nefarious activities suggested by such forces of the law. It's a game and every day the police play their part in maintaining the fiction.

But today is different. The young WPC reaches out and takes Mrs. Bentine's arm. It's shrugged aside and she stares at the girl, a girl she maybe could have gone to school with and dares her to touch her again. She hasn't grasped the import, the significance of the gesture, and waits for the story of her boys' misdemeanours and the denouement of their endeavours.

Unfazed, the WPC bends her head to Mrs. Bentine's ear and whispers. Her boys will not be coming home, not now, not ever. I watch her face change; there is a moment of dull incomprehension before the softly spoken words impact, then a scream splits the night. She collapses, her body becomes limp as if her bones have turned to dust and only the efforts of the WPC and her colleague, as they place their hands beneath her arms, prevent her from falling. They take her inside.

Doors open. Almost as if they have been awaiting events, the neighbours are there. Lights burn in cluttered halls, a crowd gathers outside the Bentine house as word spreads. And the word is death. It passes from one to another until the cry is taken up by the pack: dead, Dead, DEAD! It's like being at the movies, those flickering pictures of bygone days where grandiose gestures and exaggerated expressions left no doubt as to the mood of the players. Mouths gape, tears are shed, and voices rise in the quest for answers and vengeance. It's an outpouring of grief that makes me want to vomit.

Heads turn towards my house. Glances tinged with suspicion, minds already made up. They were thugs, vandals and I should be congratulated on removing the vermin. But I have seen it before, the unspoken thought and the essence of their grief: "The kids may have been little bastards, but they were our little bastards."

I drop the curtain quickly. Have they seen me? I do not know, but this night is done and I retreat to bed.

They try to set fire to my home.

Whilst asleep a bin is set ablaze and pushed in front of my door. I know nothing of it. My dreams are deep and sweet and only in the morning when I hear the *ran tan tan* on my door do I stir. I take my time in answering. Reducing myself to former decrepitude, I pull a blanket half over my head and leave the chain on as I open it.

Kathy! And she has brought reinforcements. This one looks more formidable. He is smart, wears a tie and a leather jacket, and together with the dossier beneath his arm, carries an air of efficiency. Over his shoulder I see a policeman standing beside my gate. A few nosy neighbours wanting to know what's going on have gathered outside.

Kathy and her colleague push inside, and quickly he scans my living room. He uses an overlong index finger to push at his glasses while making a note in his file. He has a large Adam's apple. It draws my attention. A finger hooked beneath would rip it to shreds. But no, that would be too much of a giveaway. In deference to his leadership, Kathy waits for him to sit then perches on a chair. She leans forward and fixes me with a sickly, sweet smile.

And so it begins.

A pincer movement as they try to outflank my guard, trying to seduce me with sweet words, tender promises and thinly disguised threats. Looking after the house, they say, has become too much for me, too much for my own well-being. And personal safety, they add—which is followed by a telegraphed glance to the window and the mob outside—has become an additional issue.

I see the sly smile that is exchanged between them. The attack is well planned. Kathy's face goes into sympathetic meltdown.

"We could send home help," she says, "but even that is fraught with difficulty." She shakes her head. "So many hours left alone."

Then he leans forward and peers at me over the top of his glasses. "Think of all the things that could happen."

Yes, tell me what could happen? Am I senile, am I bereft of the faculties that make me function? My head swivels from one to another. Can't they stop talking, can't they give me a moment of peace? I place my hands on my head and squeeze. I want to scream. But no, that would only give them satisfaction, confirmation of their succinct analysis.

But I am not stupid and insist on maintaining my independent status. Their advance is stalled. And when I refuse to cooperate, they play their final hand: a court order. *They* have decided I am incapable of looking after myself. *They* have decided I am not eating and my home is a pig-sty. And the final insult: I am not attending to my personal hygiene.

I! The man who once bathed with the Marquise de Paiva and dined at Bernstorff's table? I want to laugh. Lack of nutrition making me ill? Hah! I feel the sneer of contempt that so far has remained hidden begin to emerge. Thank you, but I have had all the nourishment I need. I fix them with my finest, steely-eyed gaze, rise from my chair and try to show them the door. But it's too late. My arguments are to no avail. They have decided and I am lost.

Kathy goes to the door. My WPC is there. She looks at the floor and will not meet my eye. Outside my gate, and flanked by another, unsmiling constable, a car awaits. My transfer to Autumn Lodge, a care home filled with the anaemic and blood-less, is arranged. I look from one to another, from Kathy to her colleague to the police who stand like a guard of honour and realise that I am sunk.

What kind of monsters are these?

C.M. Saunders

C.M. Saunders is both a journalist and fiction author who began writing in 1997. His early fiction has appeared in several small press titles and anthologies. After the publication of his first book in 2003, *Into the Dragon's Lair – A Supernatural History of Wales*, he worked extensively in the freelance market, contributing to over forty international publications including *Fortean Times*, *Bizarre*, *Record Collector*, *Maxim* and the *Western Mail*.

Saunders' fiction has appeared in *Screams of Terror*, *Shallow Graves*, *Dark Valentine*, *Fantastic Horror* and *Siren's Call*. His novellas *Dead of Night* and *Apartment 14F: An Oriental Ghost Story* are available on Damnation Books, while *Devil's Island* has been published by Rainstorm Press.

In 2012, Saunders released his first mainstream novel *Rainbow's End*. Most recently, his work has appeared in *Morpheus Tales: Apocalypse Special*.

THE ELEMENTALS AND I

BY C.M. SAUNDERS

I remember now.

I remember how it started.

Until not so long ago I had a respectable, influential job at a pharmaceutical company. A very large and successful international pharmaceutical company, with factories and development centers in five countries and commercial outlets all over the world. Our products were sold everywhere from corner shops to cruise ships. We had an annual turnover in excess of £100 million, and employed a total of over three thousand people, most of whom were happily slaving away in our Asian production plants. We carefully applied finance and media manipulation to turn the whole package into an unholy alliance covering virtually the entire spectrum.

We manufactured lots of drugs, many of which were designed to treat common psychological ailments like schizophrenia, dementia and Alzheimer's disease, forging a holy trinity of biology, chemistry and psychology. As such, most of our research was heavily subsidized by the governments of the world. This was no accident. Mental degeneration in the aged is something that affects most people sooner or later, either directly or indirectly. If you don't fall victim to it yourself, the chances are that your spouse, parents or close friends will. It's the time-honored law of averages and cannot be avoided. When we gave the people that mattered the hard sell we emphasized this fact, giving a little presentation complete with fictitious stories about "poor Aunt Drusilla," crocodile tears and heartbreaking footage of various old folks going ever-so-slightly mad.

By design, this terrified not only the executives of the big retailing and distributing firms—our link to the consumers—but also wealthy individuals and all sorts of other potential backers. Most of the people responsible for handing out grants and research development bursaries were, shall we say, long in the tooth. Young people just didn't walk into jobs like that. And because they were getting on a bit we simply played up the fear factor, showing them films of gibbering wrecks in nursing homes to drive the point home. The financial rewards for finding a cure for degenerative mental disease, delaying the onset, or even just slowing the debilitating process down, were enormous. Apart from psychological illness, the other main threat to mortality was cancer, and that wasn't our area.

When the money was safely in place we were free to juggle our resources. We could divert funds here, there, wherever. Expand this area, scale this area down. You get the picture. Running a business of that size was complicated. Being a chemist in a big pharmaceutical firm was a bit like being a member of an unsigned rock band. Try as they might, most bands never quite made it big. They never had all the components in place at the same time. They lacked charisma, chemistry, or never had what it took to write that one hit single that would pave the way for success, ensuring that they were snapped up by a major record label and cementing their status in the Hall of Fame.

In that respect we were quite lucky. We employed some good personnel, and with their collective experience, nous and track record, we were the medicinal equivalent of Metallica. We had a dedicated, hardcore following that had increased in size since our inception and gradually made inroads until really making it big about a decade later. Novaline was our *"Black Album."* Our masterpiece, our biggest success and the benchmark against which all our future work would be compared. In a nutshell, Novaline—definitely not to be confused with Ovaltine—sped up and improved communication between the different hemispheres of the brain, eliminating confusion and fatigue, and repairing any damaged or fatigued receptors.

It wasn't just a hit single, or even a breakthrough album, Novaline was our multi-platinum seller. The magazine *New Science*, the industry's equivalent to *Rolling Stone*, called it, "The most significant discovery in medical research in over a decade," and it won our top chemists accolades and awards all over the world. There were Nobel Prize nominations. This meant more power and more money than even we ever dreamed of, most of which we pumped back into the business, refining Novaline and launching side projects.

One of the new drugs we launched was a derivative of Novaline we called Pirifinil. It was basically identical to Novaline but with a powerful added amphetamine. We marketed it as a stimulant and concentration aid, and it proved very popular across the whole spectrum, with everyone from stressed-out students to jaded executives. Quite simply, it improved performance both physically and mentally. It made you stronger, better and faster than you could ever hope to be in your usual Pirifinil-free incarnation. From the moment we introduced Pirifinil to the international marketplace it wasn't just the old and infirm taking our drugs, it was virtually everyone.

There is something unsavory about modern society that necessitates the use of drugs, either legal or otherwise. It's almost as if they served as post-adolescent security blankets. From cappuccino to crack, we find it virtually impossible to function properly without them. Maybe it's the inherent insecurities; or maybe it's the constant drive to succeed. Within two years, on the back of a series of very expensive public awareness and advertising campaigns, market research suggested that as many as one in eight people in Western Europe either took one of our impressive arsenal of drugs or were related to someone who did on a regular basis. That was a lot of generated sales.

It takes a long time and a lot of money to develop and refine a drug. After the many research stages, if the new drug is deemed worthy of the risk involved, it enters the testing phases, ominously known as 'the trials.' Much to the chagrin of campaigners and, indeed, the general public who, it has to be said, often get their wires crossed, we start on animals. It is a common misconception that we use monkeys and guinea pigs. In most cases this simply isn't true. I'm sure some facilities *do* use monkeys and guinea pigs, but we don't. They are far too expensive. We use lab rats instead.

Many people would disagree, but I have a heart. Of course I do. I don't like to see animals suffer unnecessarily. But what most of the campaigners don't understand is that these animals are bred for this specific purpose. If it wasn't for us they wouldn't even exist. We bring them into the world. They have no other practical function and probably wouldn't last a day in the wild. In the laboratories they have meaning, and they never die in vain.

Contrary to popular belief we don't have mad scientists dissecting them with scalpels for their—and our—amusement. All our research is properly validated. Rest assured that every animal that dies in our facilities does so out of dire need, not any sadomasochistic urge. We give their lives meaning. The romantic view would be to say that we turn them from vermin into martyrs. They suffer so people don't have to. It isn't as if we rub shower gel and make-up remover in their eyes. We leave that for the toiletries and cosmetics companies.

The reasons we use rats for experiments is simple: their respiratory systems and internal organs are virtually identical to those of humans, so any adverse effects that our products may have on people are duplicated in animals. We administered doses of Novaline, Pirifinil, or whatever else we were working on at the time, in conjunction with various other chemicals that people using our products may feasibly come into contact with, from aspirin to hair dye. Then we attach the rats to heart monitors and, more importantly, we attach electrodes to their brains so we can monitor cerebral activity. We make them comfortable. Only after rigorous animal testing, sometimes lasting years, do we move on to what we call the 'human phase.'

For this we use agencies who advertise for willing volunteers to offer themselves as test subjects in return for generous monetary compensation. You may not think it, but people can earn a damn good living doing this. Obviously there are some risks involved, but they are minimal. All they have to do is pop a few pills and spend some time in our facility where we can keep an eye on them. First they are screened. We get a lot of cranks and time-wasters attracted by the money offered, and these undesirables need to be weeded out. We also have to identify and refuse people who have criminal records, take recreational drugs, drink too much or even smoke cigarettes regularly, all of which could have adverse effects.

On arrival they are given a thorough health check. Scans and samples of bodily fluids are taken, they are weighed and interviewed, and all the results logged in a database. Then we make them sign a disclaimer stating that if the unthinkable happens, and they suffer any trauma or lasting damage, they won't sue our asses. We also add confidentiality clauses, just in case they have any big ideas about going to the press or trading us off against our competitors.

Then the tests begin. Again we attach monitors and elec-trodes to observe effects and bodily reactions, but this isn't es-sential at this late stage.

The biggest advantage about using human test subjects over dumb animals is that they can actually tell you about any ad-verse effects that may occur, and describe them fully. Unfor-tunately, unless you happen to employ Dr. Doolittle, there is a very obvious communication breakdown when testing on animals.

While they are in our care the subjects are given serial num-bers, which we use to identify them instead of using their names. This makes cataloging easier for us and ensures ano-nymity. It also strips away any personal connection, desensitiz-ing our staff.

To counteract this, when in their company, we call the test subjects 'clients' to give them a false sense of importance, when in reality they are little more than human guinea pigs. Or, lab rats. To further disguise this fact they are treated very well and given the very best of everything; they get private sleeping quarters, we offer them good food, support, monitor them, and we even provide a games room for their enjoyment, neatly kitted out with a pool table, dartboard and several state-of-the-art gaming consoles. To all intents and purposes they are free to do what they want, except leave the facility. We won't let them go until after they have been thoroughly debriefed, assessed and evaluated.

Because Pirifinil is a stimulant, these particular trials led to the games room seeing most of the action. The clients found it hard to sleep. The gaming consoles witnessed marathon, forty-eight-hour-long sessions, the clients only tearing themselves away long enough to take more pills or satisfy the regulatory fifteen minute hourly breaks. Then they were back on it, blowing things up and shooting hoops like people possessed.

We also discovered that Pirifinil is an appetite suppressant. This wasn't a great surprise, as this is a side effect of most amphetamines. It's the nature of the drug. Ephedrine and its extended family have long been linked to weight loss and eating disorders. It's usually one of the things that keeps supermodels so thin.

What we are on the lookout for, above all else, are allergic reactions. These can be unpredictable and dangerous. The human body is a complex mechanism and sometimes things happen that we just can't compensate for. The delicate chemical balance is upset somehow, or the electrical impulses searing through the brain are momentarily disrupted and all hell breaks loose. Strangely, the most awful symptoms are often triggered by the most innocuous circumstances.

In the early days of testing Pirifinil on humans, one of our subjects, D2244, was eating a salad sandwich on brown bread, the first solid food he had eaten in two days, when without warning he started convulsing. His throat closed up, his eyes rolled into the back of his head, his body was wracked with spasmodic episodes and he started frothing at the mouth like a rabid dog.

After the nurses on duty brought him back from the brink of death, D2244's medication was discontinued and the client underwent extensive testing. We had to find out what caused the fit. Eventually we discovered that there had been a reaction with the mayonnaise on his sandwich. The fucking mayonnaise, of all things. Under normal circumstances the guy probably wouldn't even notice, it wouldn't cause a violent reaction, just make him feel under the weather for a few hours until his body grew accustomed to the new imbalance. The presence of Pirifinil in his body made all the difference.

During the subsequent interviews, D2244 admitted that ordinarily he wasn't a great lover of mayonnaise and had only eaten it a handful of times in his entire life. This was probably an inherent defense mechanism recognizing that the stuff was bad news and trying to avoid it. He just wasn't aware of it on a conscious level.

As I said, the human body is a complex mechanism. Even after all this time, all this scientific evolution, no one is entirely sure how some of it works. It is entirely possible that the foods any individual doesn't particularly like could be harmful to them in some undefined way, and their fussiness is just one aspect or manifestation of an elaborate and effective defense mechanism. Our tests revealed that Pirifinil exaggerated the negative effects the mayonnaise had on him to unmanageable and dangerous levels.

Unfortunately the story didn't end with the convulsions. There was partial damage to the liver and kidneys, which led to blood-clotting, with the end result somehow being an amputation below the knee of the right leg.

Client D2244 didn't sue. Even if he had tried to he wouldn't have had a leg to stand on—excuse the pun. He had one good leg left—again, excuse the pun—but having one good leg is not much good in a fight. After all, he had willingly signed the release papers. Game over.

Physical problems were one thing; psychological problems were quite something else.

The human mind is basically a dark labyrinth of unmapped territories. The greatest brains in history have absolutely no idea what goes on in there. With the aid of our research, we can understand what causes physical effects and can then begin to treat them, modifying the drug if necessary, but the intricacies of the human mind remain a complete mystery to us. It has a lot to do with perception.

Most people are crazy to a certain degree. Most of us hear disembodied voices and have thoughts that frighten us from time to time. It's almost as if someone else is planting alien thoughts in our heads. Dark thoughts. It all comes down to where you choose to draw the line. What is crazy? What is normal behavior, and is there any such thing? Or are we all just socially conditioned to curb our natural instincts? That was definitely a question for the university professors with too much time on their hands. The harsh truth of the matter is that even though they have far more fun, those who surrender to their primal urges have always been deemed less cultured than those who abstain and show a bit of restraint.

As the tests continued there were some worrying developments with regards to Pirifinil, even after the debacle that surrounded D2244. First there was significant sleep loss; then the test subjects—clients—started reporting what can only be described as altered thought patterns. They were saying that after taking Pirifinil for a few weeks they started thinking about things in entirely different ways. They said the drug gave them greater insight.

It wasn't a big deal at first; we just put it down to the change of surroundings, change in diet, lack of sleep or stress caused by the tests, all of which can have subtle influences on the thought process. We noted and logged all the complaints but didn't see anything worrisome. In fact, there was a lot of positivity in the early stages.

People seemed to function just as well on a fraction of their previously normal amount of sleep. They could complete all the aptitude and intelligence tests we set, and most of them even scored higher than they had before. If we could sustain the same levels, this would be great news for the business. Everyone could do with a few hours less sleep a night. It was like having four extra hours in a day

In addition, on the surface, people became more optimistic; they found new solutions to old problems and worried less. Less worry means less stress, and stress is one of the biggest killers in the twenty-first century. A silent assassin. We even thought about remarketing Pirifinil as an anti-depressant. It wouldn't be that big a jump—more of a sideways shuffle—as it was already a dedicated member of the 'upper' family. But then matters took a much more sinister turn.

First came the dependency. When the test programs were over and the test subjects were free to leave the facility, some of them simply refused. They would literally burst into tears at the mere thought of their plentiful supply of happy pills being discontinued; reacting the same way a child would if you took away its favorite toy. One client, PB2724, suffered some kind of breakdown and tied herself to her bed with rolled-up sheets in protest, while another, CS1974, managed to trick the staff and lock himself in a fortified supply room. It was four hours before we could get to him, and by then he had swallowed literally hundreds of Pirifinil capsules. The man was a rambling, twitching mess, frothing at the mouth and ranting about all sorts of things.

It was technically an overdose, a deliberate overdose, so we had him sectioned under the Mental Health Act, and pretty soon the men in white coats came to collect him. That was months ago. He took so many pills that he'll be lucky to have slept by now.

In the wake of that unfortunate incident it was becoming clear that there were some teething problems surrounding Pirifinil, in particular the psychological side effects. But by then it was too late to go back. The wheels of big business were firmly in motion. Millions of pounds were tied up in research and there were literally hundreds of people working on development and sales. If we pulled the plug it would decimate the whole company. We would have to start from scratch. People would lose their life savings, we would have to repay loans and grants, and our reputations would be in tatters. So we decided to persevere. We covered up all that could be covered up and ploughed all available extra funds and man hours into solving the problems. It was a gamble, but it was our only chance.

Then the clients started having hallucinations. They would lie awake at night, their pained, bloodshot eyes darting around the room, and their terrified screams reverberating around the walls. Invariably they would need to be restrained and then quarantined while we weaned them off Pirifinil. Then it took many hours of counseling and rehabilitation before we were able to release them back into society. That meant added expense.

The strangest thing of all was that in all the test subjects the hallucinations were the same. Mental illness proved to be a great leveler. No matter what ethnic, geographic or demographic group the client belonged to, sooner or later they all experienced the same disturbing symptoms. Their vivid descriptions were identical. They saw shadowy figures dancing along their peripheral vision, figures that moved too quickly to be properly seen. Usually they were little more than flickering shadows. The clients could not distinguish features, or even defined shapes at first, but they all agreed that the figures were all dressed in long, dark, flowing robes with hoods or veils obscuring their faces. And along with the terrifying figures came the deeper insight, the more fundamental understanding of the universe in which we live.

Despite often being segregated, the test subjects all gave the figures the *same name*. They called them The Elementals. Apparently they had always been with us in some shape or form, inhabiting some kind of parallel dimension. They are immortal; they neither live nor die as we know it and have no sense of time. They just exist. They just *are*. They don't interfere too much with people, mainly lurk in the background and watch us, sniggering as we continue our humdrum lives, dominated by banal acts, oblivious to their presence.

The Elementals were surprised at first that large doses of Pirifinil rendered them visible to their human counterparts. They had not been visible for centuries. Then they seemed to accept the fact, more as a novelty than anything else, it seemed. And then the communication started.

They wouldn't speak as such; instead their thoughts would permeate the mind spontaneously, unbidden and unrestrained. They would eavesdrop on your thoughts and conversations and plant seeds in your subconscious.

They knew things. They knew *everything*.

They knew every dark secret you had. They knew the history of the world. And they knew the future.

All this was very unsettling.

The case files built up, and I began doing more research about what the drug made people see more so than what it actually did. I formulated a theory that if these Elementals truly existed, they didn't look like anything much, least of all the mysterious shadowy figures described by clients such as OC2774.

Why would they even need a physical form? To all intents and purposes they had transcended the physical form and now operated on a higher plane. Personally, I thought that if they existed at all, they were just playing with him, trying to freak him out. And it had worked. We had two days of gibbering, incoherent statements and interviews, during which he talked about demons and the Devil and things that went bump in the night.

Then he made a dramatic and startling recovery. At least, he seemed to. So we let him go. He seemed to be acting normally; he was off the Pirifinil, had finally started making sense again. And, apart from some dark rings around his eyes, looked ready to reclaim his rightful place in society. His records said he was an estate agent.

Unfortunately he won't be selling any more houses. He was found hanged in his shed three days after he was discharged. We don't provide aftercare.

Nobody attached any blame to us. As far as the outside world knew, he had simply had enough and decided to end it all. We provide our clients total anonymity and are prohibited from making our records public, and this works both ways. No one had known he was ever here. Except us, of course. On the surface of it the poor man's wife had taken his kids and left him, and he also had money worries. The bank was on the verge of repossessing his home; that was why, some suspected, he had offered himself to us in the first place.

But we knew otherwise. We knew what had really happened to OC2774.

In their own inimitable way The Elementals told us about his last hours, when they had stood around him in his shed as he made a noose and tied it around his neck. They mocked him and egged him on, showing him things and telling him things he didn't want to know. Things about his estranged wife, things about the world. They even showed him how to make a hangman's knot.

You hear all the stories, listen to the test subjects ramble, try to reassure them and make sense of their inane gibbering. And we clean up after them, always wondering just what the fuck was going on. Was our drug making people crazy or just opening their eyes, lifting the veils from their vision? Did The Elementals exist? If so, what were they? And if not, how and why did so many people suffer the same delusions?

Mass hysteria was a possibility. Although after the symptoms started we tried to keep our test subjects in isolation so they wouldn't infect each other's minds with gossip and rumors. It was difficult and they always seemed to find ways to interact. This could have an impact on the subconscious. They could hear stories and then their imaginations would run wild. In theory, that's how mass hysteria works. The power of suggestion.

Of course there was the distinct possibility that Pirifinil or something else we gave them either triggered or compounded the delusions; and that was what we needed to investigate. Soon, the hallucinations became the focal point of our experiments.

We had to learn more, and not only from ignorant volunteers trying to make a few extra bucks for Christmas. We needed dedicated servants with no hidden agendas. People on the inside, so to speak. There was no way around it. Some of our charges were going to have to undergo treatment.

We decided the best way to do it was to send somebody in covertly, and have them infiltrate the next intake of test subjects. We couldn't let the other subjects know their identities, or even the scientists conducting the tests. This was the only way we could perfectly replicate the conditions.

For some reason I put my name forward for selection. Looking back, I don't know why I did it. A bit of recognition perhaps, a chance to impress the executives with my dedication,
or maybe it was just plain curiosity. I wanted to see for myself.
I have been questioning my decision ever since. Sometimes ignorance truly is bliss.

After the obligatory hoo-ha following my arrival, I was
started on a course of Pirifinil, and true to form I soon stopped
eating and sleeping as much as I once had. I actually felt good,
confident and assured. But it didn't take long before I started
seeing The Elementals myself.

It started happening just as the previous test subjects said
it would. After a few weeks I began noticing fleeting images
in my peripheral vision. Then The Elementals seemed to grow
bolder and more powerful, planting images and…thoughts
into my head, disturbing my internal monologue. Strange, alien
thoughts that I had no control over. At first they were muddled
and abstract. I saw burning buildings, screaming children,
crowds rioting. I saw rivers of blood and severed body parts.
Armageddon.

Initially I couldn't make any sense of it. I still don't understand everything, but I know much more than I used to. I now
know more than I ever wanted to know. They showed me what
killed the dinosaurs, the *real* root of all evil and what the future
held for mankind.

This is the future. What I see, what they show me; the pain,
the suffering, the destruction, the carnage, this is what will
happen to us. It is our destiny. And it is unavoidable.

I wanted to know why they were showing me this. And
then I wanted to know *who* was showing me this. It somehow

seemed a lot more important. I wanted to know what they looked like, so I asked if I could see their faces. They showed me. Oh God, they showed me.

One night, instead of dancing just outside my line of vision, one of The Elementals manifested itself right in front of me and slowly, ever so slowly, pulled back its hood. It had no face. Instead the black hood hid a grinning skeleton, with vicious, elongated fangs protruding out of its mouth instead of teeth, and there were black holes where the eyes should have been. They are monsters.

I didn't sign up for this.

Now they mock me. I can hear their wicked laughter deep in my subconscious. They know that I know, and I know that *they* know I know. But it doesn't matter. They also know that I am powerless to prevent the spread of Pirifinil. It is too late. The rewards were too great, and it found its way to the market-place prematurely. Plus, its active ingredients are in a hundred other products.

I don't know what is happening on the outside. Access to television and other media is forbidden in this facility. But I have a suspicion that since we released Pirifinil to the general public, murders and suicides are on the increase. And nobody knows why. Except The Elementals and I. Hey, that rhymes. Maybe I could forge an alternative career as a poet, if I had time. And the right frame of mind.

But I don't have the right frame of mind. And there is no more time. No more time for me to be a poet, no time for any-one to be anything. We are all on the path to destruction.

I cannot find a moment's peace. The walls of my mind are closing in and I am powerless to prevent them. I don't sleep anymore and time has no meaning. There are old fixtures in my mind that I cling to; memories, habits and things I just *know*. One of them is the knowledge that I should be doing something to stop this from happening.

I tell the doctors here that I am an undercover executive with the firm but they don't believe me. Nobody does. People are so dismissive that now I even doubt it myself. Maybe the memories I pour over are not my own. But if they're not mine, then whose are they? And where are *my* memories?

I try to block the nastiness out, but The Elementals are too strong, and it never ends. It never ends. It's like a bad dream, but I know I am awake. I know I am awake. I am awake.

And I remember how it started…

JANE BROOKS

A native of the southern United States, author Jane Brooks ultimately escaped from her birthplace below the Mason-Dixon line to the general safety of the West Coast, where she now makes a living turning numbers into stories for a large software company.

Brooks keeps a zombie apocalypse bug-out bag in the hall closet that contains both propane and condoms.

PETER WHITLEY

Peter Whitley is a skateboarder, artist and (by many accounts) a functioning cretin. He is the author of *Mastering Skateboarding*, the *Public Skatepark Development Guide*, and several award-winning memos. *Release* is his first published work of fiction.

RELEASE

BY JANE BROOKS & PETER WHITLEY

Keys. Protein bar. Water bottle. He filled his pack.

Revolver. Crowbar. Hand sanitizer. Wallet, mostly useless but comforting—he felt naked still without it. Folded duffel. Routine things for a routine day.

He spun the cylinder on the snub-nosed .38 to count the rounds. Six. *Check.*

He patted his pockets for more. *Check.*

He filled his bottle from the rain barrel, sniffed it for contaminants. Still good. *Check.*

He knelt to tie his boots.

Goals today: food and hardware, fresh linens, more warm clothing. Lumber. Batteries. Always need batteries. Stay alive.

As he crossed the bedroom to the door on the way out, he touched her shoulder gently. "Hold down the fort." He almost smiled when he said it.

She turned her head and snapped at him, but not angrily. The curiosity of teeth. He looked down and quickly tested the straps that held her to the wall. "You're not going anywhere today, are you, babe?"

A soft groan escaped from her as he dodged her reaching hands. Outside, he mounted his bike and slowly pedaled away.

* * *

There was the day it hit the news, and the week when they started to realize something was very wrong, and the month when they watched red blotches spread across glowing world maps. There was the moment when they realized it had all fallen apart. The night they stayed up planning a path to survival. The day it happened, a stupid mistake—the wrong word and the wrong argument, the wrong place, the wrong weapon, and she didn't come back—and the nights afterwards he stayed out looking for her, frantic and blinded by denial.

I can find her. She's out here somewhere.

And the night she returned.

You learn to smell the air when your life is constantly in danger, and it was the air that told him he wasn't alone as he turned the corner on foot into the driveway. Unholstering his revolver, he walked carefully into the yard, swinging wide to cover a circle around himself. Nothing behind him. Nothing to the left or right. He crept slowly, twirling towards the porch, the smell of *wrong*—carrion, blood, fever—drifting around him. And then the sound. A soft, breathy moan, wet and snagging.

In the shadows by the porch steps, an unmistakable curve. His heart skipped more than one beat.

* * *

She had, rather *has*, the most beautiful face. Even vacant and pale, her face is a perfect—oval, soft, delicate. Her eyes had been wide and blue and liquid. Now cloudy white, they still penetrate him. Her shape—the sloping curve of her neck, the softness of her thighs, the wild rollercoaster described by her hip—perfect. Nearly perfect still. He sits at night in bed sometimes and traces the curves of her with his eyes, remembering. Even absent the clarity that used to live in her features she is still his, traces of the woman he had loved blooming through the damage.

Alive, before, when the world was still right, she had affected an air of amused disinterest in him even after she'd given him her body and her apartment. *There are tasks to be accomplished*, said her tone. *Your play is trivial. I can take you or leave you.*

But she never had. Left him, that is. He expected it sometimes, when he stupidly lied about where he'd been or she disapproved of his choice of friends, or when she felt his desire for her and pushed him away because she was too busy, too focused. Her occasional criticism cut at him in ways that only slowly healed. He always thought that there was a part of her she held separate, that she wouldn't give him. He felt the absence of that thing, whatever it was, and wondered if she would ever really give herself over completely to him. She had always been focused on the pragmatic march of life, dismissing nonsense, but he was the one who spun her, tumbled her, laughing, metaphorically, onto the floor. Ass over elbows on the floor—not a position she let herself get into except in metaphors, where she was frequently upended by the things he did.

He used to try to please her, a game they would play, and she would be satisfied but never delighted. She enjoyed his devotion, and being perpetually unimpressed kept him coming back, offering gifts and deeds, like some mating ritual seen on a nature program.

His affectionate approach and her affected disdain: that was the relationship then. Now, in this inverted world, her need for him was absolute and unwavering. This is the difference in her now—her constant attending to him. Behind the marred, graceful slope of her hairline, her senses register him. Her sharp dryness is dulled, moistened—hunger is an itch, he imagines, desire an aching, slow-motion skid on a damp floor that doesn't result in a fall—but she knows him. Wants him. Needs him.

When he fucks her, he tries to be gentle.

* * *

He had kept a tight rein on his enthusiasm to enter the fray of those early days, when many thought this was a problem that could be solved, a war that could be won. Their neighbor with the ridiculous car, the self-proclaimed "biggest fan" of all the local sports teams who was also a regional manager of various plumbing and electrical retailers—the neighbor she would preface with, "I suppose we should probably invite..." whenever they had a barbecue—this neighbor tried to convince him that it was a grand adventure, a generational call-to-arms like no other. In his grand vision they would transform the cul-de-sac neighborhood into the Ponderosa Court compound.

"Thank God for the 2nd Amendment," the Biggest Fan had said. Giddy smiles masked primal fears in those early days. He gathered a small cadre of like-minded folks to help realize his vision.

These neighbors, brazenly naïve, chubby warriors on blood-pressure meds armed with guns they'd recently bought but never shot, formed ad-hoc patrols led not by the steadiest but by the most foolhardy. These neighbors never looked back at the arguments over Christmas decorations, at casual driveway conversations, at the pride in a spotless gutter. They joyously egged each other to their deaths in a sheen of unhealthy sweat and random bullets pinging off sidewalks that were once swept clear of lawn trimmings. These neighbors fell apart only at the much unexpected end, trapped in convenience store parking lots and intersections by the truly criminal or the truly dead. It was freedom and it was chaos.

He'd finished the neighbors first, once they'd been turned. He remembered every one. Mostly it was an aluminum bat. They would walk up to him with their mouths open, not even their hands out. He would wind up and clock them. The first five were like that. He pushed cars around until they formed a kind of pen in the middle of the street. This was before she turned... And she watched, worried and anxious, from the yard, armed with a shovel from the garden.

He drew them from their homes in twos and threes, into the alley of neighborhood vehicles, then hopped up into the bed of a truck and finished them as they scrambled for purchase. It was simple, almost orderly, and produced few surprises. They shared a sense of accomplishment, even a bit of showmanship. She brought him a glass of lemonade once while he was clearing battered corpses from the street, and they laughed.

It was a mistake to think this might be okay.

Of course some neighbors hid and lasted longer. They hid from the undead, then they hid from the lawless, then they hid from each other. They died of exposure and malnutrition and self-inflicted wounds—among other things—in their hiding places. And that's where he found them: in meat lockers, closets, behind washing machines. He found a child, dead— though not clear how—in a pillow fort. He found them under cars and next to cars and in cars in airtight garages. But mostly he found them in bed next to prescription bottles with mouths caked in dried puke and bile.

When neighbors didn't return or didn't come out, he and she made their way through the neighborhood, peeking through backyard fences, from house to house, creating food caches near driveways and back patios, marked with a soggy newspaper or an uprooted shrub, visible to them but invisible to looters. They survived those early days on the bloody coat-tails of these neighbors.

He expanded his definition of home ownership to include all the yards, every stockpile, every safehold and hedge against starvation and want. Meanwhile, she reflected on the profound tragedy and waste of it all, not seeing what was new but rather what was missing.

The world is profoundly different now. It has transformed into something grotesque and simple, and there's something appealing in it too. He feels the tug of Boy Scout bravado, drawn to the Rube Goldberg approach to survival, the pride of outwitting the undead, even though they are little more than carnivorous tortoises. But most of all, he likes being essential and doing essential things. Not brave, not heroic, not fierce, but essential. To himself. To her.

* * *

You can't really say what she is *thinking*. Even if she is host-
ing cognitive processes, they're alien to the living. We assign
human motivations and thoughts—even language—to pets all
the time, spelling their words cutely to simulate their quaint
misunderstanding of the human world, to make them seem
relatable and warm. But her... It's difficult to imagine what a
once-sharp mind does when robbed of the chemicals that drive
and feed it.

What is clear, though, is her *want*.

He sees it when he crosses the room, her drawn head swiv-
eling to match his movement. She wants him. No, it's not clear
what she wants, but the lack of him and the need for him show
in her body and in the ever-so-slightly shifting rigor of her face.

He hears it in her voice when he leaves, almost words cracking out into the near silence, possibly beckoning him back,
possibly simply protesting the change. He talks to her as he's
preparing to go, just so the shock of her croaking isn't the first
voice he hears in a day, and because it feels kind.

"Need extra water today. It's hot. I know—weird for Au-
gust, right? Let me check that collar. It can't be comfortable.
There, that's better. Where did I put the buck knife? Yes, right,
next to the bed..."

Sometimes he sings, bits of songs from when they were
younger. He can't tell if it calms her. It calms him.

When he is close to her, against her, inside her, she struggles
into him. Not a struggle of no—an awkward and animal yes,
he thinks. He can't know. He could be fooling himself, whistling past rape dragons. This is a thing he tries not to dwell on.

When he is close, her hips turn towards him as well as her eyes. Her shoulders square with his. Occasionally her legs rise to wrap around his, pulling him more tightly into her. Her bound hands reach for…something, her fingers curling and uncurling rhythmically like a violin exercise. This is a gesture he's seen many times before from his favorite vantage point tucked between her thighs.

Her mouth seeks purchase in his flesh, a thing he scrupulously discourages, sometimes with his hand on her chin, sometimes with a scarf tied around her face. It feels brutal to him to do this, but there is a reward: his now free hand can tenderly trace the outlines of her, a thing he used to do, before.

He misses their tenderness, those moments of physical warmth they shared and took for granted when she was alive: her head on his shoulder, his hand on her belly or thigh, her body nestled against his in sleep, the way she pressed her cheek against his whenever she said goodbye for more than a day. That tenderness is gone, replaced by her vacant, needy stare. He chooses to assign tenderness to her vigilance because it is comforting.

* * *

They atrophied together. She, her front tooth chipped, a lesion on her calf that would never heal, her fingernails splintering and turning black. And her eyes, graying, milky sacs shaped by her beautiful structure. She became gaunt. Two blades of hip bones peered over her slung shorts, and he remembered being fixated by their shape in the dim, morning light of their earliest romances, when he would sleep for an hour then be aroused into erect attention by this impossibly foreign creature in his bed. That was before.

They had called in sick together to extend those lost weekends years ago. He remembered bringing glasses to the bedroom, kissing her mouth cooled by orange juice, and the rings of condensation on the small table near the bed. That was before. There was no more orange juice forever, but she was there, still, with her hips. He knew she would never survive this.

He atrophied with her. He, his sense of global good, of certainty, of safety. It used to be, somewhere, at any given time, someone was taking care of it, things, the world. That faith rotted and fell off as the weeks passed. In its place grew a suspicious self-reliance. He saw it fall off and even glanced back at it to briefly consider if it might be useful. Logic, dignity and his pride in doing something right stopped being exercised, and they were eventually replaced by obsessive-compulsive rituals. Look up, right, left, up…take five steps…look up, right, left, up…take five steps.

He still checked useless expiration dates. He still wore clothes that he thought he might look good in, yet only wore new socks, but always for three days in a row. And in those moments where he could do nothing else, he sat on the roof with the ladder pulled up and surveyed his kingdom…his honeymoon suite…his own private Idaho. Those moments were like passing Go; an inevitable, powerless movement that still ends up somehow flashing a little sense of accomplishment. Another day, another donut. He knew he would never survive this.

* * *

It's tempting to think of the zombie problem as a war, but it's fundamentally different. The hallmarks of past conflicts—organized strategic goals, targets, supply chains, uniforms, budgets, even guerrilla tactics—are largely missing. At best, this is an extremely disorganized siege, with a big buffet table, at which only one side can eat.

And of course, at its most basic level, it is profoundly more personal. In war, losses are common, expected, but there are segments that a war will rarely touch except in the worst parts of an urban conflict. The elderly. If you're lucky, children. School teachers. Priests. Dentists. Instructional Designers. Not so when your foe is the undead, because you could easily be facing down your grocer, your neighbor, the guy from the copy room at work, your child, your mother, your lover.

So it is for him, this morning, waking up from a dream of her—his lover turned foe, there in the room with him. In the dream she had been present again, fresh, looking straight into his eyes. It was like it had been, before the danger and the struggle, before the fear, before... In the dream she had handed him something—a box, green ribbon, the size of a small book— and said his name. She was clear-eyed and beautiful. The sun blazed too brightly as it does in dreams like this, as if the extra metaphorical weight is necessary to drive home a point he already gets.

Now when he opens his eyes, fuzzy from sleep, and looks up at her leaning towards him from the wall, she almost looks alive again. He remembers the night before, inside her, moving, butting his head softly against her collarbone, concentrating on the hug of her around him and the memory of her when she was warm. Moving inside her, taking her, taking himself.

Carefully. She could tear. Filling her with the only thing he can give her.

And when it was over, the well of grief opening up again.

On the way to the backyard latrine and the beginning of his day's practical realities, he touches the skin of his enemy. Moments later, he wills a set of ideas not to form in his mind. Outside, alone, he takes his stiffening cock in his hand and mechanically finds a rare moment of blankness, without her eyes watching him.

* * *

It is this rhythm that defines his days now: waking to her, being watched by her, dressing and securing the house, leaving and scavenging, returning to her, her eyes on him and her head bent always in his direction.

He supposes she doesn't know him anymore for who he is, only what he is. He, to her, a vague impression of gravity constantly, gently, drawing her.

Her? Not "her." Her was gone, stubbed out, replaced by This. This, in this place in space, drawn to that, in that place right there, as absolute and constant as an astronomer's law. A love, of sorts. An existence defined by need.

Need for this, he, there, constantly orbiting and never colliding. Wanting, perhaps, the sweet, terminal collision of oneness, union. Please. Closer. Let me taste you, become you, and you become me. The ache of desire, unbearable and eternal. Like a gold coin that the fingertip can only just brush and never seize. Unrequited.

And for him, the presence of her. The shape of her in the

dim light. The eroding curve of her ass, the slow turning of her head when he enters the room. Devotion he never earned from her while she lived.

* * *

With winter coming, he decides to move more of their cached supplies into the house. No sense burning calories staying warm outside when he can hole up for weeks on the supplies he can store in the spare room.

Like all spare rooms, this is the grave where forgotten things are buried. Boxes of ill-fitting or impractical clothes never taken to Goodwill. Empty picture frames. Old birthday wrapping paper, torn at the ends of the roll. A broken chair he'd intended to fix. Books from college. He has already scavenged this room for batteries, flashlights, penknives, weapons. All that's left is the debris of a suburban life.

He briefly considers what to do with it all, then postpones the decision and begins to box it up. Organize first, things with like things, then make a plan. This is how she'd have done it.

In the one neat corner of the room is her desk, once the hub of her household command. Tidy stacks of opened bills wait on the blotter to be filed. The old computer tower that once hummed quietly is now coated with a faint veneer of dust. Its monitor is dark. A coffee cup of pens lies overturned next to it. Briefly he wonders how that happened, then turns away. He will move everything else first.

Books are heavy. They go in the smaller bins. Because they can burn he moves them into the living room by the fireplace.

Also the chair. He begins to organize the other things that can burn. A few useful things—a sewing kit; an old watch cap; small, needle-nosed pliers—are collected and set aside. The less utilitarian things, the unburnable, along with broken things go in bags and bins to be taken…somewhere else. The basement for now, he thinks.

The desk will burn, he tells himself as he turns toward his last task of the day. *Her desk.* Choosing a sturdy box, he breathes deeply and begins emptying the drawers into it. This box he won't throw away, not immediately. He begins to stack the detritus of her pragmatic life. What they are, these things, doesn't matter. They are hers and he will save them for now.

In the middle drawer on the right he finds a book. It is cheaply ornate, a bookshop brocade binding colored a dusty blue with embroidered roses at the corners. Tacky, she would have judged it. She must have gotten it on sale. He opened it. Of course: her journal. A bright green ribbon marks her place.

His throat constricting, he begins to read the notes she's written to herself. Reminders of priorities she might forget, observations on the motives and actions of friends, a few complaints here and there about her mother, her job, the weeds in the garden—mostly from the time just before everything fell apart. Threaded through all of that there are also passages about him, her observations of incidents he remembers, her questions and her anger and her desire. He is surprised by this, though he shouldn't be. A picture of the man she saw orbiting around her, a man he only somewhat recognizes.

* * *

He isn't always gentle. Tonight he is raw and fucks her out of anger, lust, perversion, shame. For not being what he should have been, and being now what he shouldn't. He fucks her hard and quickly and abruptly. Later, he will wash the drying streaks of cum from her thighs and wrap her hair in a stained scarf she once loved. And smell the clothes still hanging in her part of the closet. And dwell on what it was like before, though before is being replaced with new memories of after, and he feels he is losing her again because he couldn't let go when he should have.

* * *

He sees the end coming before the end comes, of course. It is predawn when a slurching sound snags and tears at his sleeping consciousness. He hears it, tussles, then smells it. It is an odor he is familiar with, even accustomed to, but more intense, more pervasive.

Before turning on the lantern he grabs the holster from the nightstand, removes the gun, and quietly moves to the edge of the bed, listening and gently finding his footing on the floor. Then a switch and the lantern pushes back the darkness. She is there. As always, her head turns slowly to face him. He walks carefully around to the foot of the bed to face her.

A raccoon-sized heap of intestines and spoiled organs lies slumped at her feet, cords of sinew, mucus and intestinal ropes hang from the cavity between her legs. He impulsively steps back.

"Oh God. Oh God. Oh God, honey. I'm so sorry."

He had evicted this idea weeks, months ago—he, who wouldn't buy emergency batteries for fear of summoning a tornado—but just as much as it was unthinkable of course it was inevitable. All roads lead to this fork.

How does this part go again?

She stares at him with her cloudy, eternal, beautiful eyes. He steps forward, kicking aside the gore with his bare foot. Loosely gripping the gun, he reaches to smooth the hair matted against her forehead with the back of his hand.

"Honey I'm sorry."

She groans. It sounds like wind through an empty barn.

It had never occurred to him to wonder if she felt any pain. The gravitas of the question nearly doubles him over now. Bound to the wall, dead, breaking, lost… Does she also in all of this…hurt?

The questions he has not allowed himself to ask now crowd into his throat. *Is now the time? Do I finish her? Is there misery that I should put her out of? How much longer can this last? Do I join her? Do I even remember how to be alone?*

He cups a breast in his unarmed hand and moves still closer, leaning his face into her neck. She snarls and bucks, her body begging for him. To devour him? To receive him? It's not clear, has never been clear.

He breathes in the air close to her and considers his position, his options. *Eternity, here, with her? Transformation and sanctuary, freedom, relief, release? Or the grief, once more, the loss, the emptiness of once again being without her?*

He searches in the familiar stench of her for a single note of her living scent. Locating it, he brushes his cheek against hers and finds her lips.

This time a kiss, nudging open her mouth with his tongue, savoring for the first time the bitter flavor of her teeth.

When she bites into him he feels his blood heat up and his mind clouds with the pain. He knows how quickly this works. He's seen it before. He takes a moment, pressing his cheek against hers again, pressing his temple against her, willing himself to breathe, to consider it once more.

After a moment he whispers softly in her ear, "Okay, babe. Let's go."

He places the barrel of the gun against her temple and squeezes the trigger slowly. A wet bang he never hears.

DAVID MURPHY

David Murphy is an Irish author whose award-winning fiction has been published worldwide and translated into several languages.

Murphy's short fiction includes two chapbooks and a short story collection published in 2004. His latest novella *Bird of Prey* was published in 2011. His previous novella *Arkon Chronicles* appeared in paperback from Silver Lake Publishing in 2003. Murphy's well received *Longevity City* was published in hardcover by Five Star in 2005.

WATER, SOME OF IT DEEP

BY DAVID MURPHY

Memories of Henry swirl in my head like sawdust at a woodcutter's. In his fifties, he seemed a man with everyday interests: backing horses, model aircraft, writing poetry. Not to mention canoeing. Or was it kayaking? I do not know the difference. He could be wonderfully entertaining. Words tumbled from the magnificent shambles of his mind, his mouth never slow with an opinion. He brimmed with conversation and a bubbly wit too complex for most of the locals. They disliked his shuffling demeanour, the intensity behind those round-rimmed spectacles, the brooding hints that beneath that chaotic, grey hair lurked depths they could not fathom. Around here they prefer their ageing hippies to be simple, readable and predictable, something to lend a little colour to the landscape. Henry was none of those things.

I first met him six years ago after Fiona and I moved west out of the city to live by the coast. We had always wanted to live by the sea—she to paint, I to write poetry. Or as the real world would have it: she part-timed as school secretary, I worked nixers in interior design. Our community here was small, a few hundred souls in a scattering of houses nestled along a cove. Three pubs, a couple of shops, a street of sorts that looked well in summer, though not many tourists veered off the main drag to come here. We were off road and, more often than not, off season. On dark days, especially in bad light of winter, our houses and street, no matter how brightly painted, took on a drab, nondescript look.

Henry's wife, Ursula, had become friendly with Fiona despite a generation gap. My wife was twenty-nine, Ursula fifty-one. Henry had nineteen years on my thirty-eight. We shared four-sided dinners in their cottage, sometimes in ours. He loved a good intellectual exchange. So did I. We sought each other out, for a while. People left us to ourselves. In my early days here, one of our few mutual friends let slip that his pals had asked him, when he had returned to their company after half an hour drinking with Henry and me, why he bothered 'talking to those fellas.' So we were known as 'those fellas'— with the emphasis on 'those'—as if we were a newly discovered social disease. Henry did not care what people thought. Neither, at first, did I.

Sometimes people asked me on the street or when I was holding up a bar, "How can you stand yer man?"

I shrugged my shoulders, made vague replies.

"He's not too bad."

"He's not the worst."

One night in bed, a few years ago, after dinner at Henry's, Fiona lay in the crook of my arm. "Henry's fixated by the financial crisis, isn't he?" she said. "Did he lose much in the crash?"

"I dunno, love. He hates bankers."

"He has lots of pet hatreds."

Pet hatreds? They were becoming more like Rottweilers. Fiona's comment struck me as rich, considering how friendly she was with the sharp-tongued Ursula.

"He hates bankers," I said, "because he's a child of the sixties who can't stand greed and materialism. He's just a cranky old hippy."

"Cranky is right. Listening to him giving out about the world tonight was worse than spending an hour watching a current affairs programme on economics."

"And it lasted just as long," I said, putting my hand on her shoulder, pulling her close.

* * *

Now I sigh and stretch in my empty bed. Dust of memory comes at me in a blizzard. I wear no goggles to keep stinging, eye-gouging memories at bay. I wear, as I have worn for years, a pair of blinkers. I should have seen that he needed to be in control, not mundanely as a control freak, which he was, but because his mind was growing erratic to the point of demanding control over everything, not just his own life but of the world around him. No aura of creepiness clung to him, though I see now that I was complicit in the evil that lurked beneath his chummy veneer. His intensity, his combativeness, his need to confront, led to him becoming unable to pull back. I should have read the signs and seen it coming because over the last few years of our friendship he had begun to paw the ground intellectually, looking for arguments, seeking out spats, putting his head down in such bullish fashion that it culminated in four arguments in two hours.

On the night of those arguments, twelve months ago now, I had known him less than five years. Several times in our history I had considered dropping his friendship, our relationship having gone through more than one cooling-off period. Each time I allowed him back in because I would warm to him again by convincing myself that life would be poorer without him, which it would have been in the same way as war would be poorer without all those deaths.

The first disagreement must have been a trivial matter. I cannot recollect it. The second argument began when I said I liked the latest piece of popular music sweeping the land. He called me a 'musical ignoramus.' I thought that a little strong and argued the toss before veering the conversation to another topic. He made equally strong comments on the state of the country. I considered what he was saying to be dangerous generalisations. While I can take criticism of my country, there are still a few nationalist hackles—genetically installed at conception, I believe—that rise when the dressing-down comes from the lips of an Englishman. I looked around the bar, wishing for someone, anyone, to join us. It was the fourth and final row that clinched it. At closing time I began telling him of poetry readings lined up to coincide with my book launch.

He said, "It just goes to show that you don't need a high standard of work to get a collection published these days."

I felt that my innards had been filleted. It may only have been a small, independent publisher in the city, but it was legitimate and arts council funded, paying me a pittance, unlike the two vanity presses he had paid to bring out his collections in England. I would get reviews and invites to arts festivals and be regarded as a genuine player on the circuit. He never would. He knew that and it killed him, and he knew that I knew how he secretly felt, but it still killed *me* to hear him say those ugly words. I sat there like an imploded corpse, wondering where the Henry I had met five years ago had gone, the man of wit and charm, replaced now by an intellect cold, judgemental, willing to say something that he should never have said, to jettison the friendship of half a decade, and for what? An opinion? In one of those fate-ordained moments, Old Maurice stood behind the counter with his hands on his hips.

"One for the ditch, lads?"

"Why not? Two pints of your finest stout!"

"I'm okay," I said. "I've had enough."

Henry grasped the seriousness of his final insult only when I refused an after-hours drink.

He and Old Maurice stared at me, both stunned into silence.

Over the next minutes Henry tried to shallow-gossip about everyday things. I finished my drink and lifted my jacket off the back of the stool. He downed his pint and accompanied me to the door as if nothing had happened.

Stepping outside, I looked at him and said, "See you around, Henry."

We parted and went our separate ways. My belly sloshed with the slop of sour stout. My mind tipped over with the firm intentions of never allowing myself to sit in that man's company again.

Next day he went out in his canoe as he did most days.

I often visualise him in that pathetic, little vessel. I prefer that to picturing him in other activities those final, awful weeks. I see him now on his last day. I replay that day over and over, not wanting events of other days to come into my mind. I give him thoughts to compliment his actions—harmless thoughts, zany actions—merely harmless, merely zany. Early symptoms of an insane mind. His or mine? Sometimes I wake up in a sweat and think: *I am no longer sure.*

I see him launch his canoe. He jumps aboard, glimpsing from the corner of his eye a page of his logbook hanging loose on the prow. He recalls yesterday's entry, remembering it word-perfect: *From Bramble Head to Bluff Harbour. About three and a half miles. Light sou'westerly. Otherwise flat calm. Must remember to stow sun-cream on board in future. Fished for codling on the drift, no luck. Went ashore at Dudgeon Cove. No annoying jet-skis today.*

He pulls hard on the paddle before the swell pushes him back onto sand. A few strokes take him beyond suck of beach. With his paddle across his midriff, he strains forward to tuck his precious logbook beneath its plastic cover to protect it from what salts and sprays the sea might throw. He has not revealed the log's existence to anyone, not even to Ursula, and certainly not to me. Ironic that I, months later, should gain access to all his writings, nautical, poetic and otherwise. I make him look forward to thinking how tonight's entry might look. I imagine it for him: *Along the curve of Two-Mile Strand to Ratchett Head. Across the bay on a rising tide.* Already the sun has burned holes in lace-curtain mist hanging over a flat Atlantic. *Ideal conditions for ocean-going.* He turns, pursues a course parallel to the shore. I make him sail slowly. I want to prolong it. With his long, grey hair he glides through the mist, a pony-tailed Neptune caressing the surface with a double-ended blade.

The red cab of a tractor flashes at him from behind trees on the shore road. A silhouette in the bouncing cab salutes him, whether in jest or mockery Henry is not sure. I make him unsure because I want him to feel nervy, uncertain. He waves back, though he suspects that the salute must be one of mockery. Because of his canoeing, locals had taken to saying, "Here's Henry the Navigator!" whenever he entered Old Maurice's, a habit he had got out of in the year since our arguments. Deep down, Henry had only contempt for the locals. I also have nothing but contempt for those around me, then and now.

'Navigator' was merited. "You're canoeing more as a career than a hobby," Ursula had said to him, her acid eloquence reminding him of why, in far-off college days, her fellow students had given her a nickname of her own: 'The Knife.' This I know because he told me back in our friendlier days. What Ursula said was right: he had a compulsion for water, for the sea. If the weather was poor he paddled on wind-sheltered lakes and rivers.

He imagines a sea-area forecast in a plummy, old-fashioned BBC accent. *Fastnet: cloud increasing. Pressure falling. Wind strong to gale force. Visibility zero. Small craft warning in operation. All ferry services cancelled.* Hugging the shoreline that last, fateful morning, his mood sours to match his imagined shipping news. I make a dread feeling stalk him in a vital, hidden spot. He must have experienced it many times, this dangerous imitation of dangerous weather. *Henry: Happiness falling. Storm clouds gathering. Outlook gloomy. Prospects zero. All future services cancelled.*

A sudden lurch almost topples him over. Concentrate, he tells himself, looking around for the rogue wave that had caught him unawares. He sees a swell so gentle he has to look for it.

He suspects there might be something beneath his hull. Guilt?
He looks over the side. Nothing but shelving sand scarcely a
fathom deep. He begins to feel his blood warm up and thinks
of what might have been—and had been, twice—tucked in the
storage space behind him. There is nothing there now, nothing
to slip sideways and unbalance his canoe. I make the sun come
out. It warms his back by the time he turns seaward at Ratchett
Head. *Across the bay on a rising tide*...to his last port of call. That
special spot, a hiding place on the southern side of an east-facing cove. Henry feels better where beach surrenders to a rocky
coastline of caves, coves, stacks and sea arches. So much more
interesting than endless sand are these overhanging cliffs to
paddle under. Little chance of eyes prying from above, many
hiding places secret and inaccessible.

He looks around. No lobstermen out in boats this ripple-
free morning, no nosey trawlers or kayaking tourists. Good.
He canoes close to bearded rocks, no longer part of the servile
world beyond the cliffs, the land of greed, selfishness and materialism; the world that had robbed him of his wealth in the
recession, and turned its critical back on his poetry. One lot had
cheated him of his money. The others would not know good
poetry if it rose up and bit them in the arse. This, he thinks.
This, I know. He said it to me. Fuelled by resentment and paranoia, ignited by a double blow—one financial, the other artis-
tic—his head had tipped over into rage, vengeance and an all-
consuming need to strike out at what society held to be its most
precious cargo: its future.

I can only think that his toxic, slow burn had smouldered for
months, years, before bursting into fire those last crazy weeks.
On this sunny final day he no longer feels as if his brain and

heart might explode with fury and violence at any moment. Now he feels light-headed because he is sailing away from the world of greed and fear. Looking up at the sky beyond the cliffs he believes that the world beneath that cruel, blue lid is no longer real. This is what is real, he tells himself: the bright seaward side of the cliffs—ocean, sun and sparkle.

He sees spray of sprat on sunlit surface, mackerel chasing them from below. He witnesses visions of garfish in pursuit, of wrasse wrestling with weeds and crustaceans. He is glad to have left his rod at home. This is no morning for fishing. No day for interfering with the natural order. I imagine another entry for his log, one that turns out to be true: *a day of consequence, of restoration and reparation, a time of atonement after weeks of insanity. Funny how the mind behaves under pressure. Now the pressure recedes.*

He paddles on, leaving fish to consume themselves. He thinks this is how it is up and down the food chain all the way from gannets squealing overhead to molluscs slugging it out on the ocean floor. And larger predators too—sharks and killer whales, not to forget those gliding along the surface in hulls long and sleek, the width of a coffin, the same colour as a coffin, pointed at both ends for stealth and sleekness. He hugs the coastline. He glides around a series of rocks to slide under a vulva-like arch, a portal to another world. Scrag Rock hoves into view, beyond it Tern Island.

He is close now, within a gull's midnight scream. On his port, sunlight illumines the sea with a glare to hurt his eyes. He blinks, keeps his gaze forward; slides past familiar boulders and kelp beds drowned in rising tide. He looks around, spellbound. The sea is a heaven-sent mirror reflecting the beauty of nature.

That last morning was a morning made for canoeing, a morning sent from God. Henry had often gone looking for God. He had been looking for God a long time. He wanted to talk to Him.

To his starboard, rocks open up, revealing a small creek in the cliff, a tiny stream-hewn cove inaccessible from above. *Two strokes of the paddle take me across an ocean of pain. I should have been a terrorist, a mere terrorist. I would have preferred that, and willingly taken it, had You seen fit to give me a choice.*

A small crevice, big enough to line himself up with the confidence that a canoeing man will fit. An expert swish of the blade, a stoop of the head; he is in. He stops the canoe and turns smoothly through three-sixty degrees. Reflected sunlight from the entrance creates an eerie dappled effect on a small, dome-shaped cave just large enough for his twelve-foot craft. He looks down on dark blue water full of anemones, invertebrates, blennies, shrimps and other harmless creatures. He checks the state of the tide. He has ten minutes before he will have to leave. He looks up. The dancing light from the entrance stipples the rock above the waterline with the ghostly marbled echo of light and all things bright. This is a wall haunted by algae, limpets, winkles, crabs and other scavengers. They climb with advancing tides—and sometimes of their own greedy slithery crawl—to a ledge above the high-water mark, a ledge you would never think was there unless you knew where to look, a place large enough to hide something from the eyes of all the world.

Henry's narrow, brown eyes adjust to the dim light of the cave. He lifts the paddle over his head and places it behind his back at right angles across the canoe. He feels his breath come shallow and fast, not from exertion but because he is about to see his handiwork. Pressing down on the paddle with his wrists he straightens his arms, lifts his buttocks off the canoe-seat and raises his head to ledge level. He opens his mouth to drink in the damp air. His eyes widen. He has to have one last look.

I no longer want to think about that day.

* * *

If I said I had not spoken to him since the Night of the Four Arguments, it would not be true. Our paths did cross. Whatever words we exchanged were polite greetings, nothing more. He took to staying in his cottage, so it seemed. I realised then that it was mutual, the desire to end our friendship. I was glad of that. So was Fiona. She had always found him hard to stomach. She remained friendly with Ursula, though we dined no more at Henry's. They met for coffee or went shopping in the city. I rarely found myself in Ursula's company. The same could be said of Fiona and me. We passed each other by in the narrowing confines of our lives. Though the cottage was small, its rooms may have been wide-open spaces for all the companionship there was between us.

For some time I had felt her growing resentment that she was carrying me, her salary paying for my poetry. Her family felt the same, frittering away her life and money on a semi-bohemian waster of a husband. Whatever Fiona and I had in common had eroded to little or nothing. She no longer painted. Watercolours had been for her a hobby, but for me poetry was a compulsion. I had to write. She worked full-time as a local school secretary now, the idealism of our earlier hopes buried among the dried-out colours in her paint-box. She no longer slept in the same bed as me, never mind in my arms. In those last twelve months my marriage plumbed like a depth charge longing to go off. During that year-long period I believed that Henry had no influence on the state of my worsening relationship with Fiona. Like so many other things those sad, dreary days, I was wrong about that too.

When the first child disappeared, the school where Fiona worked became a hornet's nest of sideways glances, accusatory looks, tension so concrete you could riverdance on it. She took the worst of it, more than the teachers or the principal. Fiona was in the foremost trench, the secretary's office being first in the firing line between school and a demented world of parent-crazy, media-driven frenzies of fear, charge and counter-charge. We thought it would die down as the weeks crawled by. It got worse. News vans everywhere, you could not walk down the street without someone sticking a microphone under your nose. Fiona was like a bag of ferrets each day after work. I saw it get to her. It got to me. I saw us all undermined as weeks slid by and the child's body was never found. Henry was high on the list of suspects mentioned in dispatches in the pub. The local know-alls had monitored how he had cut back his visits to Old Maurice's.

"Henry the Navigator's gone very odd," one of them said to me one night at the bar counter.

"In what way?"

"He doesn't come out much anymore. He's gone too quiet."

"Maybe that's because the last time he was in, you and your buddies called him 'Henry the Navigator' to his face and laughed him out of it."

That killed the conversation.

I finished my pint thinking that Henry's habit of shooting from the hip had rubbed off on me, which made me none too popular that night. I was glad because there was too much rumour-milling going on, yet I could not help but think these rumours were true. Henry had gone strange, going out canoeing in all weathers. When I mentioned this to Fiona, who throughout the child tragedy remained friendly with Ursula, she glared at me.

"God knows we've enough to worry about. Is that all you can think about? *Him?*"

All my exchanges with Fiona had become like that, short duels with verbal bullets. We were taking pot shots at each other at the end of every sentence. There was no warmth, only brief meetings over what was, or more frequently was not, in the fridge or kitchen cupboard, or use of the car and other unavoidable swapping of practical information. Then off we went, ducking and diving down sniper's alley, our rubble of a marriage demolished by years of bad communication and bad love.

Five weeks after the first, the second child was taken. Also nine years old, also a girl. The sky had fallen with the first disappearance. With the second, the gravitational impact of all the planets made my neighbours' shoulders sag, caused their eyes to ooze with suspicion and mistrust. Everyone who was still sane seemed crushed with worry and guilt. Each time I looked they stared back, faces fuelled with the fear of what might happen next—and who might be doing it. Detectives and uniforms searched everywhere, as did the locals. Teams of volunteers, including Henry, walked bogs, mountains and coastline.

Everywhere and everything was searched, but the trainee-policeman who looked inside Henry's canoe to make sure that it was empty failed to check it with a DNA kit. A single hair, fluid or skin sample would have solved it all.

Days and weeks dragged on. Fiona aged a decade those two witless months. With no bodies and no arrests, a scapegoat had to be found. The communal and police-procedural finger pointed at a simple-minded twenty-three-year-old from a nearby village, an unfortunate victim of an accident on the first day of his one and only job as a butcher's apprentice. He had hacked all four fingers off his left hand in the butcher's shop when he was fourteen years old. 'Stumpy' the locals had christened him. That he walked around with porno DVDs sticking out of his back pocket made him public enemy number one. He was arrested and dragged off, chased by a howling mob.

* * *

That last day returns to haunt me. I see him crouch. His bowed head misses the overhanging rock by inches. He is out. A swish of blade propels him from his private altar, abandoned now to its dome-shaped cathedral of stone, protected for all time by secrecy of sea, tide and cliff. He paddles across an ocean of pain. The sea has him surrounded. His mind overflows with the mother of all log entries, his canoe slowed by the weight of stones he has picked up in that creek in the cliff. *Stardate 5432 point 1…*he sniggers and considers how the human mind is capable of dwelling on gross flippancy and immeasurable regret at the same time. He wishes he could sit on a barstool and debate such matters with… It doesn't matter now. He must have felt remorse. His mind surely was tortured, given what happened next. I grasp at the hope that he did feel some shame, some twinge. He *must* have, given the log entries etched in my mind.

Mist returns. It covers him in its shroud. *Across the bay on a rising tide.* Is he paddling across the bay? He hopes not. He wants out of the bay. After all, he wrote: *Ideal conditions for ocean-going.* It is a good calm day for sailing into the broad Atlantic. Draped in mist, no one notices a single canoeist make his way out into the deep. He considers the mist to be as intangible as all the intangibles of his life, yet it is as enveloping, as consuming, as the most clear-cut, most formative events he can remember.

He recalls all those definitive events now, as if enumerating them for his log, as if allowing them to wrap him up in one last personal shipping forecast. I imagine him writing down: *Henry: Visibility zero. Pressure falling. Cloud dissipating. Outlook one of immense relief. Prospects much better for the world at large, and for the school-going population in particular.* He permits himself one last smile. His throat dries at what lies ahead. He determines to hold his course at all costs. *To thine own resolve be true,* he writes, knowing that soon, very soon, he will talk to God. He feels the swell beneath his hull and welcomes it. He knows the wind will rise, from a zephyr to a gale. He wonders what height of wave his canoe can take. He told me once, that on the manufacturer's scale of one to ten, it could take only six. With long, grey hair slung back, Henry glides through the mist, once again a pony-tailed Neptune caressing the surface with double-ended sculls.

* * *

There were no more child disappearances. A sense of calm returned to the community, to Fiona, even to my marriage. In each case it was surface gloss, false as plastic fishing lures. Cracks have a habit of staying. I should know. I tried not to walk on them with Fiona. I would have needed to be a contortionist.

One day, two months after her husband had disappeared, Ursula called to our door. She had about her a perfunctory look. There was a brusqueness in her manner that Fiona put down to the strain of her husband's suicide. We knew he had taken his own life because two days after Eoin O'Sullivan, the last person to see him alive, had waved to him from the cab of his tractor, Henry's body had been dragged up in a trawler's net. The man had made a crude attempt to weigh himself down by wrapping his paddle leash, weighed down by stones, around his upper body. Had the net not found him he might never have floated. His wife confirmed what Fiona and I already knew: they had lost all their savings in the market crash. The mortgage on their cottage was insurmountable, but there were other concerns. Ursula admitted that she was finding the going hard around here. One or two tongues wagged to the tune of how the child disappearances had stopped with her husband's death. Maybe the detectives had got the wrong man.

"Here," she handed me a folder full of spiral-bound poetry notebooks and other jotters. "You may as well have these. Nobody else would want his poetry, anyway."

I was tempted to tell her how appropriate her college-day nickname had been. What I did was look at a knife on the kitchen table.

* * *

In days that followed, I examined Henry's poetry. Though the rhythm was correct, and the language adequate, his technique was cold, flat and clumsy. The lights were on in his head but the windows to his soul remained curtained. I decided to read everything, including his canoeing logs. Ursula had handed me over the log he had written on his last day while drifting out on the tide. Crumpled and sea-stained, it was recovered from his pocket and remained legible, just, because of its tight plastic cover.

Some of the early logs were entertaining and revealing, especially his description of a freak wave capsizing him in Capalborus Bay. That day he had lost binoculars, compass, jacket, hat, pullover, sunglasses, mobile phone, boat rod, tackle box, lunchbox, hipflask, paddle, and very nearly his life, yet he still persevered with watery pursuits. My admiration for his determination soon soured. Later logs, especially the last one, bordered on the juvenile, a strange concoction of the real and unreal world inside his head, an amalgam of poetry, religion and, of all things, shipping forecasts. When I read a series of what I can only describe as poem-logs that he had called *Cargo*, it was as if a foghorn went off in my brain. I could feel his paper shake in my cold fingertips as I read what he had written.

There were hints, geographical inferences. A number of the poem-logs centred on a place on the southern side of an east-facing cove near a small creek 'two paddle-strokes' wide. Whatever distance paddle-strokes might be, his description narrowed things down. All the caves had been searched, how thoroughly I did not know.

I sat at a table in Old Maurice's the next day. I knew Shamie would be in to drink his dole money. I spread an ordnance survey map in front of me and pretended to study it. Shamie was one of those locals who loved to show blow-ins that they would never know the landscape and seascape as well as he did. The map drew him like a mackerel to a sprat.

"I have a few friends coming down," I lied. "They love hill-walking, but I was thinking cliff walks might be just the thing for them."

"A change is as good as a rest," he said with a slow belch.

"I'd like to show them something spectacular along the cliffs. Tell me, Shamie, you'd know this. Are there any blow-holes in the rocks around here?"

He looked at me from under bushy eyebrows. "There was the one at Capalborus Point. You could hear it ten miles away donkey's years ago, but it's been eroded by the waves. Still works but only on very rough days."

"I'll show them the caves and arches instead. They're not marked on the map. Where are the best ones?"

He pulled the map around to examine it closely.

I could contain myself no longer. "I know where some of the bigger caves are, looking down from my own walks. Are there any smaller ones that might be hidden by the tide?"

"They were all searched."

He had me rumbled but I persevered. "What about little ones that you'd never know were there? I bet there's very few around here." I pointed in the vague direction of Ratchett Head. A likely east-facing cove with an appropriate creek.

"Poulanconkary." He rose to it like a salmon, even putting his finger on the spot.

My Irish was rusty. *Poll an Choncaire?*—the conger's lair? The name diced my insides.

"It was searched," he repeated. "Now, my city-boy friend, do you know something the rest of us don't?"

"Who searched it?"

"The local sub-aqua club."

"Did the Garda sub-aqua or naval divers search it?"

"They worked further up and down the coast."

"So it was searched by a *club?*"

"Yes." Shamie's brow was as furrowed as Eoin O'Sullivan's field.

"Sunday divers."

The man did not get it. He stared right through me.

I wangled my way out after buying him and his cronies a few whiskies. I never darkened Old Maurice's door again. Weeks, months, after Stumpy's arrest, there was always one of them to say, "Who fingered Stumpy?" At that they would cackle like backyard hens.

I approached a local detective and told him my theory. He contacted the sub-aqua unit. They found the ledge and the remains of the two missing girls.

My life became unbearable once local papers got wind of it. When Fiona realised that her husband had been a paedophile's best friend, she was back with her mother in Cork. Whether Henry was a paedophile or a child murderer, I do not know. The bodies were more than two months dead and too damaged by decay and the crabs for the pathologist to tell. Distinctions between child murderer and paedophile are not observed or recognised around here. A rock through my front window was all the incentive I needed to move out. Stumpy had to leave also. He moved to England when they let him out of prison.

Ursula blamed Henry's financial troubles for wrecking the

insides of his head. Strikes me as simplistic. When the real identity of the culprit broke, the poor woman could only clutch at
straws. Last I heard she was walking the streets of Cork with a
piece of string around her waist to keep her coat closed. Ursula
has all the makings of becoming a bag lady.

In my case, Henry contributed to the break-up of my marriage not by the traditional act of sleeping with another man's
wife. He did worse than that, but his actions were the catalyst
for the break-up because had I not been friendly with him, perhaps Fiona and I could have patched things up. I also clutch at
straws.

His most secret character remains a mystery; his dark side
an enigma. In dead of night I wonder if a personal monetary
disaster can tip an otherwise sane man from being normal—
and normality is so relative—into the abyss? Was it like the last
drop falling into a deep and hidden beaker of turmoil that finally turned him to the more horrific end of the human spectrum, that and facing up to the truth that his poetry would
never make the grade? I don't know. I'm no expert. Experts are
not much help. Police, psychiatrists, the press, nobody has a
clue what stoked and fired him. He had never exhibited an unhealthy interest in the vulnerable or the young. He was not on
the sex-offenders list in England. He had no previous of any
sort. I must stop making excuses for this monster of a man.

I suffer recurring nightmares. All the manikin-children from
all the clothes shops become animated. They zombie-march
through the streets to my front gate, up the path, into my
porch, up my stairs… I wake up sweating, screaming, reliving
that last day through Henry's narrow, beady eyes. Could I have
saved those girls?

I miss Fiona. I fight against the bottle. I fight against myself. I have not been asked to do a reading since the murder story broke. I no longer write poetry. I keep a diary in the form of a log, of a life destroyed by the accidental alignment of two lives, his and mine. In my attempts to understand the man and his motives I wonder what it is that draws people together. Are friendships accidental alignments? For instance, Henry's and mine? Do such friendships form in an instant glance? A certain set to the mouth? An openness of the palm? A glint in the eye? A willingness to listen? A mutual interest? That last bit worries me. I have no interest in avenging myself on the vulnerable or on the young, but I feel cheated by circumstances that make me also want to gain revenge by wreaking havoc on all those happy people who surround me but stay well outside my walls. I am a loose cannon. There is madness in us all. It lies there, deep down, waiting its moment, itching to be switched on.

I live in the midlands now. I avoid tabloid journalists. I no longer read newspapers. I sit in a dirty, one-roomed flat flexing my wrists, unable to remove from my mind the tragedy of those girls. I stare into the mirror at eyes narrow and brown, just like Henry's. I feel his pain.

There are lakes around here. I walk their shorelines.

I am beginning to like these inland expanses of water. I am drawn to the sheen of the lakes, as Henry was drawn to the sparkle of the sea.

KENNETH WHITFIELD

Author Kenneth Whitfield has been terrifying horror readers for years with his work that has been published in numerous comic and prose publications.

His writing credits include scripts in the comic anthologies *Death Rattle, Trailer Park of Terror* and *When Drive-Ins Attack.*

Whitfield's short stories have been published in the horror anthologies *Demon-Minds*; *Undead Dixie*; *You Can't Kill Me, I'm Already Dead* and *Steamy Screams.* Online publications include *Horror Garage, Dark Eclipse* and *Gore Magazine.*

He was a contributing writer and editor to *The Horror Show* and *New Blood* magazines back in the day. He currently lives with his beautiful, supportive wife, eight chickens and an asthmatic cat in a log house in Tennessee.

ACCEPTANCE

BY KENNETH WHITFIELD

So here we are in a human cattle line being slowly herded forward to begin our dream vacation. A vacation from the mundane, a chance to recharge and rejuvenate—at least that's what the online ad said. I'm nursing a hell of a hangover from the fifth I downed last night while Maggie was packing and complaining of all the things she had to do to get ready for this trip. Luckily I put several of her painkillers in my pocket to help me get through this check-in ordeal. As we shuffle forward, I look around for suspicious towel-headed people and wonder if this will be the cruise ship terrorists decide to attack.

We are here because I was surfing the net a few months back, on a good high after my Prozac and bourbon, when I ran across the advertisement for the cruise. Just a few clicks, a credit card number and here we are.

It seemed like a good idea at the time.

Inching toward the check-in desk for seven fun-filled days aboard the *Sun Runner*—flagship of Sun Cruise Lines, ocean-going castle transporting us to enchanted locales for a second honeymoon. Yeah. Right. Maggie has been in one of her moods ever since I surprised her with this trip. And surrounded by chattering yuppies and their ill-behaved offspring. If I see one more bronzed face with glistening white teeth yelling into a cell phone as if they are the only people around and what they have to say is oh-so-interesting, I think I'll snap. Bunch of self-absorbed assholes. We're herded forward and Maggie's whining about how tired she is and her feet are swelling and she's getting a migraine and why can't this line move faster and…

God, I need a drink.

Looking around for terrorists, but seeing only the self-absorbed yuppie assholes shuffling forward, I smile and utter "moo" under my breath. I think it is witty. Maggie rolls her eyes and accuses me of having a manic episode.

I was once diagnosed as potentially bipolar. A chemical imbalance in my brain causing extreme personality changes at times. Wide mood swings. I don't really think so. I just have a bit of a Jekyll and Hyde personality when it comes to drinking. And Maggie's mood really affects my mood. Though she refuses to see that. If she would just get off my back…

I shrug.

A young, bronzed boy about eight years old peeks out from around his tennis-skirted mother and tennis-shorted daddy, flashing a toothy smile up at me. A big smile, too big for his face. He looks weird, like an abstract painting. His smile stretches to his ears, too large for his mouth, with teeth that are too big. Mommy and Daddy should have the maid or nanny or whoever take this kid to the dentist. Or maybe a plastic surgeon. Don't think he'll grow into those huge chompers. I "moo" again, thinking about cows chewing their cuds.

"I wish you'd stop that. You are embarrassing me!" Maggie whispers loudly and angrily in my ear, through clinched teeth, drawing more attention to us than my mooing.

The big-mouthed kid grins more broadly at me.

We finally get to the check-in desk. The lady is all smiles and pleasantness, in a *Stepford Wives* way. She is on robotic auto-pilot, or maybe on some good meds herself, and just wants to move the livestock along.

I debate asking her some smartass questions, "So, what's Gopher up to? Isaac? Is Captain Stubbing available? Has Julie the cruise director got a bunch of exciting events planned for us?," just to see if I can get her to break from the script she is reciting. But she's probably too young to get the *Love Boat* references, and I know Maggie would jump all over me. It's just not worth the effort.

I listen and smile passively at her as Maggie asks about the doctor and pharmacy availability onboard. Thankful that, at least, Maggie's whining hasn't escalated to full-fledged bitchiness yet.

We walk through security, where they X-ray and then hand search our carry-on bags. They take away my dull Swiss Army pocket knife and Maggie's small sewing scissors. Dangerous weapons indeed. I know I feel safer. I notice not one of the self-absorbed yuppie assholes is searched. The little kid who smiled at my mooing earlier keeps looking at me, grinning. He's beginning to freak me out.

"Maybe I ought to tell his parents that they need to teach their brat that staring ain't polite."

Maggie rolls her eyes at me again. I hate it when she does that.

"Yeah. Why don't you do that? After his Gold's-Gym-going daddy mops the floor with you, I can enjoy the rest of the cruise without your comments."

There it is. The onset of full-fledged bitchiness. I wonder where the nearest bar is on the boat as I surreptitiously take two painkillers from my pocket and swallow them dry.

Any port in a storm.

* * *

We pause under a cheesy banner for a Welcome Aboard photo op. A cute, young lady in hot pants—or are they called booty shorts?—snaps our picture. I'm sure we look adorable. Me in my too-small aloha shirt with buttons straining across my belly and Maggie being swallowed in a too-big matching aloha dress. Fat man and Lil' Bit? I look at the smiling, almost artificially perfect, beauty of the photographer. Turning, twisting her tight butt and tossing her hair at the same time in a practiced move, she tells us the picture will be available for purchase tonight in the photo gallery on Deck Five. I imagine she is telling me alone and suck my gut in a bit. Maggie looks extremely…apathetic. A tuxedo-clad young man with a microphone and clipboard—looking like a lounge lizard with big mouth and all—wets his lips and announces us aboard.

"Ladies and gentlemen, please welcome aboard Mr. and Mrs. Jonathan and Margret Coltrain."

Naturally this is met with resounding silence as we walk down the gangway to the ship proper. More folks meander inside, wondering like zombies in a mall. I spy the ship's duty-free shop with its affordable alcohol as we stroll by. It should be open once we reach international waters. I salivate a bit.

We find our room with relative ease—didn't even have to ask Gopher or any of the crew—and Maggie continues her bitching.

"Where is our luggage?"

I shrug. "They said it would be delivered before 8:00 pm."

"Well…this…this is unacceptable! My medicine is in the luggage and my head is splitting. Not to mention my aching feet and ankles."

"Not a whole lot I can do about that," I protest.

"Well, you could be more sympathetic! You could be more caring! You used to be so sweet and concerned…"

And this is the stage where I tune her out. We've had this *discussion* hundreds of times. Maybe thousands. We met twenty years ago. Have been married eighteen of them. Yet she thinks I should be the all-caring, all-compassionate man I was when we first met. When we were courting. When all I wanted was to get laid and *was* getting laid regularly.

I detach and play out the whole argument in my mind, her voice droning in the background like white noise. The soundtrack to our lives.

I used to bring up how amorous and down-right horny she was back then. About how *she* had changed. But she would deflect that with how if I cared more about her at this point in her life and was more concerned for her well-being, then she would be more amorous *now*.

So, of course, it was all my fault.

It's that kind of circular thinking that drinking helps me cope with. You can't be reasonable with an unreasonable person. It drives me crazy. Seems no matter what it was, it gets twisted until it is all my fault. Everything. Certainly nothing was ever *her* fault. It was always something I did. Or didn't do. Something I said. Or didn't say. No matter what happened—it was always because I couldn't accept things the way they are and wanted to be lord and master of all. So she says. So say most therapists and all twelve-step groups I've been involved with.

It was infuriating, having that type of illogic thrown at me. What about ambition and drive? Was that self-centered and selfish? What about anger? Was any form of righteous anger inherently wrong? The Bible even says 'Be ye angry and not sin,' but Twelve Steppers say 'Better leave that anger to someone else better suited to handle it.'

I get so confused, running into so many contradictions and doublethink. It's like George Orwell's *1984*. It seems most people believe any number of conflicting ideas at any time without any problems. Am I the only one who cannot hold two contradictory thoughts in my mind simultaneously and accept them both? Let go and let God! But also, to thine own self be true! That's crazy! What am I supposed to believe?

I need a drink.

The ship's intercom announces everyone must grab a lifejacket from their stateroom closets and attend the mandatory emergency lifeboat drill. Maggie is less than thrilled by this.

"I can't believe we have to put these stupid things on and go out in this hundred-degree weather and stand around sweating while they tell us the procedure for abandoning ship. And not having a change of clothes! It's worse than the stupid airlines showing how to use the oxygen masks. Morons."

I locate the life jackets, her whining just so much white noise buzzing in the background. My thoughts were on drinking, her meds in my system just barely taking the edge off.

We find our assembly area without too much trouble, one of the crew assigned to our section checking our name off a list. I try to make small talk, impressed with the lifeboats. Nothing like the little rowboats in the *Titanic* movie. These were totally enclosed, like miniature cruise ships themselves.

Maggie sweats and bitches and whines the whole fifteen minutes it takes.

Back in the cool cabin, I let her rant for a while and blame me in every way she can for being stuck on a luxury cruise ship in a luxury cabin without her medications. After she finishes, I produce the last two of her painkillers from my pocket and give them to her. She doesn't question this. Seems grateful, in a junkie needing a fix sort of way.

"Well, I guess this will do until the luggage gets here. I'm going to lie down awhile and hope my head stops hurting."

I nod in a way she doesn't like, which she seizes upon.

"What? Are you blaming me because I have a migraine? It's not my fault."

I let her go on for a little about how the doctor prescribes those addictive painkillers and she is just following doctor's orders and she can't help it if she has to take medications and I should be more understanding and it's nowhere near as bad as my drinking…

"Then I'm going to go look around while you rest."

She gives me the stink-eye.

"Fine. Try not to get too drunk to find your way back to the room. I need someone to show me how to get to the dining room and—"

I close the door on her in mid-sentence, salivating for the relief I know is nearby.

* * *

I find an open bar at the sail-away party. After four double shots of Beam I am feeling better. On the Beam. The booty-shorted girl is here taking pictures of dancing cruisers. The steel drums of a Caribbean band playing next to the bar sound pretty good. I see many smiling, bronzed yuppies with umbrella drinks and toned partners on the dance floor. They look the very picture of health and fitness.

I feel soft and pudgy. At least my skin is not quite as pale as some others on board. I order another double, telling the barkeep to just show Jim the chaser, which I think is extremely witty, but doesn't even rate a smile from him.

I look around, sipping, watching pale, middle-aged, sour looking folks sitting around tables sucking down margaritas. And Jim Beams. The pale women fall into two categories: skinny to the point of anorexia, resembling walking skeletons wearing bikinis, or trying to stuff too much body into too little bathing suit. The pale men show off pot bellies in Speedos or flabby bodies in too-long swim trunks supported by chicken legs.

Welcome to my world.

Maybe it's the mild buzz I have on, but some of these folks are beginning to look a little strange. The yuppies' are all wearing high-dollar sunglasses, the red, sinking sun reflecting in them. Their smiles seem too big, too animated. Too real. The pale people are also a little…off. Just occupying space, more animal than human. The puffy ones complacent and sedated cows. The skinny ones frail and weak sheep.

The horn sounds long and loud, the ship setting sail.

I watch bikini-clad, bronze beauties dance around, wondering how they maintain that perfection. All trim and tanned and toned. Firm, silicone-enhanced breasts jiggling to the steel drums. Watch their barely-covered, tight, sculpted butts. Playboy bunnies hopping. Feeling very envious of the god-men bopping these beauties. Sculpted bodies fitting together as works of art. Each an Adonis and Aphrodite—Greek gods and goddesses at play.

I watch the pudgy, pale people. Wonder if they will head back to their rooms shortly for some grunting and squealing. Watch the skinny, skeletal people, wondering if you'd hit bone screwing chicks like that. If they'd holler in pain or ecstasy.

Think of Maggie back in the room, dressed in baggy, flannel pajamas, sleeping blissfully in a sedated haze.

I order another double Beam. I stopped counting a while back.

* * *

Through the years, I've been involved with many programs and groups that claim to help with coping and understanding. Accepting life on life's terms. Mad, contradictory, circular thinking cults of conformity.

Self-help groups. An oxymoron.

One thing I've learned in my rounds of alcohol education is that anyone who does some serious drinking inflicts brain damage to a degree. Said brain damage can manifest itself as either incoherent or incredibly lucid thoughts—hallucinations, both visual and auditory. Blackouts—not passing out—but fully functioning and interacting with amnesia of the entire event. I've experienced pretty much all these symptoms at one time or the other, and right now I feel pretty damn lucid.

And happily high as a kite.

Braving the listing of the ship, I navigate through the dancers, guarding my plastic cup. While making for the rail, one of those Gold's Gym graduates, listening to an iPod, bumps me hard as he jogs by. We've been under sail less than an hour and this jerk is already jogging! Asshole fitness freak. I drop my drink—which luckily was almost empty so there wasn't any alcohol abuse, *ha ha*—and he doesn't say a word. Doesn't even acknowledge me. No 'Excuse me' or 'Kiss my foot' or anything. Worst thing is, I apologize! I actually say "'Scuse me." He just keeps jogging as if I was irrelevant. A minor annoyance. It's his world and he just lets me live in it. I stand there, looking at him, and say a very loud, "EXCUSE ME!" And he looks back at me over his shoulder. His eyes shaded with two-hundred-dollar Ray-Bans. Smiling at me with a toothy, too-wide grin. Sunlight actually flashes off his pearly whites. I think of knives, switchblades. A switchblade smile. I blame it on the bright sun, the meds, the Jim Beam, even drain bamage. *Ha!* I stumble step back to get another double.

After downing the drink, I go exploring, weaving around the deck. Ship seems to be listing a lot. *Ha! Again.* I stumble across the duty-free shop. It's open for business, so I guess we must be in international waters. I purchase two bottles of Jim

Beam, a half-gallon and a fifth. The sales clerk tells me that purchased alcohol is not allowed in the passengers' room and that they will keep them in the shop until the end of the cruise. He says it is to ensure the passengers buy the overpriced alcohol served at the ship's bars. At least he's honest.

"And that's why I want this. I'll go broke getting drunk at the bars every day!"

The clerk laughs at this. We chat for a while, until it is just the two of us in the store. In the end, I give him a twenty and he agrees to drop the bottles off himself at the cabin when the store closes at midnight.

I head back to the sail-away party, inhale a couple more Beams. I figure I've already run up one hell of a tab and use that to rationalize my purchases.

The sun is sinking lower, shimmering red on the water. A lot of the partiers are drifting away. The bronze people look copper-skinned in this light, sunglasses removed with slit, red eyes casting about, scouting. Snake-like and predatory. Copperheads. Playfully nipping each other, tongues flicking, touching on partner's lips. Strangely sensual. The pale people look pitiful and helpless and oblivious. I look away, shake my head to clear it, look back. Everyone looks fine. Lots of scantily clad ladies with beautiful bodies. I head back to the cabin.

When I finally locate the room, Maggie is awake, and not happy.

"You've been gone for hours!"

"I…uh…got lost."

She looks at me. I think she is more disappointed than pissed off.

"Found the bar OK though, didn't you?"

"Uh, well, yeah." I notice that she is dressed in a simple, short, black dress. And she looks nice. "I guess the luggage came?"

"Yes. They dropped the bags off outside the door, and I had to drag the suitcases in all by myself from the hallway."

I look at her and think about saying 'good job' or some other smartass comment. But she looks so petite and pretty in that dress. Not skinny, sorta sexy. Not helpless, but needing help.

"Sorry. Lost track of time. You ready for dinner?"

I go into the small bathroom, fumble to turn on the shower.

"Or you wanna join me in the shower first?"

I stumble back against the wall trying to take a shoe off, almost falling down.

She looks in on me, shakes her head sadly, her eyes looking moist. Is she going to cry? I hope not. I hate it when she cries.

"I'll lay your clothes out on the bed."

She leaves me to shower in peace.

* * *

We have the late seating for dinner. I notice that there are very few bronze people present. Mostly it's just pale, pudgy people and skinny, skeletal skanks.

Our dinner companions prove interesting. Bob and Nancy are from New York City. Bob's a doctor, Nancy's in real estate. Rich folks, old-school yuppies. Empty nesters, they enjoy traveling as much as they can.

Our other table companions are young. Marshall and Sue are just out of college. Marshall does something in software—after a fifteen-minute description of what he does, I think he means he is a salesman, not a programmer—and Sue is a stay-at-home mom-to-be. They are the new breed of yuppies. Sue proudly points out, within seconds of our meeting, the tiny baby bump she is showing off with her belly shirt. Heaven forbid anyone think it was fat. And she goes on about how she is especially proud of the way the pregnancy was affecting her breasts. So full and plump. So much so she had to wear the skimpiest and sheerest top available. Heaven forbid anyone think she had had a boob job, it was all natural. And I think Heaven forbid she wear decent clothes for a pregnant girl. I bet she's still wearing string bikinis too. Her husband Marshall looks on approvingly as she rambles on about her private parts. After she has exhausted her it's-all-about-me introduction, Bob and Nancy chime in.

Bob and Nancy both lost businesses and family in the World Trade Center attack of 9/11. Bob thinks the resulting War on Terror was misguided, but supports the troops. Nancy thinks all war is wrong and that the US brought 9/11 on itself, but she also supports the troops.

Maggie looks nervously at me. I sip my drink, and then speak.

"You know, I believe we are under attack from enemies who just hate our guts for being alive. That they are basically jealous of what we have and can't understand why their god doesn't give it to them. That the attacks were unprovoked, that we are right in fighting back and denying these animals sanctuary in domestic or foreign lands."

I take another sip, watching their expressions over the rim of the glass. Bob and Nancy looking sour. Marshall and Sue looking vacant. Placing the glass back on the table, I say nonchalantly, "Oh yeah. And I support our troops."

Maggie kicks me gently beneath the table.

A confused look from Bob and Nancy, their noses pinching up. Marshall and Sue sort of smile. Least I think they do. It's hard to tell, since they are so vapid. Sue starts in about a college roommate of hers who was a Wiccan and how she thought all religions were valid and something could be learned from each.

I raise my glass and say, "Absolutely. Look at the valuable lessons from Jim Jones' Kool-Aid communion. And those Heaven's Gate folks who committed suicide so they could hitch a ride with Jesus in a spaceship behind Comet Hale-Bopp. And of course, let's give ear to the devout individual who straps dynamite on and goes into a crowded market with nothing but innocent civilians and BLOWS THEMSELVES UP! Such valuable lessons to be learned here. Let us raise glasses in a toast to all these fine, spiritual folks."

Man, I am on a roll!

An uncomfortable silence. Old Bob and Nancy look as if they just smelled a fart. Young Marshall and Sue look as if they really don't have a clue. Which I'm sure they don't.

I smile at Maggie. She gives me a pleading expression and gives my hand a gentle squeeze. I want to press my point, feel as if I am right in doing so. But I stop. Our dinner companions are so empty spiritually they have no concept of a belief worth dying for, worth killing for. No inkling how a person can actually hold such beliefs. They are totally accepting of their soulless existence. They would fit in quite nicely with many Twelve Steppers I know, since they really stand for nothing so they'll fall for anything.

We finish in awkward chit chat, Marshall and Sue mostly, extolling the virtues of birthing underwater.

It's tough to keep my mouth shut, but I manage.

* * *

After dinner, Maggie and I take a stroll on the deck. The sun has set, a silver slip of a moon rising. There are very few people out. I see none of the big-smile bronze people.

Maggie looks very nice in the moonlight, her skin a powdery glow. Petite. Her legs shapely. I slip my arm around her waist. She doesn't flinch or tighten. She actually leans into me, puts her head on my shoulder.

"Thanks for stopping in there."

I nod.

"Nothing to thank me for. Sorry I upset everybody."

"You didn't upset everybody. You just are so opinionated about politics and religion. And you know what they say about discussing them."

"Hey…they started it. I thought I did a pretty good job of finishing it."

She lets it drop and we stroll along. I notice crew members at certain doors. They appear nonchalant, smile and speak as we stroll by. But to me they look like they are standing guard. *Weird.*

Maggie looks up at me.

"Remember how we used to take long walks?"

I almost say that was before she started getting all these aches and pains and how she wasn't physically able to do that anymore—but for once I just say, "Yeah."

She puts her arm around my waist. Hugs me.

"John, I'm really worried about your drinking. Seems the liquor is getting more important than me."

I almost say that it is *my* medication, that I don't have doctors prescribing me pills to deal with things. At least, not really. Prozac doesn't count as it doesn't get me numb by itself. But I know she would say that was because I didn't have any real physical problems to deal with, that mine were all mental. We have had that conversation many times before too. So I just let it play out in my head to the no-win conclusion.

Truth is the drinking has not been working as well lately. Case in point was my afternoon at the sail-away party. What was I going to do when the drinking stopped working completely? How would I cope with…everything?

My mind is racing, but I say simply, "Sometimes I worry too."

She puts her other arm around my pot belly.

"I'm sorry I have problems. Some mornings it is all I can do to drag myself out of bed, the aching in my muscles and joints is so bad. And I really don't take as much medication as you think. The doctor actually wants me to take more than I am, and I refuse because I don't want to become dependent on it."

We pause. I kiss her forehead.

"I know. I have some…some things I have to work through myself. I feel confused all the time. I don't feel comfortable in my own skin. And the alcohol… It either intensifies or tranquilizes the feelings. I know I need to work out those feelings but it's tough."

She kisses me on the mouth, whispers in my ear.

"I'm here to help you if you want me to."

We walk and talk, and it's very nice.

Heading back to the cabin, I notice yet more crew members standing about, still appearing to guard certain rooms, or be on patrol. I don't get it. But other things push the thought away as Maggie squeezes my butt.

Back in the cabin, we are actually getting amorous, giggling like high-school kids when there is a knock on the cabin door. Maggie pulls the sheet up to her neck. I slip on my boxers and open the door.

It's the sales clerk from the duty-free shop with my Jim Beam. He grins at seeing Maggie, tips his hat and turns away. I close the door and turn to Maggie with a bottle in each hand.

Tears are silently running down her cheeks.

I absently set the bottles on the dresser across from the bed. I return, we consummate our evening, but the mood has changed. Maggie falls asleep without medication. I reach for the fifth on the dresser and slowly unscrew the top.

I look at Maggie sleeping fitfully beside me. Though skinny, she is still as attractive as the day we met. I look over in the dresser mirror and see my bloated and tired-looking body.

I start to drink.

* * *

On the second day of our cruise I awake to the sound of Maggie in the shower. She's left the door open, steam is wafting out. My head is thick. Truth be told, I'm still drunk. I feel for the bottle to see how much is left. I am shocked to see it empty. I quickly shove it in the space between the headboard and wall. The half-gallon is on the dresser, thankfully the seal still unbroken.

Maggie enters the room, steam trailing her, one towel wrapped around her, toweling off her hair with another. She sits on the bed beside me, looks at the half-gallon, looks at me.

"Just promise me you won't drink all that at once."

I look away, tongue stuck to roof of my mouth—unbelievable cotton-mouth. I start to get up, masking both my breath and the peeling away of my tongue.

"Sure. If that means you act like you did last night more often, I guess I can behave myself."

She places her small hand on my arm as I rise.

"John. Really…please…I need you."

"Ok. Sure. Just lemme get my shower, and we'll hit the breakfast buffet on deck."

As I am showering, Maggie joins me. It is almost comical, her tiny frame and my puffy body jammed into that little shower stall. Turns out it was wasted effort, the after-effects of the alcohol taking its toll. After comforting and assuring Maggie it wasn't her fault, we head to breakfast.

After eating, we hang out by the pool. Maggie orders a piña colada. I order spring water. She smiles at me and pats my hand. We sip and watch the beautiful people frolicking. Bronze sun worshippers abound.

I sip my water, looking at a thong-clad beauty.

I see Maggie looking at the little boy who was in line with us yesterday. He's now splashing in the hot tub with a little girl. Both are laughing, flashing giant smiles. I go back to looking at Miss Thong.

Maggie sees who I am looking at and playfully smacks me on the arm. A bodybuilder-type leans into the thonged beauty, and his longish tongue darts out, licking her lips. Maggie lowers her sunglasses at seeing this, turns toward me.

"Did you see that?"

"Yep. And I hope you're not going to make any comments about men who can lick *their* eyebrows."

Maggie smiles, sort of winking at me, replaces her sunglasses, rolls over and lies on her stomach. She does not see the man smile broadly, jaw almost dislocating, looking like the head of a snake. I blink, and he is once again just a blonde surfer dude with his blonde surfer chick. I shake my head. My drinking is taking its toll, short-circuiting brain cells, conjuring up my own versions of pink elephants. More of that drain bamage.

Our young dining mates, Marshall and Sue, walk by. Sure enough, Sue is wearing a tiny string bikini, even has a hand on her belly. They wave, thankfully not speaking as both slip into the hot tub.

"Ain't a hot tub bad for a pregnant woman?"

Maggie glances over, and then looks back. "Yeah. Could boil the baby if she's not careful."

I shake my head. "Idiots. Gotta go pee."

Maggie smiles sweetly. "Hurry back. After this morning, a man who can lick his eyebrows is looking pretty good."

I reach over and smack her butt, then lean in to kiss her on the cheek.

As soon as I am out of her sight I head for the pool bar and order a double vodka. Downing it quickly, I turn, pause, then turn back and order another. I watch my time.

Back with Maggie, she rises up and kisses me. On the lips. Very nice, but I know she is just checking my breath. She lays back down, smiling. Thank God for vodka.

We both doze in the beautiful sunshine. In about an hour,

we head back to the cabin. Our cabin steward, Manuel, is just leaving. We smile and nod. Inside the cabin, I check that Manuel has not moved the half-gallon from the dresser. I see Maggie looking nervously at me.

"Just checking. Wanna make sure nothing goes missing."

We fall into the freshly made bed, and this time there are no problems in the romance department.

Maggie decides to take a real nap. I decide to go exploring. Sober exploring I assure her. I hold her until her breathing becomes slow and even. I then ease out of bed, dress and head for the bar.

* * *

"Vodka double."

After my third, I take a walk. After fifteen minutes of wondering the deck, I get the distinct feeling someone is following me. Of course it could just be paranoia. That's another symptom of alcoholism. Every time I turn, I feel that something just slipped out of my vision. I almost convince myself it's my pink elephants on parade again. There are enough people milling about to make it seem I am being silly.

But I feel like I'm being stalked. *What you feel ain't real*. Another Twelve-Step pearl of illogical wisdom. I turn quickly into the lido area—lido? libido?—doors swishing closed behind me. I walk briskly by fellow passengers, forcing myself to not look over my shoulder. Silly. I'm being silly. It's broad daylight. I'm just feeling the effects of the vodkas, coupled with the fifth of bourbon last night, and some fried brain cells.

And now I've got a small, nagging fear that the drinking is starting to not work anymore.

Up ahead I see a placard near a conference room announcing the Friends of Bill are now meeting in there. Friends of Bill. I know them. They're the original Twelve-Step group. I hesitate, and then stop. Looking at the sign. Feeling paranoid. Feeling stalked. A little tipsy. Maybe, as they say, a Higher Power has led me here.

I chalk that up to more Twelve-Step and therapeutic brainwashing.

I ease open the door and step inside.

I know these halls. Have been in many similar. Smell of coffee brewing. It's dim. As my eyes adjust, I see many people sitting in folding metal chairs. A man is at a podium, a stylized emblem hanging on the wall behind him. A tall, bronzed man. He smiles broadly, too broadly, all teeth and mouth as he hisses softly at me.

"I'm ssssorry. This is a clossssed meeting."

More smiling heads with too-big smiles turn towards me. I take a step backwards, feeling behind me for the door knob, apologizing.

"Sorry. My fault. Took wrong turn, wrong room."

Someone grabs my arm, squinting at me. His sparkling gray eyes lock onto mine. Seem to look right through me. I don't like the way his eyes look. There is craziness in those frighteningly clear eyes. And he is holding my arm too tight.

"Wait. It's ok! You are welcome here, friend."

For a moment I am tempted. His eyes hold me almost hypnotized.

This *could* work. Likeminded people battling a common problem and all that. It has helped in the past, and may be the answer if I really gave myself over totally to the program and accepted my condition.

The door behind me opens. A shaft of light pierces the room, severing the spell. Off to the side, standing near a snack table, the light shines on one of the smiling bronze people with a napkin tucked into its collar turning toward me. He appears to be eating a turkey leg. But his mouth is stretched impossibly wide. Jaws are dislocated. Like a snake eating a rat. And the turkey leg looks like it has small fingers.

I'm losing it. Seeing things.

The man's grip relaxes a little and I jerk away. I turn and fumble past a crew member pushing a dining cart in through the open door. Hear laughter behind me. Hear snatches of conversation as the door is closing.

"Easy does it."

"He'll be back when he's ready."

"Progress, not perfection."

Along the railing, I see the little boy standing next to a deck chair, smiling huge at me. He is my stalker. I blink and he has his little girlfriend from the hot tub with him. They are smiling at me with impossibly large smiles. I blink again and they are both gone, but I hear them giggling. Children's laughter fading away.

The logical part of my abused brain thinks visual and auditory hallucinations. Maybe the onset of delirium tremens. The emotional part of my brain thinks since I am so far gone, it doesn't really matter anymore. Not exactly two contradictory terms—they complement each other.

With effort, I literally jog to the nearest bar.

By the third drink I have convinced myself it was all a trick of the light. I head back to the cabin, feeling as if every buffed and bronzed person on board is staring at me, grinning at me.

Nope. No problem here. I'm OK. *They* all have problems.

Back in the room, Maggie suspects I have been drinking. She doesn't outright accuse me, but she keeps watching my every move. Paranoid? Me? I tell her I did a little jogging—not really a lie—that's why I'm flushed. I order room service, hardly slurring any words.

The crew member who delivers our food is the same guy who was delivering to the Friends of Bill meeting. He grins at me. A normal grin.

I pick at my food, thinking of lady fingers and baby arms.

I am really losing it.

That evening, we take in an early show—a loud musical about sissy, prissy pirates. I beg off dinner, saying I have a headache, which is true. We just grab something at the buffet and head back to the room. I feel as if everyone on board has their eyes burning holes in me.

At least all the copperhead snake people with red eyes...

That night we turn in before the sun sets, pulling the curtain to make the room dark. I lay awake a long time, just staring into the darkness. Worrying about my mental health. Knowing there's a half-gallon of relief on the dresser. Maggie tosses and turns, restless in a medicated sleep. But I do not touch the half-gallon.

* * *

I lose the battle of the bottle around ten the next morning.

Maggie sleeps in, and I'm sucking down vodka doubles at the pool bar, enjoying the scantily-clad, female scenery in the beautiful, bright Caribbean sunlight.

It is amazing the effect alcohol is having in convincing me that all is well. It seems to be working again. The thought passes through my mind that this is just temporary, that I am just having a *good* high—but I don't dwell on it. Take a drink and don't worry about it. Right *now*, which is all we have, as the Friends of Bill say. Right *this* moment, everything is fine.

An announcement comes over the ship's intercom system.

"Ladies and gentlemen. This is your captain speaking. I want to once again welcome you all aboard and wish you a pleasant vacation."

I raise my glass in toast to the speaker.

"I want to thank each and every one of you for cruising with us. I especially want to thank our special guests."

Special guests?

"Twice a year we sail with these folks, and they are truly unique people. This is really *their* cruise."

So why did I have to pay then?

I smile at my returning wit, taking another drink. Maybe they're a band or something. Murmuring from other guests. Seems I'm not the only one wondering.

"I now request that all confirmed crew members reveal the sigil at this stage to avoid any *accidents*."

Many of the crew remove their hats and wipe away thick makeup from their foreheads, revealing a tattoo of a third eye. A cat-eye sun, flames all around, staring at us. Not all crew have these tattoos, these sigils. The crew without the tattoos appear to be as clueless as us cattle.

More murmuring, a subdued form of panic beginning to take hold. A quiet panic. Something seriously weird is going on here.

"Now ladies and gentlemen, without further ado. Let the Feastiva Feeding begin!"

I see an Adonis bite the ear from one of the pale ladies.

An Aphrodite sucks an eyeball from a pudgy, pale man.

The kid who laughed at my moo joke smiles at me from the pool. His mouth is definitely bigger, stretching to his ears. Snake-like. Young copperhead. Other bronze beauties—male, female and their children—are also smiling switchblade smiles, mouths stretching to accommodate rows of razorblade teeth.

The kid moves toward me with incredible speed. He appears to be in a strobe light. One blink of my eyes and he is out of the pool. Two blinks, he has covered half the distance, still grinning. Three blinks, he is at my leg. Smiling up at me. White, knife-teeth sparkling as he licks his lips, grinning broadly.

I do the only thing I can. No heroics, just pure reflex. I raise my leg quickly and catch the kid cleanly in his chin. His teeth chatter together. The kid sprawls backwards, clutching at his bloody mouth, howling and crying.

I actually hurt him. It takes a moment for that to register.

His bikini-clad mother appears, squats beside him, comforting him. Her bronze butt is firm without a trace of cellulite, accented by an orange thong. She strokes the boy's forehead, quiets his sniffling. She looks up at me with fire in her eyes.

Her switchblade smile is huge, bisecting her dark face. Red-speckled bleached-blonde hair falls along the brown leather of her cheeks. Pieces of flesh and bone visible in her sharp teeth. Blood spills from her mouth, runs down her chin, down her neck, washes over her ample silicone breasts.

She screams, "You asshole! You hurt my Billy!"

She propels herself forward, impossibly fast, a strobe effect again. Her hands draw back. I see those long, sharp, manicured fingernails. Dripping blood. My arms go up instinctive.

"You hurt my baby!"

Her nails rake my left forearm and plow furrows across my right cheek as she slaps at me. Red wells in the deep gouges, running, my blood splattering to the slickening deck. I look dazed and confused at her. She stands fuming, ready to attack again. A leather-skinned male walks up beside her, designer tennis outfit all bloody, chewing on a dismembered arm like a chicken wing. Little Billy walks up between them, licking his bloody chin with his tongue. A family of vipers. They all look at me, the male shaking his head as he tears at the arm meat.

From a distance I hear: "He's drunk."

I stumble away, wondering if this is it—the final break with reality my alcohol abuse has been leading to. I slip in a bloody puddle beside the hot tub and land hard on my ass, teeth clicking together from the impact. I look into the bubbling, red broth and see young, pregnant Sue from dinner floating face down. She bobs in the hot jets. Her body slowly turns, and I see she has been gutted, her tiny belly bump a bloody hole. A teenaged blonde boy pops up from the foamy, syrupy waves, jaw dislocated like a roadkill toad, chewing happily on innards. I tell myself it is heart or kidney. It's too big to be what my brain insists it is.

Someone grabs my ankle. I panic, stomp down hard, crushing her husband Marshall's hand. Both his legs are bent at impossible angles as he pulls himself along the red, wet deck. He doesn't scream, just makes unintelligible sounds as he looks up at me. I see his nose and lips are gone, teeth missing, his mouth full of blood. I back away from him just as a topless woman pounces on his back, her blood-soaked breasts firm and thumb-sized nipples erect. Grasping his forehead with one hand, she pulls his head back. Using the razor-sharp manicured fingernails of her other hand, she effortlessly slices his throat, blood spewing. She moans in orgasmic delight, looking at me, licking her lips, grinning like a razor-mouthed jack-o'-lantern.

The lady photographer, smiling her own switchblade smile, snaps a picture of her at her climax.

It'll be for sale tonight in the photo gallery on Deck Five.

Time slows down. Everything is distinct and clear. Surreal. I look slowly around. I hear everything from the snapping of bones to the slurping of body fluids. Screams and shouts. Scenes of carnage abound. Dismemberment. Disembowelment. Decapitation. Sharks on a feeding frenzy in human chum. I see third-eye-tattooed, armed crew members strategically placed, no way in or out of the pool area without going by one of them. I see others smoking, laughing as they roll out fire hoses, gather buckets and mops, preparing to wash down the decks.

I see a bleeding, flabby, pale person crawl beside one of the armed crew members. The guard watches amusedly, makes no move to stop him. The bleeding man makes it past the guard, continues crawling slowly, leaving a red snail-trail behind him.

It's old Bob from dinner. I wonder where his wife Nancy is.

A Snakehead charges for the wounded Bob. The guard puts

up a hand, stopping him. I see the Snakehead turn, hissing angrily at the one that got away, then grabs a fleeing small-chested, pale-skinned lady, chomping a goodly portion of her right breast off. Several crew members rush to wounded Bob with a first aid kit and start administering to him.

A few feet to my right, a crew member turns to an approaching lady and her young girl. They are dressed in matching mommy-daughter outfits for the pool and smiling broadly. I see it is the little girl from the hot tub yesterday, the one that was with Billy. Billy, the little copperhead whose nose I smashed earlier and who is now behind me with his family. The guard stops mommy and daughter from entering the bloody arena.

"Sorry Madame and mademoiselle. The festivities have already begun. There are more fun and games planned throughout the week, please check your ship newspaper."

Daughter looks as if she is going to throw a tantrum.

"MOMMY! I WANNA GO IN!"

Mommy tries to negotiate while daughter squirms and squeals.

"But, but we're only a few minutes late. Couldn't you let us in? This is precious Julie's first cruise, and she skipped breakfast waiting for this."

"WANNA GO IN NOW!" Julie makes a snapping lunge at another badly mangled guest crawling past the guard. Her mother barely holds her back.

"Madame! You must restrain your daughter. We have strict rules of promptness and discipline at all shipboard activities. If by chance any Normal makes it out of the gaming area, we must have absolute control to treat them and ready them for other events."

Precious Julie wriggles from mommy and darts past the crew member. The crew member is pissed. He and mommy head after the girl who is hollering, "Billy!" and running…

Straight for me. *Shit!*

Billy and his family pause, turning back toward me. Someone stumbles roughly into me. I grab them by the shoulders. It's Nancy, Bob's wife, our other dinner companion. We stand face to face. Missing chunks of hair, scalped in places. In a strobed, time-lapse photographic way, with each blink I see her face change. *Blink.* Her nose is gone. *Blink.* She has no ears, just bloody holes on each side of her head. *Blink.* She is gurgling, blood running from her open mouth and mangled lips. *Blink.* Her tongue is missing, ripped out by its roots.

Blink. Time resumes. Shock takes its toll. My knees give way and I drop to the deck like a rag doll, leaving Nancy standing alone, swaying. I hear flesh rending as Billy and precious Julie tear into Nancy like rabid dogs. Rabid puppies. They snarl and bite and gnash and even snap at each other. A feeding frenzy.

Bits of flesh and bone and blood shower down on me as I taste salty fluid and rubbery meat, my mouth open.

Then precious Julie's mommy starts arguing with Billy's mom and dad, and it begins to sound like a parental playground dispute.

"Lady, can't you keep your little brat from butting in!?"

"I'm sorry, she's just so excited. Hey! Who are you calling a brat?"

As a crew member intervenes, I crawl away. Slowly, then faster. Slipping, cracking my chin several times on wet wood planking and furniture. Chunks of flesh and entrails all about. Fading out, then snapping to, senses heightened to the point of an acid trip. Slaughterhouse smell. Tasting blood and flesh in my mouth. Touching sticky, thick, red wetness. Hearing screams and laughter. Thinking of Maggie. Getting to her and then escaping on a lifeboat. Crazy thoughts. Whole thing's crazy. Struggling. Keep crawling. Get to Maggie. Escape.

Once outside the perimeter, I struggle to my feet and start running, holding my bleeding arm. Running drunkenly. Crew members asking, "Sir, do you need medical assistance?" I start screaming as I run.

Winding through the decks and stairwells. Stumbling through a nightmare. Numb from shock and alcohol. Finally, dazed and out of breath, unable to shout or scream anymore, throat hoarse, I fall against our cabin door. Fumbling for the electronic key, holding my wounded and still seeping left arm, I bump my shoulder repeatedly against the door, whispering loudly in a panic.

"Maggie! It's me! Open the door! Please! It's crazy! *They're* crazy! Insane. Blood and stuff everywhere!"

I hear shuffling behind the door, can sense the disapproving look on her face. Hear the long-suffering tone in her voice. And it really doesn't matter anymore.

"John! What have you done now?"

She opens the door at the same time I get the card reader to give me a green light. I fall inside, pushing the door closed hard behind me with my back. I pause. Everything freezes again.

Everything is so bright and well-defined. I am having a moment of perfect clarity. An epiphany. What Friends of Bill and Twelve-Steppers might call a religious experience.

Maggie's accusing look and tone disappear. Her carefully made-up, beautiful, blue eyes open wide as she sees my torn and blood-spattered clothes. Her sweet mouth opens, forming a perfect O. Her delicate, ivory hands, with perfectly manicured nails, reach for the deep scratches on my cheek. She strokes my cheek with the back of her fingers, looks at her clear fingernail polish now dripping red. Her short hair is tousled, looking very sexy. She is wearing a short, white slip. Bare feet. So petite and delicate. She looks beautiful. Sexy. A China doll. How could a doughboy slob like me end up with an angel like that? Behind her I see hairspray and make-up scattered on the dresser, next to my half-gallon. She was getting ready for our date. For our dinner date.

I pitch forward, passing out.

* * *

"How long was I out?"

"A few minutes. Ten at most."

Maggie is on her knees, cradling my bloody head against the soft coolness of her silky slip.

A thumping in the hallway. Yelling. Then silence.

I rise slowly, wincing at my pounding head. Maggie stays on her knees, looks up at me. I have never seen her look so tiny and helpless. Never seen her look at me with such intensity, such an honest, pleading look.

"*What* is going on?"

I offer her my good hand. She takes it, rising to stand beside me. I reach over and take the half-gallon from the dresser, twisting the cap off, take a long pull. I wipe my mouth with the back of my hand and am honest with her.

"I don't know."

Our door jumps and thumps as something large hits it, or is thrown against it. Maggie clutches me. I gently push her to arm's length. The blood flow from the wound on my left forearm is thickening, slowing.

"We have to barricade the door. Keep them out."

She looks at me with panic in her eyes. Eyes darting from my eyes to the half-gallon I hold and back again. Panic and worry.

"Keep *who* out!?"

I look deeply into her eyes, trying to retain some semblance of being in control, of *not* being crazy. Trying to assure her I have not had a total break with reality. Not yet.

The door handle shakes.

"I think I left the key in the door."

Loud click of the lock being deactivated by the card key. The door swings open.

Our steward, Manuel, is standing there holding our room key card. A large, Hispanic man, he has the sigil tattooed on his shiny forehead, bald head gleaming. He is also out of uniform, being stripped to the waist, wearing dark suspenders. Splotches of red and yellow and other unidentifiable fluids are drying on his white pants and bare torso. He is carrying a 9mm Glock in a tactical holster on his right hip.

He enters the room fully, leaving the door open behind him. Muffled sounds of music and revelry mixed with screams from up on deck. He hands me the card key.

"You may wish to be more careful. The staff can access rooms with a master key, but a key left in the door may invite unwanted cruise guests at inappropriate times."

He acknowledges my confusion as I automatically and stupidly take the key. I take another long pull from the half-gallon.

Maggie nervously shuffles beside me, trying to understand what is happening.

"Oh. Por favor. Forgive my appearance. Some of our honored guests get a little…excited, and it is a constant struggle to keep them in the designated areas as well as keeping facilities and amenities in a clean state. We are allowed to be more casual as it helps with the swabbing of the decks."

He smiles. A normal-size smile with normal-size, nicotine-stained teeth. I smell cigarettes and coffee on him. He is a Normal that has betrayed his kind. I think the grinning idiot is expecting a tip.

Maggie lays a soft hand on my shoulder.

In the doorway behind Manuel, looking like a deranged, drunken spring breaker, a college-aged boy-monster appears. Wearing swim trunks, his brown leather body bathed in crimson. He is smiling that impossibly huge smile, shaking his head side to side, tongue lolling out, making 'bugga, bugga, bugga' sounds. Manuel turns and addresses him.

"Sir! If you please. The current festivities are limited to the pool area on the forward deck."

As he turns, I move as fast as my soft body will allow, bringing the heavy liquor bottle down with all my might on top of Manuel's head. Unlike in the movies, the bottle does not shatter. But Manuel's head does. He falls like a pole-axed cow, blood streaming down his forehead, following the fault line of his fractured skull. Stunned, I look up at the drunken monster, who is staring wide-eyed back at me. Both of us shocked at my action, both wondering what to do next.

Maggie's scream breaks the tension.

The monster blinks, startled, then turns and scurries away.

I look at Maggie. She has both hands to her cheeks, eyes wide, shocked, chanting the mantra: "Oh my God, Oh my God, Oh my God..."

I take the pistol from Manuel's holster, looking gingerly into the hallway after the young monster. Nothing. Look in the other direction. From the stairwell a young female copperhead appears. Tan and bikini-clad. She's wearing earphones attached to the MP3 player clamped on her hand, eyes closed, bopping to unheard tunes. Blood runs from her mouth down her ample cleavage. I raise the pistol and fire, missing her head by a good foot. She stops, eyes wide, seeing the body of Manuel, seeing me holding a smoking gun in one hand and a rapidly emptying half-gallon of Jim Beam in the other. Her mouth slits from ear to ear. Full of razor-sharp, shark teeth. She leans forward and starts a strobe-speed run toward me.

I forget the headshot stuff and lower the pistol, aiming at the middle of her silicone chest. Center of mass at ten feet, I squeeze the trigger gently twice. I read all that somewhere sometime: *center of mass; squeeze, don't pull the trigger.* She disappears. I feel her cold breath on my cheek for a split second, and then her mouth is on my ear whispering.

"Careful, old man. You might hurt somebody."

She licks my ear.

Then she's gone, and it takes me a few seconds to realize I no longer have the pistol. She took it. I absently bring the half-gallon back up and take another long draw, ignoring the fresh blood on the glass. I am doing some serious chugging when Maggie tries to forcefully yank the bottle away from me. She can't do it. She elbows me viciously in the stomach, knocks me back. I trip, landing on the bed. Still holding onto the bottle, spilling very little.

The room spins. I could be entering a blackout, or already be in one. But if I was in a blackout, how would I know? I actually chuckle at the paradox my poisoned brain is presenting. Maggie is furious. I hear the thumping and bumping, screaming and music from outside. I bring the half-gallon up and drink like a man dying of thirst. Maggie slams the door, leaving Manuel and his shattered skull just outside the door. She is scared, and I am of no use. Her eyes are flashing red as she turns on me, screaming.

"What in the hell is going on?"

Then everything fades to black.

* * *

I awake to the sound of silence. My head is throbbing, my mouth dry as sandpaper. A hurting, familiar feeling. Wondering what in the hell I did last night. Lying immobile as images dance in my mind, trying to separate the real from the imagined, what I did from what I dreamed. It's all a nightmare blur of copperhead snake monsters and blood and panic and fear. I open my eyes and the room is grey. Sharp moonlight filters in through the porthole window. I feel cautiously about the bed. I am alone. My hand closes on the neck of a half-gallon bottle. I heft it. It's empty.

It's also sticky, tacky with red molasses.

Oh God, what did I do?

Laying there, the dread and fear bubbling up in me. Petrified.

Wondering where Maggie was, wondering if I had hurt her in a drunken rage. Praying it was all a dream, that I had simply stayed in the cabin and drunk until I passed out and it was all horrible nightmares.

I'm sweating. Anxiety oozing from every pore. Panic seizes my very core, contracting my stomach into a knot of terror, undulating, a big, black oozing tumor being slowly pushed up my esophagus.

I roll to the edge of the bed, in physical agony, grabbing a little white plastic trashcan placed nearby. My thoughts tumble over themselves. Maggie must have placed it there. Maybe she is all right. Maybe she is not mad at me. I heave, great floods of fluid issue from me, splashing into the basket.

Red.

I strain and bellow and vomit until I am spent. Tears run down my cheeks and clear snot from my nose. The wastebasket is a third full of rich, red broth. Chunks of meat and unidentifiable fleshy objects floating inside. This is it. Something in me has physically broken this time. Surely I cannot survive this.

I hear the toilet flush. Maggie appears in the bathroom door, pausing, looking at me sadly. Eventually she pads over and sits on the bed beside me, cradling my gray, puffy body into her clean, white, terry cloth robe. My head on her shoulder, I hear her sniffle, feel her move as she reaches up to wipe a tear.

"It'll be all right. We can get through this."

I think she is talking to herself as much as to me. We've had this conversation many times before. I mumble that I know I have to accept things. I will get help. That I will learn to like myself so I can love her.

I look at the empty bottle of Jim Bean lying on the bed beside us. Clotty blood on the outside. A little amber fluid beckoning inside. I look at our reflections in the mirror atop the dresser. My beautiful, long-suffering wife hugging me, rocking me like a baby. Tears streaming down her cheeks. Her perfect, razor-smile glistening from ear to ear, shark teeth sparkling. My own switchblade smile, dull and dingy, teeth yellowish with bits of human flesh still clinging.

God, I need a drink.

A.A. Garrison

A.A. Garrison is a thirty-year-old man living in the mountains of North Carolina, USA, where he writes and landscapes comfortably above sea level.

His short fiction has appeared in dozens of magazines, anthologies and web journals, as well as the Pseudopod webcast. He is the author of the campy, post-apocalyptic horror novel, *The End of Jack Cruz* published by Montag Press. And his shocking tale of religious fanaticism was published in *Splatterlands: Reawakening the Splatterpunk Revolution* from Grey Matter Press.

VARIATIONS OF SOULLESSNESS

BY A.A. GARRISON

It was evening when Easter called on the fortune teller. The sign's neon hand threw candy colors into the settling dark. There were no other customers.

The woman exploded any stereotypes—a young blonde with no Mediterranean to her. The foyer offered two chairs and a table, a draped door in the back wall. Easter darkened the front doorway; the two fixed one another. It was full seconds before he spoke.

"Hello," Easter said, his eyes like the night outside.

The woman said, "Hello," motionless.

"I would like a reading."

"Reading," she said, on autopilot, lost in his gravity.

"A palm reading." He threw his head to the sign. "Twenty dollars. Yes?"

"Yes." The fortune teller stood to the draped door, trailing a black dress struck blue in the neon. She peeled back the portiere and extended a hand. "After you."

Easter came fully inside, pulling the door closed. Scents of incense, pine, terror. His steps were silent for all his size.

The back room was dark, expectedly pagan, a constellation of eyes down the walls. A fern of incense smoldered on a black-covered table. No crystal ball in sight. Easter dragged out a chair and sat politely. His eyes tracked her.

The portiere closed, and the fortune teller asked his name.

"Easter."

"Easter?"

"Easter."

"Interesting." She joined him at the table. "And are you right- or left-handed, Easter?"

"I am ambidextrous." He stared at her.

"Okay. Well. What hand do you write with?"

He could see the girl she'd been, the old woman to come. It evoked summer. "My left hand."

"Let's see."

He submitted an enormous hand, hers so small. Frail fingers worked at the palm, touching where blood had been. He saw her lick her lips, her breathing grow.

"Have you had, um, an injury? On your hand. Plastic surgery?" Almost hopeful.

Easter shook his massive head. "No."

"Oh." She gave back his hand.

"A problem?"

"No." Her eyes wouldn't meet his. "Your other hand, please."

He sent over his right hand, the woman accepting it as one might a gun. She pointed into it, tracing the vein-colored lines, and her breath caught. She let go of the hand like it was dirty.

"Leave," she said in a thready whisper. "Please leave."

Easter did not move. "May I have my reading first?"

"Empty. You are empty," she said to the table.

"Soulless, you might say?"

She nodded the slightest bit. His hand remained out, her eyes glued to it.

Easter returned her nod. "Yes. I just wanted to be sure. It's good to be sure." He stood hugely and opened a wallet. "Twenty dollars?"

No answer. The woman kept staring at where his hand had been.

Easter removed bills and laid them down. She made no move for them. The front door thudded closed, shaking the neon into dance.

* * *

Easter interrupted the department-store crowd, incongruous with his size and toting a filled basket. The people evoked rainfall, severed ears, a beetle-man seen in dreams. Approaching the least-congested checkout, he nearly collided with another shopper.

They mutually stopped, Easter looking down, the man looking up. The man's throat moved, his fingers white over his cart.

Easter stepped aside, extending a hand of extraordinary length. "Please."

The other man sped into line. Easter filed behind.

The cashier, a young man, chewed gum loudly. "Howdy," he said in between snaps.

Easter said, "Hello."

The cashier scanned barcodes with gusto. Rope. Bolt cutters. Flashlight. Pliers. "Forgot the ski mask," he quipped, hunched over the apparatus.

"Excuse me?" Easter said, his monotone only intimating question.

The cashier smiled through his gum. "Need a ski mask when you're robbing someone." He winked and rung up a latex apron and matching gloves.

"Not robbing," Easter said. "Invading."

The cashier nodded mightily. "Ah. Gotch'ya." Hammer. Field knife. Hand lantern. "No duct tape?"

"No. They will be free to scream."

The cashier gave pause. He punched a button and the register worked. "Twenty-nine eleven," he said, the wit gone from his voice.

Easter tendered the precise amount, two coins atop the bills. He was as tall as the counter was long.

The cashier accepted the money and printed a receipt, interesting himself in the floor. "Have a good day."

Easter said, "All days are good," and accepted his receipt and his purchases.

The parking lot evoked larkspur and grey, deadfall trees.

* * *

Morning, no sun. The unlit sign read "$$$ CHEAP BOOKS $$$." Easter watched a man unlock the store and go inside. The sign lit.

Above the door hung an obnoxious cowbell. Easter found

the clerk behind the counter like a bartender. "What say?" the man asked rhetorically.

Easter walked the length of the bookstore. Empty. "Hugo Perot," he said to the room at large. Perot was an author.

After a brief, assessing pause, "Humor, right'n front of you." The clerk's voice evoked playful winds, the sound a guitar makes when bumped. Easter entered the aisle in front of him.

So many books. Most shelved so that only the spines were in view, but some were turned out, the images persecuting, invasive. The man Perot's was one of these, *Hooligan's Hymn*. Easter took it in both hands, perhaps weighing it. It made a pulpy thud on the counter.

The clerk again interrupted his read. "That all?" he said through a beard.

Easter's eyes burned holes. "Perot. You have read him?"

"I have."

"This?" Easter nodded down, his eyes stationary.

"Umm-hmm."

"I have read this, too."

The clerk waited for more, searching the strange Goliath before him.

Easter's eyes closed; opened. "A comedy it is, yet violent, graphically so. Cruelly so. You found it funny?"

"I did. Perot's a genius."

"The violence." Easter sounded to taste the word. "It was… made light of. Poked fun at. Exploited for comic value."

"Burlesqued," the clerk supplied.

Easter lightened, activating his mock smile. "Thank you. 'Burlesqued.' Perfect. Mister Perot *burlesqued* these violences, for humor's sake."

"You could say that."

"You laughed?" Easter asked, more accusation than question.

"Yes. Of course. Perot's a—"

"Genius."

"Yeah..."

A ghastly silence. The store was at the edge of town, out of the way.

Easter parted *Hooligan's Hymn* and flipped to a page he seemed to have picked out. *"Roberts broke the beer bottle into a little sierra,"* he read aloud, *"and bent his hostage ass-up. Her panties needed changing, and he told her so. She wriggled around to see, handcuffs clinking. 'Not even gonna buy me a drink, first?'"*

The clerk had laughed a note before seeing that he was not supposed to laugh. His face blanked.

Easter's eyes quit the book, rising once more to afflict the clerk. "Mister Roberts proceeds to rape her with the broken bottle. The woman provides comic relief throughout. She and the reconstructive surgeon fall in love."

Question filled the clerk's face, yet he said nothing.

"I appreciated the writer's wit," Easter said. "He has in fact demonstrated quite an intellect. But I did not find it funny."

The clerk said something like, "Well, uh…"

"Would you laugh upon receiving broken glass in the anus?" Easter asked.

A crystalline pause. Then: "What the hell kinda question is that?"

"Would you?"

"It's just a book, mister." The clerk shifted his feet. "Don't take it seriously."

Easter was both implacable and composed. "Perhaps for you, it's just a book. Perhaps now."

"You gonna buy anything?" the clerk said, trying for outraged.

Easter pointed down. "Yes. This novel. Hugo Perot."

The clerk totaled the sale without looking at his register. Easter paid cash.

Outside evoked tiddlywinks and fresh-mowed grass.

* * *

The convenience store specialized in discount cigarettes, according to its windows. People conspired in the parking lot, looking at Easter and then away. The inside was as soulless as he.

The store offered only six-packs of beer. Down the road, Easter consigned five bottles to a dumpster. The glass made breaking sounds.

* * *

The author lived near a farming town one hundred miles away, in the mountains. Easter drove there that day. By the time he arrived, the beer was very warm.

He waited until night, then drove to the address he'd paid money to learn. It sent him up one of the many mountains, on a road blackly paved. A sign read "SERENITY ACRES," followed by a spatter of upscale dwellings, each named like streets. The house in question terminated a long driveway, sited grandly on the mountainside, just visible by its own light. Its name was *The O'Conner*.

Easter's stolen sedan was straight-stick and heavily muffled. He drove up past the property, then U-turned, killed the engine and lights and drifted tacitly back to a gravel pit just before the author's backwoods home. Easter wore all black and painted his face the same. A white trash bag went in the car's window. His things fit in an army-surplus rucksack.

The dark woods were navigated very carefully, then the house emerged, as to be all he saw. Around the corner, lit windows threw cross-haired squares of day. Stink of humus, summer life; a dull bass drone that could be music. Unseen insects harassed Easter's skin. The mountain, like he, was very quiet. It was 9:45.

He spent an hour learning the tall, Georgian home, correlating it to the memorized floor plan. The cars in the driveway were jimmied, disabled. Easter was ready by 11:00, but the subjects were still awake. He stationed himself beneath the unlit bedroom window and closed his eyes, seeing prophecy in the warm red there.

It was midnight before they took to the master bedroom. Through its window, the author looked only vaguely like his jacket photo, smaller, less substantial, as a monster does by daylight. His wife was pretty. They shared an off-white powder, grinning. Easter did not watch their sexual encounter. The lights were out by 1:00. He waited until 3:11 to intrude on their home.

The power was configured in an unexpected way, but he defeated it and the phone. His sneakers came off on the back stoop, the alarm inactive as he solved the backdoor lock and whispered inside, his Santa's sack of tools in hand. The home smelled of cinnamon and dinner, womanish, arousing vaginal imagery. Carpet alternating with hardwood, the sour warmth of space inhabited. The flashlight stayed in his palm but for brief semaphores, more sonar than visual.

The stairwell was heavy shag, and made not a sound as Easter scaled its edges. He found the couple at the end of a hallway, sleeping in a pale rug of moonlight. He stood studying the besouled—the woman wrapped desperately around the author, a multi-limbed numeral one, nude but for scant sheets. Easter noted a chair at a nearby desk.

He set his tools soundlessly to the floor, first removing the chloroform.

* * *

Vincent Young, pseudonym Hugo Perot, awoke after some respectful slapping.

"Hmmm?" he said from his chest, his face bunching.

"Vincent Young," Easter said, towering over the bed. The hand lantern burned from the corner desk, an orangey chiaroscuro.

"Vince? *Vince!*" The woman. Her voice came funny, from the angle. Her chair creaked.

The author's head came up slow, as though on a long string. He spoke unintelligibly, and the woman shrieked his name in answer, stressing her restraints.

When the woman quieted, Easter said, "Vincent Young. Wake up, please."

Blind eyes rolled his way, the lids equalizing. "The shit...?" The author tried to sit up but was chastened by the ropes, kept in his star-shaped posture. "The shit!"

"*Vince,*" the woman mewled, bent candidly over the cap-sized chair. Her legs made parentheses, like a frog's.

The author at last realized the gigantic man at his bedside. "Hello, Mister Young," Easter said to him. "You have a lovely home."

All at once, the author grew wise. "Who're you?" he asked.

"My name is Easter. Pleased to make your acquaintance."

The author looked himself up and down, at the ropes restricting his arms and legs. He blinked a single time, very fast.

"Relax, Mister Young. Please," Easter said sensibly. "We have business to tend. You must relax."

"Vince…" the woman sobbed, head hung. Her hair touched the floor, tears dripping out.

The author regarded the strange mating of woman and chair—arms roped to the rests, a foot to each rear chair-leg, rear end staring at the ceiling. "Sheila," he whispered, then looked to Easter with new eyes.

"I've read your books," Easter said.

The author said, "Oh, God."

Easter went on. "You've a great imagination. A firm grasp on life's humors, wit. Such tales!" His voice raised without facial consequence. "But I fear I cannot appreciate your work fully, for you disregard the sanctity of life. The sanctity of pain."

"Wha'd'you want?" the author asked, and swallowed deep.

Easter ignored him. "I was born into this world lacking a soul, thus I am incapable of love and happiness or their derivatives. Do not question these facts. Only listen. Receive. Might you receive?"

The author said he could.

Easter lit over the bed. "What God creates a man with no soul? A thing that can know pain and fear but not the love to conclude them? Do you believe in God, Mister Young?"

The author only stared.

"I do," Easter said. "And isn't that peculiar? A soulless thing aware of his maker and his spiritual nullification? God has revealed Himself to me, as he does to each of us, soulless and otherwise."

The author said, "What's your point?" Perfectly neutral, a phone voice. The woman said "*Vince.*"

Easter looked skyward, deep in thought. "The point is, I and my kind know only pain and its inflicting, and this is our purpose, to dispense such amongst God's greater creatures so they might learn by it." He darkened very slightly. "But you, you make light of this, in your fictions—you *burlesque* this process. This presents an imbalance, you must understand. Imbalance must be righted, and I am the vehicle of this."

"I don't…I don't follow," the author said, trying to be interested. He shouldered sweat from his face, not quite getting it.

Easter looked at him in a unique way. "Pain, violence, suffering—these are my passions, Mister Young, what I am to share with this world. My version of love, yes? But you have burlesqued my love, my gift—*invalidated* it, and for entertainment."

"They're just books—"

"Nonsense," Easter said, voice unraised. "We are both enlightened individuals. Let us not play games. You know as well as I. If you think it, it is real. Not physically, no, but in the minds of men, which is ever more relevant."

The author shook his head.

"You have corrupted thousands, *millions*, with this travesty," Easter said. "How would they, then, know to accept my offerings? Know their value and lessons? Do you not see your *transgression?*"

The woman moaned, "He's *cray-zeee...*"

Easter stood, the woman watching him from her child's vantage. He unzipped his bag and produced the *Hooligan's Hymn* purchased just that morning—a preacher with his Bible. Easter parted the book and read aloud the sequence he'd shared with the clerk—the broken-bottle sodomy, the unlikely romance. The author was silent throughout, his face contorted, older.

Easter closed the book after, snapping it like a trap. "Glass in the anus would be painful, yes? Unpleasant?"

After a long moment, the author agreed.

A solemn headshake. "Oh, but you lie. You find it quite funny, I think."

"It's just a boo—"

"Just nothing. Burlesque the world, and you burlesque yourself, Mister Young. Do not resist, you have made this bed."

The author watched Easter select the beer single and bring it down over the desk, yeasty foam pouring out. As Easter's intent became clear, a silence fell.

The woman screamed when Easter did as was written, her wildcat notes stressing the windows, the author looking on. She offered no jokes.

* * *

Seven years later.
The third morning show in as many days.

JULIUS FAIR: It is my pleasure to be sitting with the re-nowned Hugo Perot, celebrated author of such classic novels as *New Country*, *Hooligan's Hymn* and *The Odd Bunch*. I would like to thank you for this opportunity, sir.

HUGO PEROT: Yeah. Yes. You bet.

JF: Mister Perot, your much anticipated new novel, *Variations of Soullessness*, is to be released next Tuesday. The reviews, however, have been mixed, and I am not alone when I say it is a departure. Gone is the snide Falstaffian voice that won you a place amongst literary royalty, in its place a dark, often strange view of reality. Please comment.

HP: It's simple, really: I write what I see, like anyone, and I've been seeing things different since *Hooligan's*. I'm sure it'll disappoint a lot of folks, but what can I say? I deal with things by writing them out of me, and *Soullessness* is a product of that.

JF: Your home invasion, seven years ago this summer, when your wife was attacked. Did this have bearing on your sea change?

HP: It did. Certainly.

JF: Any elaboration there? And please, tell me if I'm over-stepping my bounds.

HP: No, no. The attack, eh, it was food for thought. I'd writ-ten about such things many times—parodied them, profited from them—but the actual experience, after seeing it firsthand, it felt wrong, filling my reader's heads with those perceptions. The ugliness.

JF: And how is your lovely wife?

HP: Sheila's doing well. [Curt]

JF: Wonderful. Now, your last comment, I find that interesting. You don't want to fill your reader's head with "ugliness," yet your new book is decidedly violent, the saga of a soulless man employed by God to bring about balance in the world's affairs. Torture, mutilation. Prosthetic limbs. Scarography. Not the prettiest of pictures. [Points] Comment.

HP: It's true, yeah, not pretty, at first glance—but you gotta read between the lines, see. The guy's victims, they all learn from the violence, grow from it. It's really a positive piece, when you read it right. Very hopeful. And it's real, I think. I've always held that the writer's charge is to expose some facet of reality, and I simply wasn't doing that in the past. Before, I was...*burlesquing* people and their pain, twisting it into entertainment, and that's just not real. Pain is sacred.

JF: Fascinating. I believe you once said the same of humor, regarding its holiness.

HP: And I still do, I still do. Humor is sacred, but only within the confines of respect. I know that now, since Eas—since the attack. It was very humbling.

JF: And, for the record, there is some marvelous humor in your upcoming book, albeit of a different kind.

HP: Yes. I think the reader will find their funny bones engaged, if they don't mind some home truths here and there. [Smiles.]

JF: Indeed. *Variations of Soullessness*, Hugo Perot, from Jupiter Books, November eleventh. Anything you would like to say in closing?

HP: Yes. Burlesque the world, and you burlesque yourself. My book in a nutshell. It's sappy as hell, something I might've parodied once, but try and prove it wrong. Thank you.

JF: Thank you, Mister Perot.

RHESA SEALY

Rhesa Sealy is a Canadian auhor who is a graduate of the University of Waterloo where she studied English Language and Literature. Sealy has been a writer throughout her life, ultimately serving as a publicity assistant with a Canadian publisher.

Sealy has always had a special interest in fiction and her writing career began as a contributor to *Beginning of Line,* a fan-fiction blog dedicated to continuing the story of *Caprica* following the cancellation of the television series of the same name.

CHAPELSTON

BY RHESA SEALY

There is a sickening awareness, churning, twisting and rising up from my stomach as we walk towards Saint Mary's Cemetery. Needing a drink desperately, I want to be anywhere but here. It has been twenty years since I walked the streets of Chapelston. Twenty years of trying to drown my memories in a bottle. Jack was always my responsibility. His sudden death was simply the final act. It is only fitting I be the one to bury him, seeing his short, tragic life to its completion.

I suppose that is why Kara tags along, even though I don't see the need. She's probably afraid I might try to kill myself. I have thought about suicide. Have seen good, brave men crumble under the weight of images they could not shake from their mind's eye, blowing their brains out to escape. I have seen it all, too much in fact. But I am a coward. I ran. There is no word to describe absolute evil. No word to provoke the type of madness and horrors I saw all those years ago. All I know is that I had to go. I needed to save what little of my sanity I had left. Those were dark days. They broke my soul.

"Connor." Kara points to a man walking towards us. He waves.

"He means us," she whispers.

He is dressed in an all-black suit, ready for a funeral. His face seems vaguely familiar. It's old, like mine, and bears the reminders of the past.

"I think I know him," I say.

"What's his name?"

"Can't remember."

He reaches us, a thoughtful expression fixed on his face, eyeing us more carefully than I'm comfortable with, which makes me more protective of Kara. I take her elbow and draw her close.

"Connor Mason?" he asks.

"Yes."

"I'm Father Francis. I knew you back in the days when you were a detective, during those frightening times."

He makes it sound like back then we had been waiting for a bomb to drop or war to be declared. Those times had been unspeakably evil, *beyond* frightening.

Kara jumps forward, hand extended, "Oh wonderful, Father, I'm glad you're here. I'm Kara Michaals. We spoke."

"Yes, good to see you both," he replies.

Father Francis eyes me again as though he has something to say; instead he pulls his collar out of his pocket and slips it on. There is a smile on his face. I can't see what is so wonderful about this moment and am happy when he and Kara begin to speak again. Stepping away for a moment, I look up and down the street.

My hands shake. I'm not feeling very well. I believe I'm hallucinating. I can literally taste the cold bourbon in my mouth.

I can picture the glass in my hand, the cubes of ice suspended in the glow of the auburn liquid. I glance around to see Kara and the priest chatting as I fumble for my cigarettes. I swear, remembering I kicked the habit long before my wife died.

"Can we hurry this along? He's dead. Jack won't care what we say."

Seeing their reactions, I realized I snarled more than was needed. Kara frowns. I feel a gut-punch to my insides. I hate seeing her look at me like I'm a mental case. I brace for a scolding.

"I know this is hard, but hold on, it's almost over," she says.

She kisses my cheek, and all the jitters I had moments before are gone. Unfortunately, the guilt returns.

It's strange how guilt works. It's been five years, and I still feel as though I am betraying my wife. I have enough guilt to wrap around the world, and I live with too many ghosts. I'm toxic. Kara doesn't realize, or maybe she refuses to accept it, but I know what I am.

"Come on," she says, walking ahead urging me forward.

Taking a breath is bullshit; it doesn't help. It only delays the inevitable. I've spent more than my share of time in this cemetery and laid to rest too many innocent souls in this god-forsaken plot of earth. However, this is where Jack's family is buried, and I have brought him home. So I plaster a fake smile on my face and enter Saint Mary's.

Kara explains the format of the service. I don't really care. My eyeballs are throbbing, and all I want to know is that smooth burn of bourbon slipping down my throat.

I want out of Chapelston. This is my stubbornness continuing to inflict its torment upon me. That's when it dawns on me that my life is meaningless.

"Shall we begin?" Father Francis asks.

I nod.

"Then in the name of the Father, the Son and the Holy…"

God and I have an understanding from years back. He keeps out of my way, and I never ask him for anything. I can't accept any suggestions or excuses. I know too much.

As he finishes praying, Father Francis reaches for a Bible. He flips it open to a page and reads. It's a nice passage. Gazing into the hole—the dark, deep pit of nothingness—part of me wants to fling myself into it. Maybe the ground will open, swallow me whole, and perhaps the peace I desperately fight to maintain everyday will finally be everlasting. Jack, I realize, is a lucky son of a bitch. He has solitude.

"Connor?"

It takes a moment, but Kara and the priest are looking at me.

"Sorry."

"Would you like to say something?" Father Francis repeats.

Kara touches my elbow, encouraging. I clasp my hands in front of me, afraid my shaking might be visible if I leave them free.

"Jack Cullen was a good officer. He did his profession proud. And I was honoured to have worked alongside him. In the end, he has found his peace. Amen."

"Amen," they both reply.

I realize that "Amen" is a stupid choice of words, but what is done is done.

"And so we send your soul back to your Father above and the flesh shall return to the land, ashes to ashes and dust to dust, in nomine Patris et Filii et Spiritus Sancti," the priest intones, crossing the air in front of him.

Kara walks over to shake the priest's hand as I look around the cemetery. I hear the ghosts of the past moaning, calling out to me. Where was their justice? I have no answers for them.

"Connor, we can go," Kara says. "And what about the lawyer?"

I check the time. "We meet him in an hour."

"Okay, what do you want to do until then?"

Drink.

"Let's get a sandwich or something."

As we head out I look back to see a grave digger shoveling dirt back into the hole. Jack is now at rest. I grow cold. I'm now the only one left.

"I was once a brilliant detective. I was good until seven women were murdered, and I lost it. Lost it all, even my mind."

"Connor."

"What I saw back then, what happened to Beatrice...I ran. I ran so fast I abandoned justice and truth. I should have done the honourable thing instead of running away like a coward."

"The honourable thing?" Kara asks, confusion in her eyes.

"In Roman times, when a soldier's actions were dishonourable, he would have fallen on his sword. That was the honourable thing to do."

"You mean suicide."

"I mean a justifiable act for my unjustifiable action."

"Suicide."

"Retribution, Kara."

"I'm glad you didn't," she says as we reach the car.

I open the door for her and she climbs in. As I reach for the handle on the driver's side, a cold sensation draws my attention to a nearby grave. What I see makes me shudder. I rub my eyes to wipe away the hallucination. It's Beatrice, eyeless and shrivelled, a mummified index finger pointing accusingly at me.

"Connor? What's wrong?"

"Nothing, I just remembered why I left here in the first place," I say. "Come on, let's see if he'll see us now so we can get the hell out of here today."

I get in, turn the ignition and pull away.

* * *

"As you can see, it's a fairly large estate," the lawyer says, pointing to Rosaland Manor. He fumbles the file around in his hands before setting the briefcase on the hood of his car.

"His mother knew she was dying, and her only living relative had been Jack. She never faulted you for what happened to him. But she knew he would not pull out of it. So, she thought you were worthy of this place. You may do what you want with it," he said, pulling keys from the pocket of the case.

I feel it is an out-of-body moment. I watch myself accept the keys and shake his hand.

"Rosaland is all yours, as are all the acres of land it sits on. Currently, it's uninhabited. Here's my card. Have a look around. I'm happy to do whatever legal work you need and assist you in whatever way I can, Mr. Mason. I've been handling this estate all my professional life."

"Thanks."

"Well, I had better be off. Oh, and one more thing. Wolves."

"Wolves?" Kara asks.

The lawyer laughs. "Yes. I know this sounds strange, but we haven't seen many in a very long time. Gainsbridge Forest is nearby. Just notify animal control if you see any. They're monitoring the numbers and it looks promising having them come back. Well, I'm off. Call me any time, Mr. Mason, and have a good afternoon."

As he drives away, Kara grabs the keys from my hand and dashes for the front door of Rosaland. I don't want to go in. I want to get back into the car and head far away from here.

"Come on, Connor, let's check this place out." She raises the keys above her head, jangling them, then unlocks the door. "Oh my God, Connor. What are you going to do with it?"

"Sell it."

"What?"

I'm not staying. I want no further connection to Chapelston. I got out once, and I want to make sure I get out again.

"Kara, let's go. If we head back now, we'll get halfway."

"Why? Don't you want to see this place? It's yours. I know you said terrible things happened, but you could actually have roots again. Raise a family here."

A family?

"No. Let's go."

I turn around to leave as Kara's hand grabs hold of mine, crushing it.

There in the threshold of the house stood four white wolves. Their fur was as pure as iceberg snow, and their eyes—bluer than any ocean I had ever seen—were cold and solid, like shimmering diamonds glaring back at us. They bare their teeth, and I slowly pull Kara back as gray mist rolls in from behind them. Moving like snakes, it pools around our ankles.

The wolves sit back on their haunches, their diamond eyes never leaving us—never leaving me. They seem to stare into my soul, as if aware of my cowardice. Perhaps they taunt me, like the shadows from so long ago. Then, in unison, they howl. Their call is primal. I don't know how long the standoff lasts, but we remain there on the threshold until the sun sinks in the sky. The mist dissipates, and I must blink, because when I look again the wolves are gone.

I grab Kara's hand and we run for the safety of the car, skidding to a halt midway as the ground breaks into fissures. Kara screams, looking back over her shoulder, and when I turn I can't believe what I see.

"Not again," I whisper.

The clear evening sky is now turning a blackish-green. Thunder rumbles and the ground shakes beneath our feet.

"The car! We have to get to the car!" I yell.

More thunder shatters the evening, followed by a loud explosion. Lightning crashes around us as I grab the door handle. That's when I see it.

I never thought I would see it again, but there it is: the dome-shaped light. I once lost a man to it and another man lost his mind. And I know what happens next.

Kara's whimpers are lost in the sound of the shockwave that follows. It lasts only a few seconds, but the heat is unbearable.

I touch the steering wheel and pull back immediately. It's hot. I tap it gently until it's cool enough to handle, turn the ignition and speed down the driveway racing away from the shadows dancing in my rearview mirror. Drifting around the turn, I accelerate hauling metal-ass and leaving Chapelston behind.

"Connor, what was that?"

"Hell reminding me there's a Devil out there."

I push the car to its limits, easing up on the engine only once

I have put distance between us and Chapelston. We are sailing down Highway 95 when Kara takes a calming breath, wiping her tears.

"I can't..." she begins.

"Don't. Don't think about it. Don't let it rest on the membrane of your soul. It'll drive you mad, I promise you. Whatever you hold Holy, now is probably time to ask for a favour."

"Was that what happened to you, twenty years ago?"

I grip the wheel tighter. "Forget it Kara. We're gone, it's over."

* * *

It's just after two o'clock in the morning when I walk Kara to the door of her house. She strolls inside slowly, as though she expects something or someone to leap out at her. She jumps a little as I close the door.

"Will you stay?"

"Sure."

She smiles sheepishly at me over her shoulder. It's happening; the slow, caress of evil is coming between us. I know that look well.

"Thanks. I don't think I could stay alone right now," she says, heading up the stairs.

* * *

Evil so unspeakable, there was no way to banish it from one's mind. I stayed with Kara for several days, doing what I could to help her cope. I knew though, what she had seen in Chapelston would bleed into her. She would never be the same, yet I couldn't stay any longer. I needed to sink into the bottom of a good bottle of bourbon.

Back at home, I head into the living room, wanting to feel the bourbon burn in my throat. I remind myself I'm not in Chapelston as I crack off the cap, raising the bottle.

"May your soul be at peace, Jack, and to you Chapelston, f—"

As I lift the bottle to my lips, the doorbell rings.

"Conner Mason, open up, this is the State Police!"

The bottle slips from my hand, crashing to the floor.

From the other side of the door, I hear someone yell, "Break it down." I raise my hands over my head just as a group of angry State Troopers crash through, guns pointed.

"Slowly, drop to your knees, interlace your hands and place them on your head," one officer says.

I do as told and they swarm me immediately. I'm shoved to the floor as someone's knee is planted in my back, cuffs slapped on my wrists.

"Looks like he dropped a bottle," an officer says. "Take him."

"Where are you taking me?"

"Chapelston."

"Why? You can't do this," I say, resisting the urge to struggle as we near the patrol car. "What am I being charged with?"

A burly trooper is about to shove my head inside when I see the shadow. It's dark and formless. The thud of the door seals my fate. I press my face against the window. The sickening feeling I had days ago returns as I sink into the seat.

"I need to make a phone call. I get to make a phone call," I say.

They ignore me, driving on.

Kara.

* * *

I'm back in Chapelston and in a cell for hours before I hear the door clang. A man in a blazer and dark jeans walks in. He pulls his credentials, holds them up and snaps them shut just as quickly. "I'm Detective Thomas Bourne. You're Connor Mason, a former detective of Chapelston PD I've been told," the man sneers.

"I guess."

Bourne leans against the cell wall. "Samantha Briggs, know her? She went missing a week ago. So there was this strange lightning storm on Tuesday. You were here on Tuesday, right?"

Son of a bitch.

"Well, a hiker looking for cover swears a dome-shaped light was trying to kill him. He headed over to the drainage tube near the ravine. He found her after, near the top. Odd, huh? Check this out," he says, pulling out his cell phone. He holds it up for me to look at the digital image. It has been twenty years since I'd seen a similarly gruesome sight. "I'll confess it shook me, and I've seen limbs blown off, men cut in half. I've seen it all."

"Military?" I ask.

"Seventy-fifth Ranger Regiment. You?"

"I served."

He hikes an eyebrow. I say nothing. He chuckles, but it is filled with malice. I know what he is thinking, but I do not have to justify anything to him.

"Guess you've seen this thing before," he says.

There is a firm accusation in his words. I will not let Chapelston take me.

"You see that dome of light?"

Death is clawing at my insides. "Yes. Scared the shit out of us."

"Us?"

"My friend Kara was there too. Look, I need to call her, let her know I'm okay."

Bourne folds his arms, looking me over. "In a minute. Mind telling me why you were even here? I was told you ran. I mean…left. Decades ago."

He thinks he knows, but he doesn't. "Officer Jack Cullen died. I brought him home to Saint Mary's Cemetery."

"And you inherited Rosaland?"

"Yes."

Bourne looks down at his shoes.

"You show up and women start dying. It's not a coincidence, is it?" he asks softly.

I need a drink.

"I didn't kill her."

"Yet, you being back now, when this is happening, is suspicious."

"I'm a suspect?"

"Person of interest," he counters before suddenly jabbing his phone towards me. "You're a piece of work. Not stopping this killer when you had a chance. Now, I'm left cleaning up your shit. So the way I figure it, this is your opportunity to right your wrong, or I'll throw your ass to Death Row. You're going to help me stop this sick son of a bitch. Or, I'll arrest you as a serial killer."

Serial killer.

I have long suffered with the knowledge of abandoning those women. It has become a disease in my body. I know they have not received justice.

"I didn't kill them."

* * *

"You shouldn't be there, Connor. Come back, please just come back," Kara says over the phone.

"This detective wants to nail my ass to the wall for these murders. I've no choice. I have to stay and help. And, maybe, right my wrongs."

"You're not some ancient Roman—"

"Kara? Is everything okay?"

"Sorry. I thought I heard something. Connor, you don't have to make this sacrifice."

But I do.

She fights with me over this for a long time, but when I hang up I have managed to keep her from returning.

I find Detective Bourne sitting in his office reviewing a file and he glances up, the look of contempt still etched on his face.

"Thanks for letting me call her."

"How long has it been since you had a drink? I know withdrawal when I see it."

"I'm not in withdrawal."

"Whatever. So you were some hotshot detective, but you never found this," he says, dropping the file onto the desk.

"What is it?" I take it up.

"Made a few inquiries when this body showed up. Seems it's not just a Chapelston event."

I read. There's an email from a detective in Shadwell, England. He writes about a case more than twenty-four years old, a series of murders, twelve in total. The women were found in the Entertaining District. It was brutal. Autopsy reports indicate unknown cause of death, though the use of fire is suggested.

He writes that it seems like mummification, but no suspects. The case went cold. It stills haunts him.

"It was a different time. E-mail was not yet popular," I say, dropping the file.

Bourne shakes his head, "Well, I've made other inquiries, so we'll see…"

I'm not ready for this, to run into the wall that is the Past. I need air.

"Where are you going?" Bourne yells, "Don't you go and get drunk you bastard."

I slam the door, exit the police station and head down the street.

* * *

Morgan's Irish Pub is where I end up. Sliding into a booth, I order a whiskey. I keep it at arm's length as my heart races.

"Connor?"

It's Father Francis, holding a glass of Guinness. He smiles. "Want one?"

"No thanks."

I move the whiskey away and invite him to sit.

"You should join me," he says, pushing the whiskey back. He stops my waitress and orders me a Coke. "I hate to drink alone."

"Did you once tell me you lived in England?" I ask.

"Yes, before the Lord called me here. So, you're back to help Detective Bourne?"

"Ahh…"

Father Francis nods. "It's a small town; we know about Samantha. It's troubling."

It was *some*thing.

"Well, I must go. This tragedy is stirring emotions. I'm offering a prayer circle and small vigil this evening. You're welcome to come. I remember when you came that last time. You found strength."

I remembered. We had spoken for a long while until I found the courage to continue.

"Come around seven," he says, heading out.

I grab the whiskey, twirling the glass in my hand. I want to drown in it, but mummified corpses and ghosts tear at me, screaming for their time, their justice. I pay and leave the bar.

* * *

The group looks up as I enter. Father Francis smiles, pointing to a chair near the front of the room. There are whispers, but I ignore them.

"Come now, this is a place of Holiness. Now, I know this feels frightening, but the Lord will give us strength."

I look about at the people, wondering if any have another reason for being here. I must have been exhausted, as soon Father Francis is shaking me awake. He chuckles next to me.

"Long day?" he asks.

"Yeah, sorry about that."

"Not at all, detective."

"No," I say shaking my head, "Just consulting."

He smiles. "Just like Sherlock. You're chasing a Moriarty?"

I shake my head. "I think you made that joke before, or something similar, the last time."

"Really? My mistake. How can I help you, Connor?"

I look down at my hands before leaning back. There's Christ, nailed to the cross, looking back at me. I shrug.

Father Francis nods, patting my shoulder. "We will weather this as we did before. I will never forget their eyes, but grand work is not the job of the police. Theirs is with dedication to the evidence and the facts, but we know this killer's game, don't we?"

"What?"

He leans back, interlacing his fingers. "Do you remember that vow you made when we talked all those years back, when you attended a similar vigil?"

I try to recall. "I believe I said I would give Beatrice and the others the justice they deserved."

"Yes, but you also said you would give your life, be the force of good needed to stop this killer, send this evil back to where it had come."

The memory returns to me. "I was overzealous, cocky to the point of melodramatic with that one."

"It made people feel safe. I believe this time you will stop him."

"Why? Do you think he started up because he thinks he won't get caught, again?"

"Only God knows."

I stand. "Son of a bitch. Sorry, but do you think he did this deliberately?"

Father Francis shrugs. "I do not know. I am not a detective, only a humble servant of God, but redemption comes in many ways my son."

I nod. "I have to go."

* * *

Even though it's late when I return to the station, there is lots of activity. Bourne looks up at me. "Another woman is missing," he says.

"Have people searched the forest?"

"Why?"

"Twenty years ago all the women were found there. Maybe we'll get lucky and catch the killer in the act of disposing the body."

We all stop as thunder cracks the sky. I am still.

"Goddamn thunderstorms," Bourne says. "I hope it doesn't rain."

I want to say no, but then I hope it does. I know what will happen if no rain comes. The dome will arrive, and a body will be found. It's always the same. So I pray, oddly enough, for rain.

* * *

It is too late when we get the call that the second victim has been found. She is discovered behind the same hill where I found Beatrice years ago. I don't want to be here, but Bourne thinks my observations are needed.

He is crouched beside the woman's body. He's unfeeling, cold, detached, but out of the corner of my eye I see that the other CSI agents and officers are not handling it as gracefully.

"What do you think made these holes around her eyes" he asks, "and why these slices on the abdomen? Ritual or something? Kind of reminds me of something, the wounds on the abdomen that is, not these around the eyes."

I never take my eyes off the shadows. I know what they can do.

"Connor?"

"Don't know. Some crescent-shaped tool for the eyes, but a blade of some sort for the abdomen. They're the same wounds made to the victims from twenty years ago. We left those details out of the public reports, along with the fact Beatrice was missing one of her shoes."

"Why?"

I glance at a shadow. "Seemed like a good detail to hold back on. I always thought she had run from her attacker, the fear being so great she had to leave it, to keep running."

"Okay, so not a copycat," he says. "And this?"

He points to the fading green glow around her wrists, ankles and waist.

"Never got it identified. There was a theory of it being mystical reside. I disregarded it."

Detective Bourne arches an eyebrow at me. I shrug, looking around. My stomach twists into knots.

"Look, we need to get this body back to the coroner's," I say, noticing the shadows move.

Detective Bourne chuckles before shouting orders. I start climbing up the embankment as fast as I can.

"Back to the office?" he asks.

"Yeah."

As we drive back into town, I notice the church in the distance and recall a memory of a conversation I had with my old captain.

"Father Andrew's new assistant priest is having a vigil for Beatrice and the others. I'm going to go."

"They say serial killers like to embed themselves into their investigations. That's a good call, Detective Mason."

"Thank you, sir."

As I get out of the car to follow Bourne, I whirl around feeling the ghosts of my past walking over my grave. I shudder.

"What?" he asks.

"I thought…never mind."

"Well, any clue on suspects?"

"Maybe it's the same person. I mean, it could be, because, maybe…" The word escapes me.

"Anniversary," Bourne offers. "Well, we know serial killers take significance from dates. Twenty years could be significant. And if it's not a copycat, then it's our—*your*—killer."

I think back to my conversation with Father Francis. "Maybe," I say, climbing the steps.

"Jack the Ripper," he says, snapping his fingers.

"What?"

"What that scene reminds me of," he says, "I'm somewhat of a Ripper enthusiast; I remember it from reading 'The Macnaghten Memoranda.'"

I laugh. "And you think I'm nuts. The man's dead."

"Yeah, well, it's what it reminds me of, but worse," he adds, pulling open the door.

* * *

"Problem?"

"I think Kara's upset. She's not picking up her cell. Keeps going to voicemail."

Bourne smiles. "Maybe she got smart and dumped your psycho ass. Want pizza?" he asks, holding up the menu.

I sigh, hoping he's wrong. "Sure."

* * *

There's something in the distance. Hazy, but soon it begins to come into focus, and I see…

Her eyes are bright and filled with agony.

"Who are you?" I ask.

She says nothing, only floats in midair. Translucent and soft, her features are delicate. The room is small, but a light at the far end draws my attention. I move towards it, coming to a stop seconds later to look upwards. In the ceiling there is a large, stained-glass skylight, and beyond it the dark blue evening sky is dotted with large, cotton-swab clouds. The stars appear like the eyes of ghosts, filled with unquestionable torment, far away, a shimmering aura of white light surrounding each. The sight is beautiful, but I feel a presence that is dark, unsympathetic, without hope. It taunts me as I notice the altar. The woman reappears.

"Where am I?"

She drifts behind me, dry, shrivelled and mummified. I turn, stumbling, and see her eyes are missing. Dark, clotted blood oozes from her mouth. I notice the shoeless foot. It is Beatrice.

"Give. Me. Peace…," she moans through the blood.

Before I can respond, the shadows attack. They hold tight as one breaks free. Mist, like tentacles, reaches out and swirls around me grabbing for my eyes. Blanketing the floor, it latches around my ankles and drops me to my knees. It flips me onto my back and binds me around the waist and at my wrists. I gasp for air, drowning in the mist.

In the distance I hear the howling of wolves as the mist continues its attack. I want to tear at the tendrils that now burrow into my head. My eyeballs bulge with the pressure. I fear they will pop out as the heat becomes unbearable. As my sight begins to fail, I hear the chanting begin. I dig my fingernails into the cement floor as a new pain seizes me. I want to cry, but tears won't come as my eyes feel like they are being pulled inside my skull. Through the howling of the wolves I listen to the distant chants, trying to focus on the words.

"Vitae est anima et spiritus sit perpetuum."

I feel a hand on my shoulder. It is comforting, but the heat is too much to bear. I want to scream, but only a feeble garble comes. My skin tightens and I cannot fight.

* * *

"Connor, Connor! Wake up you drunken bastard."

I bolt upright, startling Detective Bourne. My hands go to my face as I fall off the couch. Rushing to a mirror, I see my face is old and etched, yet my eyes appear to be fine. My hands are bruised and sore, with grit underneath the fingernails.

"What's wrong with you?" Bourne asks.

I wince in pain.

"What the…?"

Bourne grabs my wrist. I try to pull free, but he wrenches my sleeve up. He lets go, and I can hear the cracking of my mind. I can't find a word to express how insanity feels. I only know there's a measure of loneliness that hurts even my broken soul. I fumble with the other sleeve. There too is a green hue.

"Take your shirt off," Bourne instructs.

I want to refuse, but he glares at me. I lift it up, and it's there too. I look at him.

"What the hell?"

"Exactly," I reply.

"Bullshit. It's some friggin' dumbass prank. Shove your evil up your ass, Connor. Hell my ass. God you're a nut job. I should lock you up."

God is not involved in this. I know that for certain. It is Chapelston taking hold. I think about the dark pit of nothingness, about wanting to fling myself in. It hasn't been a nightmare, it's been real. The shadows are trying to kill me just as they killed Beatrice and the others. The air in my lungs burns and I cough. Blood is on my palm. I look over at Bourne. I can now see his fear.

"Sir!" an officer in the station screams. "The sky! The lightning!"

We stare at each other.

"When someone goes missing there's always lightning and thunder. Why?" Bourne asks.

"You know," I say.

We say nothing until someone else shouts. We bolt from the room to find the officers crowding around the windows in the back of the building. Bourne heads for the door, pulling it open. *Boom!* A crack of thunder rumbles in the sky. I'm too afraid to move. Others involuntarily flinch. The ground shakes. It's coming. I hear the faint sound of howling.

"Earthquake!" someone shouts.

Detective Bourne looks back at me. I know he's beginning to see the link with the storms. He drops to his knees upon noticing for the first time the formation of the dome in the distance.

"Close those windows and blinds," I order. "Take cover."

The officers follow my instructions without question. The shaking soon halts, but not before the wave of heat blows the windows inwards. There are shouts as some catch glass. I look around at the chaos while helping Bourne to a chair.

"They're connected," he mumbles.

"I know."

"The dome of light, it's…it's…"

"I know," I say.

Bourne's rational mind is crumbling, and his brain, the magnificent thing it is, is adapting, building walls, erasing the trauma; but he cannot, does not want to believe in other-worldly evils, so his brain flips a switch. I don't think he'll survive. I know that look, the far off delusion of escape.

Outside, everything has returned to normal. I look back to see many frightened boys. They are men, yes, but now reduced to boys, as there is no handbook for understanding evil.

I bang my fist on the table to gather everyone's attention. "I've been here before. I know many of you want to walk away, but you can't. None of you signed up for this, but it's happening, and I need you all to pull together for Detective Bourne."

"Are you taking lead on this sir?" one of the officers asks.

No, I'm out of here.

"Yes. I'm going to follow up on some leads." They appeared relieved. I think about my cowardice and breathe. "I need some of you to take calls because we're going to be flooded shortly. Help the injured. I need some of you walk the beat and keep traffic clear, as people will be fleeing, and some to handle the other emergencies. Call a doctor for Bourne."

"What was that noise?"

Evil.

"An explosion," I say, heading towards the front of the building.

I'm a wreck as I exit, yet the speech felt remarkable. It seemed like an old version of me, when I still had strength and logic. It is a good feeling, seeing a reflection of the man I had once been.

I decide against going directly to Gainsbridge Forest and instead walk in the opposite direction. I come to a stop outside a toy store. I'm surprised to see it's still around. And I once again remember a fragment from my past...

She rocks gently in her chair. Her eyes are dull, but Mrs. Holden had a knowing look.

"He doesn't come to see me anymore," she says.

"Who doesn't?"

"Father."

"I see. Mrs. Holden, please try to remember when you last saw Beatrice, your granddaughter?"

"Skinny, too skinny. He sends that other one. The Devil can cite scripture for his purpose. He does, you know. Shakespeare saw the Devil too," she murmurs.

* * *

I'm startled from the memory by the reflection of Father Francis in the shop's glass.

"Oh, Father, I didn't hear you."

He smiles. "You seemed lost in thought."

Glancing to the street, I watch as a car packed with a fleeing family speeds by. The frightened face of the young boy inside chills me.

"People are leaving," I say.

"Yes. Like before. Is there anything I can do?"

"The CPD is doing all they can to catch this killer," I say.

"Perhaps, but a little guidance can always help," he replies.

I look about, people are scared, running, and I don't know why it's happening again. "Do you think there's such thing as magic, Father? Dark magic?"

"I can believe in evil, but I believe magic is mostly something that many fall to when they are unwilling to seek a logical meaning."

"Father, do you remember Beatrice, before her death?"

"Mrs. Holden's granddaughter? Terrible, what happened to Beatrice. Her family suffered a great loss. I believe the father suffered most. Something with the male condition. Some men aren't as strong as they hope they will be in dark times. I think it was seeing her with only one shoe. Something about that tore him to shreds. But I do remember her a little. I would see her when I did blessing and prayers with Mrs. Holden, before she decided to see another priest from her hometown. Why do you ask?"

"I just remember something about a conversation back then. It's probably nothing"

"Well, I'm here if you need anything."

"Thank you, Father."

As I walk away, I look over my shoulder and Father Francis is nowhere to be seen.

* * *

It takes an hour after I arrive at the Town Hall to get a twenty-year-old map of Gainsbridge.

"What are you looking for, sir?" the clerk asks.

I honestly didn't have a good answer, but I quickly give him a description of the ornate room from my dream, hoping I might get some sort of clue as to what it was I was looking for.

"Sounds to me you're describing what the old locals used to call Old Chapel located here in Old Gainsbridge."

"*Old* Gainsbridge?"

"Yup, this was before your time, but Gainsbridge was once two towns. It was crazy to name one Old Gainsbridge and the other New Gainsbridge, but that's how it was for a time. Eventually, common sense won out and one of the cities was renamed Chapelston."

After a few more questions about the chapel's location, I exited Town Hall with map in hand.

* * *

Forty-five minutes later, I climb out of the patrol car and pull the map from my back pocket and begin making my way down the trail.

"They say serial killers like to embed themselves into the investigations. Maybe our killer is there."

My captain's words echo from the past as I travel the once well-worn hiking trails that have now returned to their natural state. All that remained was a rotting, wooden sign.

Back when I was still an officer, I had explored these trails. It helped to clear my mind of the shit I saw while working the beat. Gainsbridge Forest put life into perspective; it helped me escape.

In the distance I hear the snapping of branches. Howling indicates the wolves are nearby.

I take a deep breath, trying to maintain my composure.

As I close in on Old Chapel, the shadows begin to dance. And I know the wolves are there somewhere, waiting and watching. The once manicured lawns are now overgrown and wild. The grass touches me, swishing with each step I take. The cemetery is uncared for. Creeping vines and wild flowers decorate the stone reminders of lives once lived.

I reach the old, gothic-style, wrought-iron gate and glance over my shoulder. The forest is darker and mist is slithering through the trees. I want to do what I always do and run, but instead I push the gate open. There's no expected squeal. I wipe at one of the hinges and find fresh oil. I approach the building as the mist creeps closer and the wolves come into view. Four white wolves—soldiers holding the line.

Reaching deep, I take a breath and keep going. The chapel isn't as small as I remember. I open the large, carved wood doors.

"Hello! I'm with the CPD. Can I come in?"

No answer.

The limestone floors are not covered in dust or cobwebs. The pews seem newly polished. And there's a heavy scent of incense in the air. Through the clean, stained glass windows, I see the sky is changing.

There's a tall, Purbeck Marble column at the end of the aisle. Behind it hides a spiral staircase. I pull out my mini-flashlight and shine it onto the steps. As I ascend a feeling of déjà vu washes over me.

"CPD! Anyone here?"

At the top there is a small room with a light at the far end. I have been here before. The large, stained glass skylight is there, and the sky above is filling with storm clouds.

"I see you have figured it out." I hear the gentle voice.

"Who's there?"

A chuckle fills the room as I flick my light towards it. He's holding a dagger to Kara's throat.

"Please no sudden movements, Detective."

"I'm not a detective."

"And yet you were clever enough to find me. I am pleased. You are a Sherlock."

Father Francis pulls Kara from the shadows. Tears are streaming from her eyes and her cries are muffled by the gag in her mouth. He stops behind the altar.

"Let her go. You don't need to use her."

"After I went to such lengths to collect her? I think this is fitting."

"Why?"

"Isn't it obvious?"

It isn't. I need to start thinking like a negotiator, not like an angry lover.

"You're right, it should be. Why don't you remind me?"

"It's been twenty years since your pledge. We spoke of it recently. I reminded you. I know you thought I wouldn't take it seriously, but I did. You were magnificent at the vigil, strong, stoic. I heard you. Normally, I would have moved on, but you inspired me to stay. After all, you are *my* Sherlock aren't you? I was patient. I knew it would be a special reunion. I just needed a way to bring you home."

"You killed Jack?"

"I sat with him once," Father Francis explained. "We chatted about Beatrice and that night on the hill when he saw me. Poor man, he just collapsed. I toppled the first domino to bring you back. Though I was sick for a while. Absorbing a diseased soul is hard on the body."

"A diseased soul? What do you mean?"

He smiled as he forced Kara to lie down on the altar. The mist had entered the room and was slithering towards her.

"I have spent a lifetime searching for the meaning of life. I started with the physical, slicing into them, wanting to look at the soul. I later discovered the mystical. I am not a monster. I serve those with gentle hands, and take what I need when it is time. I survive as any living creature would."

"You're not evil? It's just a misunderstanding?"

"I knew you could see that, Detective."

I want to laugh at the madness—true delusional madness—but I only see Kara's tears.

"Now you get to witness truth, Detective."

"What is this truth, Father? Talk to me. I'm listening. Tell me your side."

He falters a bit, a soft expression on his face as he strokes Kara's cheek, "It began in Whitechapel. In 1888. It was filthy place, full of ugliness and perversions. I wanted to cleanse it, yet I also wanted to understand. I still keep a bit of that past," he says, slicing Kara's abdomen with the dagger. "I was a young, respectable man, so I had to work in secret," he laughs, placing a hand on her forehead, "You are a lovely. I will not enjoy doing this to you, but I will do it."

Kara looks at me, her sad eyes, fearful, pleading. I step forward, only to have the shadows grab hold and drop me to my knees.

"I was taught how to harness the energy of life by men of great knowledge and power, so that I may live and continue to help this polluted world, Connor. You see, my first attempts were crude, grizzly, naïve. I learned from them. Sweet Polly was my first lesson into understanding the true power of the soul," he says, setting the dagger down.

I struggle against the shadowy extremities holding me in place.

"Somehow the name Jack the Ripper got out. They made it seem like my work was ugly. It wasn't. I was seeking knowledge. Women are the keepers of life, they giveth it. I soon discovered how truly powerful they were. I began extracting their souls. And their souls extended my life, my cause. A shaman taught me how to correctly harness it so that I could continue my calling."

"Let her go. You don't have to do this."

"Vitae est anima et spiritus sit perpetuum."

The mist grows thicker, creeping up the altar. I watch, struggling, begging for him to stop as he moves to the top of the altar and to Kara's head. Pressing his fingernails around her eye sockets, she screams. I shout, fighting against the shadows. He doesn't hear me.

A light surrounds Kara, brilliant and white, starting from her stomach, expanding outward. I know what it is. It is radiant. It is her soul. I can see everything then.

Father Francis keeps chanting. Kara is screaming. Her fingernails bite into the altar. Her body is arching, contorting. Her soul is being ripped from her as Father Francis watches, entranced. The shadows dance. The mist blankets her, drowning her. The gag has incinerated. She does not scream but her face begins to stretch, elongating into a hideous shape.

The world around me is like a kaleidoscope, but slowly the

shapes and images come to a stop. And I see her—beautiful, young and sad as she glides towards me, brilliant. It's Beatrice. She touches my shoulder and the shadows release me.

I'm free and hurtling towards Father Francis. Our bodies collide and I slam him against the wall. A maniacal laugh leaves him as I ball a fist, smashing it into his face. He slumps.

Kara moans, barely able to move. Her body is fragile. She flinches when I try to lift her. Her eyes are white, the irises scarred.

"Ten-One, CPD, Ten-One…this is Mason, come in. I need units and a bus at Old Chapel, now. I've also got a Ten-Eighty-Two, subject Father Francis."

"Roger that. Officer needs assistance, with units and bus dispatched."

I shove the radio into my back pocket and hold Kara's hand. She moans and my heart leaps as she squeezes.

From behind me Father Francis yells, and I turn to see him rushing at me. He's wild and unstable. I notice the dagger and grab it…

He tries for me again, but I slice him.

Then I see Beatrice. She smiles.

Father Francis throws himself at me and we struggle for control of the dagger before it flies across the floor.

He's on top of me now and punches my throat before driving his nails around my eyes.

"I suppose this was always how it should be," he says in a reflective tone. "Vitae est anima et spiritus sit perpetuum. I will relish this time, Connor."

The anxiety and pain eases when Beatrice places a gentle hand on my shoulder.

I feel the handle of the dagger with my fingertips and pull. Father Francis and I struggle, fighting for possession of the dagger. He kicks it from my hand.

"You must submit." He spits in my face.

"Go to Hell," I scream.

We fight. We struggle. It stops. We are wrapped in a death embrace until I fall backwards, collapsing on the floor.

* * *

Being swallowed by the darkness isn't as comforting as I once thought it would be. Somehow, even now, I crave a drink. I expect to hear the Devil call to me. I can't be going anywhere else, cowardice doesn't just go away, does it?

Sadly, I'm not dead. I don't get the luxury of simple, sweet death. I'm a bastard forever stuck with this life. Opening my eyes, I let the world back in, and I see Detective Bourne looking down at me.

It's bittersweet, because while I long for death, I suppose I haven't deserved that right.

"Give me a hand," Bourne says to an officer walking past.

They help me up.

"You okay?" he asks.

"I'm not sure."

He looks down at Father Francis's body. "Jesus."

Scoffing, I turn away from the dead priest. In the bustle of the room as more officers appear, time seems to slow down. I see Beatrice at the back of the room. She is no longer twisted and shriveled, but now appears in the flesh in which she once lived. A soft smile flashes and I watch her turn away, fading into a brilliant light.

Bourne says something, pulling me back to reality.

"No, not Jesus. Not him at all," I say, turning away to be with Kara.

Seeing her there, I don't know what the future holds for us, but part of it I hope will be filled with new memories and not of ghosts and regrets.

JC HEMPHILL

Writing consumes. The reader is consumed by a world of imagination;
the writer is consumed by an obsession for expressing those imaginings.

As both an avid reader and writer, JC Hemphill can be difficult to find. The words, you see, have consumed him. And if you or anyone you know goes looking for him, beware. Words have teeth and they just might consume you too.

With over twenty publications in the last two years, Hemphill's work has appeared in *Buzzy Mag*, *Stupefying Stories* and *Nameless* Magazine, with upcoming work in *Space and Time*, *Tales to Terrify* and *S.T. Joshi's Weird Fiction Review*.

Hemphill lives in Denver, Colorado with his wife and two dogs.

LAST CALL

BY JC HEMPHILL

Dennis had spent the last hour listening to *the* Maurice Townsend griping about his recent outbreak of bad luck—the scandal, the girlfriend's tearful confession on the news, the fall-out with his wife, his lost job, lost friends, lost dignity, on and on and on. But Dennis lapped it right up. After all, when would he get another chance to drink with Atlanta's hardest hitting anchorman?

As Maurice Townsend rambled, kicking back shot after shot of Captain, then Cuervo, Dennis listened and added words of encouragement at all the right times. Before long, Maurice Townsend was hugging Dennis with one arm and raising a toast to his new friend with the other.

"You, sir," Maurice said in the serious tone of a newscaster, "are the kindest person I've ever met. Ever."

Dennis noticed the anchorman controlled his drunken slur like a pro. "How so?"

"You haven't given me the look in…how long have we been friends?"

"About an hour."

Maurice nodded. "Right. In an hour, you haven't given me the who-does-this-guy-think-he-is look. Not once." Dennis tried to respond, but Maurice pushed on. "Which is good. Because everyone else does. Some people do it with pity in their eyes, but I can tell that most wish I'd turn around and walk myself straight to Hell. Nobody bothers to consider my side. Maybe I have my reasons for what I did. Maybe I didn't have a choice."

"Can't fight who we are," Dennis said. "It's human nature to want greener grass."

Maurice's eyes widened. "Yeah. Human nature. Genius. How much would I have to pay you to explain that to my wife?"

"I'm gonna let you in on a secret. Nothing will get you in trouble faster than barroom wisdom," Dennis said, adding a chuckle. "Give a man enough booze and he'll turn a stool into a soapbox. Give his *audience* enough booze and that man's philosophies will rival Gandhi's. Over the years, me and the regulars here have solved every world problem you can think of. But come next day, those solutions have more holes than a rusty pair of tighty-whiteys."

"Too true," Maurice said with a nod. "Where's the restroom in this pit?"

Dennis pointed toward a shadowed corner. "Just past the jukebox."

Without Maurice yakking, the familiar comfort of Lights Out Pub returned. He closed his eyes and thought about his own problems. Sure, Maurice lost his wife of a decade, girlfriend of six months, and overseas bank accounts, but Dennis never had any of those things. Not that he hadn't tried for them. The skin of his hands and feet were thicker than an armadillo's hide from all his trying, working in the same factory year after year hoping to get promoted, telling himself that if he kept with the grind, he'd eventually get noticed. But he never did. And year after year a little more of his emaciated paycheck funded his favorite bar and a little more of his time was spent solving other people's problems.

Ding-Ding-Ding.

Dennis' eyes popped open at the sound of the iconic triple-ring of a boxing bell. The bartender, Doug, a sickly man who skulked behind the bar silently refilling drinks, used it to signify last call. Some nights, when alcohol had melted his thoughts, the bell made Dennis imagine himself as a punch-drunk boxer about to enter the twelfth round of a fight he had lost in the seventh.

He glanced around the dim bar. Signed boxing gloves and photos of famous prizefights hung on the walls. Wooden chairs were already turned up on tables and Dennis realized that the bell had been rung especially for them.

"Last call," Dennis said as Maurice returned. "Time to shove off."

"All good things…" Maurice said, suddenly looking like a very large, very dejected child.

"You gonna make it? I can have Doug call a cab."

Maurice reached back, fumbled a wallet out of his slacks, and slapped a crisp hundred on the bar. "Can't. That's the last of my cash. Anything left over is a tip. Damn IRS froze my accounts. Didn't I tell you that?"

"What about the bus? Tell me where you live and I can tell

you which route to take. It's the only way I travel. Best designated driver you can ask for."

"BUS!" Maurice threw his hands in the air. "Me? Let me tell you something, friend. *I* don't ride the bus. Never have. Never will."

"All right."

Maurice seemed to think for a second. "You can drive me."

"I don't have a car. I told you, I ride—"

"My car," Maurice said. He shoved a hand into his front pocket. "You drive me home in my Cadillac." He patted Dennis on the shoulder with his free hand as the other searched his pocket. "Ah-ha. Here they are." Maurice pulled a modest set of keys out and dangled them in front of Dennis.

"How will I get home?"

"You'll take my car. I don't care. If not you, my wife or the government will end up with the damned thing."

Dennis glanced at Doug, who was staring at them from behind the bar. A frown creased the bartender's face. "Okay, but I'm not keeping your car. We'll figure out how to get it back to you tomorrow."

"Whatever. Let's just go." He leaned in to whisper, but forgot to lower his voice. "I'm sick of the way this dump smells."

Dennis glanced at Doug again. The frown deepened.

"We're going," Dennis said, nudging the larger man toward the door.

"You think the Crypt Keeper back there would give us some road beers?"

"You're outta money, right?"

Maurice Townsend let his wide shoulders sink. "My luck's all dried up, huh?"

* * *

After a string of carjackings in the area, property management for the bar's strip mall had decided to install high-intensity lamps in the parking lot. The thinking was that brighter light would form some kind of criminal barrier. Personally, Dennis found them annoying. He always saw spots after stepping out of the dungeon-like bar.

Maurice placed a large paw on Dennis' shoulder and leaned heavily. With his free hand, he pointed to the rear of the parking lot. "That's me."

Only one car occupied the lot, and although Maurice had mentioned owning a Cadillac, Dennis never would've guessed the car before them belonged to the anchorman.

"You didn't tell me you drove an Eldorado," Dennis said. He could see only the backend, but the dramatic tailfins of the time were unmistakable. "Fifty-Eight?"

"She's a Fifty-Nine Brougham. Cherry. Restored her myself, mostly. Had my upholstery guy do the interior, but I handled the mechanics."

Maurice swayed on his feet while keeping his hand moored to Dennis' shoulder. A belch rose in the man's chest and threatened puke. Maurice blinked, blinked again, then patted his chest with a fist.

"You all right?" Dennis asked.

"Ugh. Yeah. I think the tequila wants to relocate. Let's get going. I'd rather be hugging my own toilet if I'm going to throw up."

Dennis took the lead with Maurice a step behind, hand on his shoulder for guidance like a blind man. The car—a black slab of Detroit steel—faced Memorial Avenue and the plexi-glass cubicle of a bus stop. The street was empty except for the Number 150 bus that was pulling in from the left. The skel-eton crew of buses ran to accommodate the flood of drunks expelled by last calls everywhere. Dennis called them drunk tanks. The only passenger so far was an older man in a wrin-kled suit, sleeping with his back against the windows. Dennis was suddenly happy to drive the Cadillac. Those overly large windows always made him feel like he was part of a mobile museum dedicated to scaring children straight—"Look here kids: a drunk. Don't grow up to be *that* man. No, no. *That* man is a sad man."

The hand on Dennis' shoulder tightened, almost clench-ing. It made him wince and turn. Maurice's eyebrows were scrunched in confusion.

"What's wrong?" Dennis asked. "Sick?"

Maurice didn't respond at first. He let go of Dennis' shoul-der and bobbed his head from side to side as if he were trying to see through the glare on a television screen. "Someone's in my car."

Dennis glanced at the Cadillac. They were still about thirty yards out, but close enough to see the lights from the bus shin-ing through the tinted windows, illuminating the outlines of the car's interior. On the right was the rectangular silhouette of a headrest, but on the left was a bulbous shape. The bus released a hydraulic exhale and pulled away from the curb. As it left, so did the shadow box image of the man sitting in Maurice's car, the tinted windows returning the car to a solid black slab.

"Are you expecting someone?" Dennis asked.

"No."

"Did someone know you were here?"

Maurice shook his head slowly. Shock had sobered him. "I'm the only one with keys."

"So let's call the cops."

From the way Maurice's face contorted, Dennis could tell he didn't like that idea one bit. "Screw them. I can handle this. I'm not letting some punk kid jack my car. I'm sick of people taking things from me, of being…being *shit* on." A wild anger surfaced as he spoke. He was a kicked and cornered dog, and his car was his bone. He had lost everything else, but he wasn't going to give up his bone. Not tonight.

Maurice stalked forward. Dennis followed. He didn't like the idea of interrupting a carjacker in the middle of a robbery. To him, it seemed like a perfect way to become one of the news stories Maurice built his career on.

Dennis cupped a hand around his mouth and tried to project a whisper. "Hey. What if he's waiting for us?"

Maurice didn't seem to hear and crouched lower as he approached the chrome bumper. Dennis did the same, asking himself why. He didn't have an obligation to this guy. Sure, it was Maurice Townsend, a man once synonymous with credible news reporting, now a famously debunked loser. If the bus hadn't just left, he would've jumped on. But the next one wouldn't be by for twenty-four minutes and he was already in the parking lot; already crouched behind the car, mere inches from a man who had no friends to count on.

Maurice pointed at Dennis and motioned for him to circle around the passenger side. Before Dennis could respond, Maurice stepped along the driver side with his head ducked below window level. Dennis crept to the backseat and poked his head up enough to see in. A distorted image of his unshaven face reflected in the tint.

Dennis didn't know what to do next. All Maurice had done was point. Did he want Dennis to open the door? Was he waiting for a signal?

Dennis heard the lock mechanism engage, followed by Maurice whipping open the driver's door. The car shook on its springs with the sudden movement. The anchorman let out a scream that was half warrior's cry, half panic. Then he ripped open the door to the backseat with a second, less abrasive scream.

Dennis sprang to a stand seconds later. Maurice stood on the other side of the car staring at the interior. His skin shone with a layer of sweat and his chest was heaving. Dennis opened the front passenger door. Then the back. The car was empty.

Maurice said, "You saw him, right?"

"Earlier, yeah…er…it could've been a trick of light, I suppose."

Maurice leaned into the car.

Dennis scanned the parking lot, half expecting the intruder to magically appear behind them. The only movement came as a light breeze swept a mixture of trash and leaves across the ground, and moths swarmed at a height of fifteen feet around the security lamp near the hood of the car.

His gaze drifted to the underside of the Cadillac, and he wondered if the carjacker could've crawled underneath somehow. He took a few steps back and crouched. He saw Maurice's loafers on the other side and nothing more.

Then he noticed his shadow. It extended into the shadow beneath the car so that it looked like Dennis had no head. He looked up at the moths in their mock air battle and the lamp they fought over. Ants made of ice marched up his spine and he stopped breathing as his mind confronted an impossibility. "What the hell," he muttered.

Maurice backed away from the car and looked across the roof at Dennis. "Did you say something?"

"My shadow..." Dennis let the word drift. What he was about to say would sound idiotic. He glanced at the other security lamps scattered throughout the parking lot. None were as close as the one by the hood.

"What about it?" Maurice asked. He started to move around the trunk when he noticed his own dark silhouette. "What the—" He moved from side to side as if he were trying to escape it. "Are you seeing this?"

"Mine's doing it, too."

They both walked toward the back of the Cadillac, eyeing their shadows as if they might come to life and attack them.

When Maurice spoke, he sounded unusually shaken. "In ten years of reporting the news, I have *never* seen anything like this. I mean...wow."

Dennis backed up. Maurice did the same, and they stood next to each other with their arms dead at their sides. Both shadows were perfectly formed in height and size and so dark they looked like human-shaped holes in the ground. But the real paradox was in the direction they pointed—always toward the car, no matter where the light originated. When Dennis was on the passenger side, his shadow had defied physics and stretched *across* the light instead of away from it. And when he swung around to the back of the Cadillac, his shadow rotated with him as if the car was the pivot point and not the man. Maurice's—although taller and broader—was identical.

Dennis didn't know what to say. He scanned the light sources again, but found nothing new. The car was a shadow magnet.

"I tell you what," Maurice said. "If I still had my job right now, I'd have a film crew here in five minutes."

Dennis waved his hand and watched his outline return the gesture. He circled Maurice and approached the driver's door. The shadow never fluctuated in shape, or lack of color, or position to the car.

Then the lights went out. Not just the lamps in the parking lot, but the street lights too, and the neon signs of nearby businesses, the inner-glow of the furniture store across the street, the accent light on the Cadillac's door that let you know it was open, the moon and stars in the sky, all light everywhere died in one single dousing.

"Whoa," Maurice said from the black. "Wh— What the heck? I can't see squat."

Dennis patted the air around him, feeling for the car. He desperately needed something real to hold, something to ground him and keep him from floating off into the abyss. He found the open door and followed it to the dashboard. He groped for the steering wheel and used it to guide himself into the leather seat. What he really wanted to do was run back to the bar where he could drink until the sun came up and replaced this awful darkness with yellow rays, scudding clouds and morning traffic.

Maurice spoke from somewhere near the back of the car. "Hey, uh…buddy, you there?"

"Yeah. Front seat."

"Stay there. I'm coming—"

The world blinked back to life as every light popped back on and with them the details of the street and parking lot and rows of suburban businesses were once again visible. There was no pupil dilation. No spots from the light change. No sign that anything had gone wrong.

"I know what this is," Maurice said in his best and-here's-your-nightly-news voice. "People slip drugs—hallucinogens— into people's drinks all the time. Usually to date rape someone. But sometimes it's to rob them. Once the victim passes out, the perpetrator can take their time searching them. Some go so far as to tie the victim up in a basement somewhere so they can use the person's house keys for an easy home invasion."

Dennis had never hallucinated before, but this wasn't how he imagined the experience. He pictured tie-dye flashes and cartoon characters, maybe talking Cheshire cats and opium-addled bugs.

Maurice's eyebrows lowered in suspicion. "I'll bet that slinky bartender comes out any second." He pointed a thumb over his shoulder without looking.

But Dennis looked.

Maurice pulled a smartphone from his pocket. "We should've called the cops like you said."

Dennis wasn't listening. He had stopped breathing. His arm drifted up, seemingly on its own, and pointed at the bar. Or, rather, where the bar belonged.

Maurice already had the phone to his ear. He pivoted to look where Dennis was pointing. The phone slipped from his hand and clattered onto the ground.

Beyond the parking lot was the darkness that had blinded them. The bar and the other adjoining businesses were gone, having been engulfed by some of the densest, blackest fog imaginable.

Dennis stepped out of the car. "I don't think this is drugs."

The Darkness chose that instant to lurch forward in a great wall, erasing all existence in its path. Entire lamps were absorbed, a patch of trees and a dumpster to the far right, the concrete and yellow lines of the parking lot all disappeared as nothingness pushed toward them.

For a second, Dennis could only watch the Darkness inching forward. There was nothing to compare it to. He'd been inside it once and didn't want to go back. It was cold and lonely and gave him the sense that he'd never see light again if it caught him.

Internally, Dennis was screaming to run, but he remembered that he held the keys to a fully restored V-8 monster.

Dennis yelled for Maurice to get in the car. Then he turned and scrambled into the driver's seat. Ignoring the pain of his knees smacking the steering column, he fumbled for the keys in his pocket, panicked by the black wall eclipsing the rearview mirror. Maurice got in beside him and shouted commands, but all sound seemed padded in bubble wrap.

Dennis managed to get the right key in the ignition, and the engine beneath the long hood rumbled to life. From there, Dennis worked mechanically, depressing the brake, shifting into gear, simultaneously releasing the brake and slamming the gas and gripping the steering wheel for dear life as the car bounced over the curb and onto the sidewalk. He tensed, expecting a tire to blow. They held, but the car wobbled like a rowboat in a cruise liner's wake. The Cadillac plowed through a corner of the bus stop, bending the thin support beams and shattering glass, then into the street where Dennis yanked the wheel to the right. Memorial Avenue ran parallel to the Darkness, but they didn't have another option. Their best hope was the intersection at Thirty-Seventh where they could turn north.

With the tires gripping blacktop, the tone of the engine shifted to a deeper, angrier climb as it accelerated to thirty, forty, fifty miles per hour. Half of the front windshield was clouded in a webbing of cracks from the collision, so Dennis hesitated to go any faster. When he looked through Maurice's window at the oncoming Darkness and saw that it was less than ten yards from the road, he put his full strength into pinning the gas pedal to the floor.

Dennis' senses were returning in fragments, and he took a moment to glance at his passenger. The anchorman's palsied hands struggled to find the buckle of his seatbelt. After latching himself in, Maurice's lips began moving in a voiceless mumble.

"Mr. Townsend," Dennis said over the sound of the engine. "Maurice."

The anchorman didn't respond.

Several thoughts crossed his mind then. What about other people? Was everyone experiencing this? Was anyone? Or was it just them? Maybe Maurice wasn't real. Maybe this was a dream—a nightmare. Maybe he was dead.

As the Darkness started edging into the road, he spotted the traffic lights for the intersection. Thirty-Seventh came on much faster than he anticipated. Dennis heard himself yell, "Hang on," and then he was working the emergency brake to keep the car from skidding off the road as it took the ninety-degree turn. The Cadillac groaned as two tons of momentum shifted direction. The Darkness crossed the intersection and reached for their bumper, a mere wisp from consuming the taillights. Dennis released the brake and punched the gas.

Thirty-Seventh connected the residential areas with the highway, so the businesses were larger, the streetlamps brighter. Even at two in the morning Thirty-Seventh usually had some traffic. There were always buses or truckers making overnight deliveries. But not tonight. Tonight, Thirty-Seventh was all theirs.

"It's still coming," Maurice said, surprising Dennis.

"Yeah, yeah. I see." He was, in fact, trying to ignore it so he could read the signs of the stores they passed in order to get his bearings—Daily's Coffee, Capitol City Taxes, Chomp: Hotdogs & Hoagies, the ever-present Dry Cleaners, a jewelry store next to a pawn store, another Daily's Coffee, another Capitol City Taxes, another Chomp—

Dennis let off the gas as a tingle flushed through his chest.

"Why are we slowing?" Maurice asked. "Pedal to the metal, pedal to the metal."

"I... I..." Dennis couldn't find the words. He didn't know how to explain that despite the speedometer reading eighty-five, they weren't actually going anywhere. Dennis tried to focus on the horizon in the hopes of seeing something new, but the same stores came and went in an endless cycle. Daily's, Capitol City, Chomp, Dry Cleaners, pawn store, jewelry store, repeat. It reminded him of the old cartoons where they looped the same three images in the background over and over again to show motion. And when he glimpsed the side mirror—*Objects in mirror are closer than they appear*—he saw the Darkness steadily gaining.

Maurice clutched the seatbelt across his chest as he too noticed the repetition.

Dennis tried accelerating again, but all that changed was the rate at which the background rolled. The Darkness approached with each passing second, devouring more of the world, reaching out for them, closer, closer…

A sense of intense power overran the cramped atmosphere of the car. The air gained an electrical charge, the radio came to life and blared static, the lights, both inside the car and out, flickered, the forward momentum slowed as the engine sputtered and died, and Dennis felt a lightlessness take him as the car coasted.

Before he or Maurice could speak, the engine cranked back to life and, like a thunderstorm changing direction, the energy in the car shifted.

"Stop," Maurice shouted. "I'd rather be standing outside than speeding down the road when it catches us."

Dennis eased off the gas, nodding in agreement. The car didn't slow. It continued to accelerate, reaching ninety miles an hour on its own. The cracks in the windshield began to spread and crackle under pressure from the wind. He tried pumping the brakes. The car plowed on, rounding a hundred.

Dennis yanked the e-brake. Still no response. Maurice started kicking at an imaginary brake on the floor in front of him.

A smoky odor made Dennis cough. He thought the tires or a belt in the engine was burning. But when he noticed the shadowed outline of a man in the rearview mirror, sitting just inches away in the backseat, he forgot all about the smell and the possessed car and the Darkness.

Amber light from the street lamps outside flicked across the man's face, revealing a pointed, clean-shaven chin beneath the brim of a felt bowler hat. A perpetual grin lifted the corners of his mouth.

Dennis' heart stopped beating. Every nerve in his body twitched, and before he knew what he was doing, he pulled himself closer to the steering wheel and away from the backseat. The man in the bowler hat hadn't moved or spoken, but his presence was enough to terrorize Dennis.

Maurice, alerted by Dennis' apprehension, looked over his shoulder. A stunned silence fell over him, followed closely by horrified recognition. His body went slack and his lips began to form one word, over and over again: "No. No, no, no, no, no, no…"

Dennis had a brief moment to register Maurice's reaction before the car began to drift to the left. He tried to pull straight, but the harder he tugged the wheel clockwise, the more it turned counterclockwise.

Maurice uttered one final phrase—"Not yet"—before the windshield filled with the red brick wall of the hundredth Dry Cleaners they had passed in the last three minutes. As the hood of the Fifty-Nine Eldorado Brougham struck the wall, but before the impact sent Dennis flying through the windshield and into a darkness greater than that of the one pursuing them, time seemed to stop. Shards of glass hung suspended in the air where the windshield had finally imploded. Maurice blocked his face with both hands, poised for impact. The hood, just beginning to crumple, resembled frozen waves in a black pond, and the speedometer read a solid sixty-three.

Then Dennis felt something penetrating his brain.

A voice, raspy and burned, but somehow playful, accompanied the invasion of his mind: *"Dennis Richard Fowler. I've come to offer you the deal of a lifetime."*

Dennis used the rearview to watch the man in the bowler hat. As the words scratched his thoughts, the man remained motionless, only letting the corners of his smirk stretch a little more.

"The deal is this," the voice said. *"Your life now"* — time jumped forward a beat and the car moved another inch closer to becoming one with the wall before it stopped again — *"for life later."*

The first question that came to mind — who the hell are you? — was promptly answered by the voice: *"I am nothing more than an offer. Strike a deal and all this will go away. A decade of happiness, fortune, women and life will be yours. Pass and your path ends with Mr. Townsend's — here, now."*

Dennis' next thoughts — Did you make this same deal with Maurice? Is this why the past ten years have come crashing down on him? — were answered by time and the car pitching forward another fraction. The sudden restarting of momentum was enough to drive Dennis into the steering wheel. The thumb of his outstretched hand caught the dash and bent back until it snapped. Sharp pain shot up his arm like a lit fuse.

With time stopped, the man in the bowler hat sitting unmoved, Dennis thought he heard a slight chuckle in the background of his thoughts.

"One," the voice said and the car moved forward another inch. The hood crinkled, Maurice splayed against his seatbelt, and Dennis was tossed forward again.

"*Two.*" Time took another skip forward. A plume of glass and brick and metal erupted all around Dennis as the front end of the car buckled and the back end lifted off the ground. Dennis was sent into the steering wheel for a third time. Numbness spread through his legs.

"*Thr—*"

Before the voice could utter the number, Dennis found use of his mouth. "Deal."

The presence withdrew from his head, and the man in the bowler hat vanished.

Dennis had just enough time to sigh, thinking he was safe, before the car completed its terrible course. Needles seemed to pierce every inch of his body as he was tossed head first into the red brick. And then there was no more. The Darkness had caught them.

* * *

Ding-ding-ding.

Dennis jerked his head away from the bar. His forehead hurt from sleeping face down and his brain felt like a bruised peach.

Dennis heard a slight chuckle in the back of his mind that made his body go cold. A shadow moved behind the bar.

"Passed out, did ya?" Doug, the slinky bartender said. He stepped into the light with a condescending grin on his face. "I can't believe you let that pussy-footed anchorman drink you under, Dennis."

"Anchorman?" Dennis repeated.

"Drunker than I thought." Doug gave him a look of pity. "You don't recall listening to Maurice Townsend drone on for an hour about his hoighty-toighty life being so damned unfair?"

"He left?"

"Sure did. Five, six minutes ago. Came out the bathroom, must'a seen you dozing, and left."

Vivid nightmares played through Dennis' mind.

Doug leaned against the bar. "Looks like your luck is finally turning up, Dennis. Mr. Townsend left a hundred dollar bill and said drinks were on him."

Dennis didn't respond. He listened to the sound of a speeding ambulance as it warbled past the bar outside.

He rushed to the front door, ignoring Doug's confused questions, and stepped into the night in search of a black Cadillac Brougham. The Number 150 bus exhaled and pulled away from the stop. Dennis was just in time to hear the ambulance as it raced toward the intersection of Memorial Avenue and Thirty-Seventh. He didn't need to follow to know it would turn north on Thirty-Seventh, toward the business simply know as Dry Cleaners, where they would try in vain to save the life of a drunk driver who was destined to make the news one last time.

Dennis stood alone in the parking lot, thinking about life and luck. But most of all, he thought about just how long—or short—ten years really was.

EDWARD MORRIS

Critically acclaimed author Edward Morris is a 2011 nominee for the Pushcart Prize in Literature and was also nominated for the Rhysling Award in 2009 and the British Science Fiction Association Award in 2005.

Morris' work has appeared in more than one hundred markets worldwide, including his collaboration with Joseph Pulver, "A Cold Yellow Moon," having been published in *The Lovecraft Ezine*, *Ross Lockhart's Tales of Jack the Ripper* and Robert M. Price's *The Mountains of Madness*.

TRENT ZELAZNY

Trent Zelazny is the Nightmare Award-winning author of *To Sleep Gently*, *Destination Unknown*, *Fractal Despondency*, *Shadowboxer*, *The Day the Leash Gave Way and Other Stories*, *A Crack in Melancholy Time*, *Butterfly Potion* and *Too Late to Call Texas*.

He is also an international playwright and the editor of the anthologies *Mirages: Tales From Authors of the Macabre* and *Dames, Booze, Guns & Gumshoes*.

Zelazny was born in New Mexico, has lived in California, Oregon, Arizona and Florida. He currently resides in his birthplace of Santa Fe.

CITY SONG

BY EDWARD MORRIS & TRENT ZELAZNY

Day and night, Portland screamed and dripped and bitched and moved along around them. The traffic was their music, and their music was their silence. Most of the time anyway.

Sometimes, the music was different. Older. Sometimes it was the kind people passed down. The kind you saved for a rainy day. It rained a lot in Portland. But Dewey remembered a lot of songs.

Pensively whistling "Baby, I Need Your Loving," Dewey presently whickered and flashed around with the rusty pair of fabric scissors, slowly trimming Ralph's hair like some kind of hedge.

Glenda sat close to both of them, as she usually did, watching the exchange as she field-stripped cigarette butts holding anything more than a centimeter of tobacco, flicking the tiny brown second-hand organic turds into a cut-down can that once held some energy drink or another. Those kind weren't coded for recycling. Oregon law. In their camp, those cans had become street Tupperware. Her harridan fingernails lovingly hulled the sniped-out cigarettes like peas, even thoughtfully flicking the papers into an old coffee can that was a third full of compost. In their camp, nothing went to waste. Not even air—okay, air did a lot of the time. But not for long.

"Hot as the hinges of Hell," Dewey observed, breaking the tune and setting his scissors down. "Wait just one second."

Ralph grunted assent, clearly not happy about sitting still.

Dewey removed his ratty, black pocket t-shirt and tossed it to the ground, then resumed cutting Ralph's hair.

"Is Jessica still sleeping?" he asked, suddenly more cautious than his usual sleepy demeanor projected. Everyone present saw him tense up like a pit bull, and they knew why.

"Out like a light," Glenda told him back right away. She always wanted to make the peace, and keep it. She had the scars to illustrate that particular need.

By the telepathy of street-camp life, natural as pigeons, everyone looked at Jessica's house at the same time. They were lucky to have carved out this much real estate under the Burnside Bridge. Campsites were becoming less and less available, following the Sit-Lie Ordinance and the rest of the local bullshit that went out with the bathwater when the Cascadian Secession took its legendary flaming shit and Portland went under martial law—like the rest of Oregon, Washington, California and Alaska. Nowadays, even space in the filthy loam and black mold under this bridge was at a premium.

Most of the gangbangers—the Bantu, Cholo and Snakehead sets, anyway—lived like ratty kings down in the old skatepark, or whatever office building they'd most recently blown to pieces over protection money. And regular people had to fight over scraps of third-hand land. Anybody who lived outside did, anyway. Since martial law came down, that was about one person in four.

But nobody fought about Jessica. They let her have her own house, big enough for a grown man to toss and turn in when he slept. Part of said house was hanging out into the river, but Ralph had made a makeshift float rig from a pallet and some old-time plastic bottles he had found. That seemed to have worked.

Jessica was special. Nobody fought about that, either. Glenda once privately wondered if Jessica could help them build some new digs somewhere, in a different campsite, but she shut up about that fast. She was the first to admit, when pressed, that Jessica was the sun in their sky, and they'd all be toast without everything she did for them.

"Tell you what," Ralph said, closing his eyes as hair fell past his face, "Soon as I get a good coupla bucks up when I go out bottlin', I'm gonna see if I can scrounge some batteries for the radio again."

"Fuck that," Dewey snarled. "I been brushin' my teeth with salt for a month. Go find us some toothpaste from the Rooshians. What's that guy's name?"

Ralph tried not to smile. "Walt. And, you got a point. But man, don't cha miss a good baseball game on the radio? Music? Real music, not this stuff now?" He almost choked on the words. "Rock and roll? Motown?"

Dewey snipped away. "Never cared much for sports," he sighed, dragging his clubbed left foot in its special Goodwill boot as if for emphasis. "And when it comes to music, Ralph, why…you know I got the whole damn discographies of more bands than you ever forgot, stored away up here." He pointed at his head.

As if illustrating this, he started whistling the bridge of "Baby, I Need Your Lovin'" again, as he lopped off the last straggling curls sticking out of Ralph's new haircut. A few more snips and he slapped Ralph on the back.

"You're all done."

Ralph ran his fingers over his head and smiled. His eyes were full of a million golden afternoons, catalyzed by a million oldies as golden as all the beer that flowed at the top of the ninth inning of the World Series.

"I always liked the oldies station best," he said out loud. "The Supremes, The Beatles. There was an energy there."

"I hear ya," said Dewey. "Got a couple dozen-hundred killer tunes from each of those bands in my jukebox. You know that, brother." He pointed to his head again, then raised his hands in the air and stretched his back.

"Do me a favor, Dewey?"

Dewey shrugged. "What do you need?"

"Sing one of those old songs. Right now." Ralph was adamant.

"Not sure I'm up for it right now, Ralph." Dewey glanced briefly at the setting sun. "Timing, Ralph. Timing." But Ralph didn't get it. He still nattered on.

"Doesn't have to be Beatles or Supremes. Anything. We need music, man. I go nuts without it, sometimes. Don't you?"

Dewey looked around. "Everything's a song. The wind. The traffic. Some fool all gacked out on the dumb shit and yellin'. Everything. It all makes a song."

Ralph looked at him. "You're perma-fried. I mean a real song."

"What, you don't like my whistlin'?"

That got to Ralph. He had to think about it. "Well, yeah, I like it okay. But it just, like...whetted my appetite, you know? I know the radio ain't much even when it works, but sometimes you can find one of those pirate stations that still plays reggae and shit. They know about soul music. About Motown."

"Know any doo-wop?" Glenda asked, launching into a hideous and phonetically irreproducible version of the Penguins' "Earth Angel" that made both men wince. She stopped quickly, though.

"A slow one," Ralph agreed, looking out across the river to the twin cities—Portland and its reflection on the still water. It was a neon rainbow that made the whole town look twice as tall, twice as clean, twice as new.

The reflection made him think about Rose's City, what they called the Portland underworld before the turn two centuries ago. A Portland where drugs were still legal and the cops were still Mob, when everything was an opium den or a hobo jungle and the government wasn't nearly as strong.

Glorious times, he often imagined. But most of the time he knew better. One kind of martial law was no better than another.

Dewey scowled. "If I wake Jessica up, she's gonna be cranky. She's not gonna want to go out tonight, and we gotta do this. That's just as regular as the rain, you know that."

Ralph looked around guiltily. "I lit off one of those M-80's that Strickland left here before he got pinched by the cops the other day. I was jack-fishin', down there." He pointed at the river. "She slept right through it."

Dewey gave Ralph a long-suffering look, but then turned his dark eyes toward the pink Dali sky that hung over Portland—a sky brighter than the neon and the skyscrapers, brighter than the reflection on the river.

"If she wakes up, that's your ass," he told Ralph finally.

"Just sing, Dewey. Please?"

"All right, all right." A first line danced across the surface of his mind, and it came with an odd organ solo, the first few bars of Shep and the Limelights' "Daddy's Home." His own Daddy had that record. On 45.

The words started coming back. He looked at the river again, watched how the waves rippled. And, softly at first, he began singing. Off key a little at the beginning, but it had been a while.

Ralph trained his ears, tuned out the city and closed his eyes. A smile grew on his face, and he giggled. At first he imagined he was sitting with the radio, but this gave way to what music was all about.

Flowing gently, his glowing, fervent soul dancing with young girls, soaring over Portland and vanishing from realities too harsh to comprehend. He was in the clouds with Glenda, Jessica and Dewey. Things were better here, even if it was only going to be for a minute.

But as Dewey neared the end of the song, Ralph realized he was thankful. He had himself some real friends, friends who did what they could for each other to keep going. When the music ended, he opened his eyes. The sun was gone. Darkness was waking.

He looked at Glenda, who studied the cityscape-reflection on the river and then each of their faces. She was smiling like a child hearing music for the first time.

"Things can still be beautiful," she told them with the open-handed, yet oblique, simplicity of a little girl. "It's never all gone." Then she set her gaze on Dewey. "Thank you."

Dewey nodded. A steady cacophony of city silence ensued, calm and tranquil in its never-ceasing mayhem. Up towards the north, a cruise ship made its way down the river. Above and around them, the bridge started going up automatically. Chances were the luxury liner would be docking downtown for the tourists to come get falling-down drunk that night.

As it came closer, Dewey dreamed of one day cruising on one of those things. Eating good food and having people bring him champagne. Watching the pretty, scantily dressed women as they wandered about. Hearing the band do Louis Armstrong and Duke Ellington tunes in the ballroom.

Yeah, maybe someday. But for now, he was here. Though things could always be better, he had a kind of freedom those richies would never know. And that thought gave rise to several other kinds of thoughts.

"Hey, Ralph. Remember the day we found Jessica?"

"Sure. You were the one that dragged her out of the water, right down there. She was barely holding onto that piece of driftwood, just about dead before we got to her. She probably wouldn't have made it without us."

They shared a look.

Dewey's brow furrowed. "We been through this a million times. Say it anyway."

Ralph sighed. "I know there's no way to find out now, but how'd she even get in the water in the first place?"

"Maybe just careless," Dewey said. "Could've fallen off a boat or something. Or got in a scrap. Hell, she might be South

American or something, for all we know." He chuckled. "Big girl."

Glenda nodded. "Big girl with her leg almost torn off. Took her a while to walk right. Even longer to…kinda shake it off, you know? It shows in anyone's eyes, for a long time after, when you get hurt that bad. Anyone…"

Ralph shuddered. "I thought she was gonna chew the ass out of me when she woke up. Chew the ass out of all of us. Sometimes, you don't want…someone to get healthy, 'cos they hate…" He had to chuckle. "They hate sittin' still. Bein' bed-bound." The chuckle even touched his eyes. "Our Jessica."

"She knew who we were," said Dewey. "She knew what we did. Same as anyone who lives out here." There were tears standing out in his eyes. Big ones. "We looked out for her. Now she looks out for us."

That was when they heard the slow scraping sounds of Jessica stirring. Two legs crept out into the fresh air, then two more, accompanied by her stout head.

"Hey, lady!" Ralph called. "Hope ya slept okay. Ya hungry?"

But they all knew the answer to that.

Jessica climbed the rest of the way out of her house that no one fought with her about—the vast, mud-gray silk bubble of her personal shanty. When she yawned, she gave them all a city-lighted frontal view through her basal, fang-tipped members and into her mouth. She raised her two large sets of forelegs and stretched.

When she lowered herself, Dewey, Ralph and Glenda all looked into her expressionless anterior eyes. Then Jessica turned back in the direction of her house, scaled it until she reached the underside of the bridge and, upside-down, strolled leisurely across towards the western side of the city.

"There she goes," Dewey remarked, "Let's get the fire started."

* * *

Later, staring deep into the flames, Ralph cleared his throat. "Hey, Dewey, would you sing us another song?"

"No, not tonight," Dewey replied. "Maybe tomorrow. I'm pretty tuckered out and my throat's feeling a little funny."

"Not coming down with something, are ya?" Glenda asked.

"I don't think so. Just hadn't sung in a while, and it's been pretty warm lately."

"I love it when you sing," Ralph reiterated. "If you sang more often, I wouldn't need to buy batteries for—" He shut up at the look.

Glenda redirected Dewey. "Did you ever try to sing professionally?"

Then all of them noticed a shape moving on the underside of the bridge, headed toward their side of the river.

Dewey thought a moment. "Back in high school, I sang in a band. Played a little guitar too. But I never went further than that. Maybe I didn't have enough interest. Certainly not enough drive. Here comes Jessica."

They watched her crawl to the end of the bridge. A large white cocoon hung close to her, from a rope attached to her spinnerets.

Reaching her web, she strung her victim up under the bridge, got herself poised, then pierced the body with her fangs. Under the light of the fire, through the silken bandages, and from the forearm wearing a fancy gold watch that protruded from the cocoon just the slightest bit, they could tell the body was male.

"That looks like a pretty nice watch," Ralph said. "I bet you if we hock that we could get us some toothpaste *and* some batteries, and probably some other stuff too. Could get Glenda here a real pack of cigarettes, instead of rollies or snipes."

Dewey sighed. "That's a Patek Phillippe watch, genius. I saw the face. We hock that, we get a lot more than toothpaste and batteries." He paused, "Well, we still got a little while before we eat. She'll be at that for at least half an hour."

"I'm really hungry," said Ralph.

"We all are," said Dewey, "but you know the rules. Jessica takes what she wants first. We'll get that watch, though, and anything else in his pockets."

"I didn't mean to sound disrespectful," Ralph muttered at the ground. I know she's lookin' out for us."

"We all give, in our own ways," Glenda told them.

"You got that right," said Dewey, looking up at Jessica, then out across the river to the western side of the city. "Well," he gave in, voice full of a long smile. "We got some time to kill. How about another song?"

"I would love that," said Ralph. Dewey closed his eyes, took a deep breath, and started in on "I'll Be There." Glenda joined in on the second verse.

Declarations of Copyright

MORE FROM
GREY MATTER PRESS

greymatterpress.com

A COLLECTION OF MODERN HORROR

DARK

VISIONS

1

VOLUME ONE

EDITED BY

ANTHONY RIVERA AND SHARON LAWSON

DARK VISIONS
A Collection of Modern Horror - Volume One

Somewhere just beyond the veil of human perception lies a darkened plane where very evil things reside. Weaving their horrifying visions, they pull the strings on our lives and lure us into a comfortable reality. But it's a web of lies...

This book is their instruction manual. And it's only the beginning...

DARK VISIONS: A COLLECTION OF MODERN HORROR - Volume One includes thirteen disturbing tales of dread from some of the most visionary minds writing horror, SciFi and speculative fiction today.

DARK VISIONS: A COLLECTION OF MODERN HORROR - Volume One uncovers the truth behind our own misguided concepts of reality.

FEATURING:

Jonathan Maberry	Milo James Fowler
Jay Caselberg	Jonathan Balog
Jeff Hemenway	Brian Fatah Steele
Sarah L. Johnson	Sean Logan
Ray Garton	John F.D. Taff
Jason S. Ridler	Charles Austin Muir
	David A. Riley

DARKVISIONSANTHOLOGY.com

 GREY MATTER PRESS

greymatterpress.com

SPLATTER

REAWAKENING THE SPLATTERPUNK REVOLUTION

LANDS

COLLECTED AND EDITED BY
ANTHONY RIVERA AND SHARON LAWSON

SPLATTERLANDS
Reawakening the Splatterpunk Revolution

Almost three decades ago, a literary movement forever changed the landscape of the horror entertainment industry. Grey Matter Press breathes new life into that revolution as we reawaken the true essence of Splatterpunk with the release of *Splatterlands*.

Splatterlands: Reawakening the Splatterpunk Revolution is a collection of personal, intelligent and subversive horror with a point. This illustrated volume of dark fiction honors the truly revolutionary efforts of some of the most brilliant writers of all time with an all-new collection of visceral, disturbing and thought-provoking work from a diverse group of modern minds.

Exploring concepts that include serial murder, betrayal, religious fanaticism, physical abuse, societal corruption, greed, mental instability, sexual assault and more, *Splatterlands* delivers on the promise of the original Splatterpunk movement with this collection of honest, intelligent and hyper-intensive horror.

FEATURING:

Ray Garton	Michele Garber
Michael Laimo	A.A. Garrison
Paul M. Collrin	Jack Maddox
Eric Del Carlo	Allen Griffin
James S. Dorr	Christine Morgan
Gregory L. Norris	Chad Stroup

J. Michael Major

Illustrations by Carrion House

SPLATTERLANDS.com

GREY MATTER PRESS

greymatterpress.com

Made in the USA
Charleston, SC
13 January 2014